BROKEN GATES

Happy Reading!
~D.J. Dyllin :)

BROKEN GATES

D.T. DYLLIN

DRAGONFAIRY PRESS
ATLANTA

BROKEN GATES

This is a work of fiction. All characters, organizations, and events portrayed in this book are products of the imagination or are used fictitiously.

Cover art by Lindsay Tiry

Published by Dragonfairy Press, Atlanta
www.dragonfairypress.com
Dragonfairy Press and the Dragonfairy Press logo are trademarks of Dragonfairy Press LLC.

First Publication, May 2013
Trade Paperback ISBN: 978-1-939452-23-8
PDF ISBN: 978-1-939452-26-9

Published in the United States of America

Library of Congress Control Number: 2013938299

For my mom,
who hid romance novels in the most random places,
like in the car under the passenger seat.
Thanks for getting me hooked.

1

We were at war. And just like in every war there were casualties. Jenna, Jeremy, Bryn, and myself were the last of our kind . . . Speaker, Gatekeeper, Guardian, and Seer . . . respectively. Only a short time ago our kind had been thriving, our numbers many, but then the alien Riders that were trying to take over our world had exterminated them . . . because of me. If not for my visions, they'd all still be alive. The revenge I yearned to mete out would one day . . . hopefully . . . help me to assuage my feelings of guilt. I just prayed that no one else would suffer because of me . . . Too bad I forgot to pray for myself.

I knew something was wrong only an instant before the bedroom door slammed open. But in life and death situations an instant can mean the difference between one and the other. "Bryn!" I gasped, sitting up in bed with a start. I barely had time to register the threatening shape outlined from the lights in the hallway before a gunshot exploded in our direction. I reacted without thinking and threw myself in the path of the bullet in a bid to save Bryn from being hit. Unfortunately for me, that meant I would be the one getting a slug buried in my flesh. A flash of white-hot searing pain ripped across my shoulder just before a blinding light erupted in my head. Everything went silent except for a ringing in my ears and the rasping sound of my own struggle to breathe. I found myself praying that Bryn was okay just as everything went dark.

"I have foreseen the outcome of both choices, and it leaves us with only one course of action. As much as it pains me, you must do what I ask of you." I stood watching as a woman that I didn't know spoke to a man kneeling in front of her. He seemed to be in pain, if the way he clutched at her dress was any indication. She was tall and regal, with long white hair that hung halfway down her back. Despite her hair color, her face was young and completely unlined. The man kneeling in front of her had dark auburn hair burnished brighter by the flames in the nearby fireplace. His build was massive and I found myself thinking that he could quite possibly dwarf even Khol in size.

"No, please. You're asking me to betray you." The man sank down further, reaching up to wrap his arms around the women's legs as if she was the only thing keeping him anchored to this Earth.

She lifted her dainty hand as if she would stroke his hair, but let it fall back to her side before she actually made contact. "If you do not do as I ask, *that* will be a betrayal to me." Her words were harsh, but there was no mistaking the anguish I saw in her glowing golden eyes.

"Send another," the man said raggedly.

"It must be you. I can trust no other with this task."

The man abruptly stood and rose up to his full height; the woman seemed almost childlike in comparison to his size. They just stood looking at each other for what seemed like an eternity to me, a battle of wills silently raging between them, until the man suddenly dropped to his knees again. "As you wish, my Queen." And with those as his parting words, he disappeared.

She remained where he had left her, as if in shock, before she turned away and crumpled onto the nearby bed, sobbing as if she had just lost something very dear to her. And maybe she had.

I took a step toward her, drawn in by my own curiosity to know what I had just witnessed. Why was I being shown this particular scene? It didn't have the same feel as my normal visions, and yet, I couldn't come up with any other explanation.

The woman lifted her head and gazed into the flames of the fire, her tear-streaked face blotchy and yet still beautiful. "Paige Joplin Stone, you are our first and last hope," she whispered.

My breath caught in my throat and I froze with surprise. Confusion about what was happening overtook me. Was this a vision after all, or something more? And if it was a vision, was it from the past, present, or future? Who was this woman and how did she know about me? She and her companion were obviously both dragons, as evidenced by his disappearing act and her glowing eyes but—but he had called her Queen, and her hair was white. I knew of no Dragon Queens, or factions of White Dragons.

"My little Seer." Khol's voice echoed inside of my head as I turned away from the woman and the scene I had been enthralled with.

"What are you doing here?" I asked, wondering if in fact, he was really here.

Khol's iridescent green eyes blazed brighter than I'd ever seen them do before. He reached out his hand toward me in an offering for me to take it. "Come back to us. You can't stay here any longer."

I tilted my head to study him. There was desperation wound into every plane of his face. "Where's here? Who's she?" I nodded in the direction of the once again sobbing woman.

"Please. We can't lose you," he rasped as if I hadn't said anything at all. *"I can't lose you."* The last part seemed to be said inside of my mind, as if I was reading Khol's thoughts.

"I'm not going anywhere. No one's going to lose me," I stated, even though by that point I was completely confused as to what it was he was talking about.

Khol's lips turned up in a grim smile. "That's where you're wrong, my little Seer; you're already here, which makes you lost, and you need to return to us. *To me.*" His thoughts echoed in my head again.

"But—" I started, but he didn't let me finish my protest.

"Do you trust me?"

I eyed him warily for a moment, wondering why he would ask me such a question at a time like this. Oh well, I suppose I could at least humor him. "Yes, you know I do."

He offered me his hand again. "Then come with me, now."

I rolled my eyes at him, but walked toward him anyways. I reached out my hand to intertwine my fingers with his and as I met his gaze, I seemed to fall into the depths of his eyes and everything washed out into a vivid green that blinded me.

"Khol?" I mumbled, my throat feeling scratchy and raw. Why were my eyelids so heavy? It felt like both of them were weighted down with fifty pounds each. "Khol? What happened?"

I heard a loud crash as if a chair had been thrown against the wall and some scuffling noises that I couldn't decipher. "I told you to stay the hell away from her." I heard Bryn's familiar voice growl with menace.

An answering growl reverberated off the walls, "I just saved her."

"I would have—was going to save her," Bryn snarled.

"I gave you a month," Khol snarled back.

"Hey," I grumbled. "No fighting." My eyelids finally seemed to shed their excess weight and I blinked them open to a much too bright room. "Bright lights," I muttered to myself, feeling like I imagined a Mogwai would . . . Just call me Gizmo.

"Oh, my God, you're awake." I barely had time to focus in on Jenna's elated face before she was on me, crushing me with a much too tight bear hug.

"Can't breathe," I sputtered.

"Oh, right, sorry," she said as she released me. "Guys—she's awake. Not just mumbling anymore," Jenna called out without breaking visuals with me.

Khol and Bryn seemed to just appear at my bedside, both of them wearing almost identical expressions of surprise intermingled with joy. I looked from face to face and couldn't figure out why everyone was just staring at me. "What happened?" I couldn't shake the feeling I was missing something pretty major.

Bryn dropped down beside me and took me in his arms, pressing his unshaved face into my hair. "Twice. I've almost lost you twice now." His voice cracked about half way through belying his strong emotions.

I looked over his shoulder and met Khol's eyes with question. "You were shot." Khol said. His gaze flicked away from me as if he couldn't bear to look at me when he said the rest. "I healed you the best I could. I couldn't do it properly with you being so close to death . . . and unconscious . . . You slipped into a coma . . ."

I gasped as the memory slammed home . . . *An image of a threatening shape outlined from the lights in the hallway before a gunshot exploded in our direction. Me reacting without thinking and throwing myself into the path of the bullet in a bid to save Bryn from being hit. White-hot searing pain ripping across my shoulder just before a blinding light erupted in my head. Everything going silent except for a ringing in my ears and the rasping sound of my breathing before everything went dark.*

"I remember," I whispered in shock. "I almost died." Yes, the words felt right when I said them out loud. Even though Khol had just said as much himself.

"I wasn't worried," Jenna exclaimed. "I knew these two big galoots wouldn't let you die." She grinned at me through long thick black bangs. I guess the more things change, the more they stay the same. Jenna hadn't dyed her hair some outrageous color but the black let me know that it wouldn't be long before the sticking to the shades in nature restriction to help her go incognito, was going to get thrown out like last week's leftover's.

"I still don't understand why I only slipped into a coma if I was so close to death, and I couldn't be healed properly." I reached up around Bryn, who was still clinging to me, to feel my head and found nothing but a whole healthy scalp and hair under my fingertips. I heaved a sigh of relief . . . No bald spots.

"It took all of my strength to heal your body." It was Khol's turn for his voice to crack. "But even then I almost failed. A part of you went somewhere else I—"

Bryn released me abruptly and turned to square off with Khol again. "I would have found her. I—"

"*You* don't have the power. I gave you a month." Khol's power snapped out and rolled off of him in angry waves. "She could have been like that for years if I would have waited for you to figure it out."

"She's *my Anam Cara*," Bryn grated through clenched teeth.

"Are you even sure about that anymore?" Khol's words felt like a slap to my face and my heart doubled in time. What did he mean by that exactly?

"What's that supposed to mean?" Bryn said, mirroring my inner thoughts.

"Your bond was shaky at best out here, and with her near death experience—"

"Holy shit!" Jenna interjected. "It could have null and voided your *Anam Cara* bond Bryn, just like it did to Khol's before!" I had been bonded to Khol as his *Anam Cara* for what felt like five minutes before I'd attempted to take my own life. Being so close to death had broken the bond, and Khol being so filled with guilt, had finally let Bryn bond with me. Could all of that have been for nothing? Could my and Bryn's *Anam Cara* bond be broken now as well?

"Exactly," Khol confirmed.

Bryn's whole body seemed to deflate with the revelation and he turned to look at me with a torrent of dark emotions swirling around in his sea storm eyes. I awkwardly pulled myself from the bed and lurched into him still feeling weak. "Bryn. It doesn't matter, we'll fix it."

He stared down at me for a dozen heartbeats as if he was searching for an answer to something in my face before he spoke. "Maybe it happened for a reason."

It suddenly felt like there was a boa constrictor wrapped around my chest as I struggled to breathe. "What—what are you saying?"

"Just what it sounds like." He looked away from me not wanting to meet my eyes. "Maybe being mated to Khol would be the best thing for you." *This isn't really happening. I must be dreaming, or still in a coma. That's what it is—I'm having a horrible coma induced nightmare. None of this is real.* "He has the power to protect you when I can't."

"No, listen to me, none of that matters! I love *you*. I want *you*. Bryn—"

"No, *you* listen to *me*. It does matter. We can't even bond all the way, and having you walk around without a full bond is like painting a sign on your back asking other male dragons to force themselves on you. And—and—" Bryn stammered as he took me by the shoulders, his eyes burning a bright dragon blue. "What if Khol hadn't been there when you were shot? You'd be dead."

I felt my face crumple up and huge fat tears began to run down my cheeks as I gulped for air. "Please—I love you." It was a miracle I managed to get even those words out.

Bryn's face softened as he cupped mine in his huge warm hands, his thumbs wiping at my tears. "I'm only doing this because of how much I love you, Peej. You tried to sacrifice your life for me once, now it's my turn to do it for you."

"No, I won't let you," I squeaked. *No . . . no . . . no . . . no . . . no . . .* The one word began to bounce around in my brain as I struggled not to panic. Bryn was just upset; he wouldn't really leave me. He'd told me he would fight for me as long as I wanted him. He'd promised. He'd told me *always*. I'd trusted him . . . in him.

"You don't get a say in this choice." Bryn then dipped his head and took quick possession of my mouth, sliding his tongue in to intertwine with mine. I clutched at his shoulders trying to pull him closer to me, and he let me for a brief moment before he broke all contact completely.

I stepped into him to try and hold on but he just disappeared. "No!" I screamed, knowing there was no way for me to follow him. My skin felt ice cold without his touch and I dropped to the ground as my vision blurred like watercolors running off the page. "No!" I screamed again. Khol's warm strong arms wrapped around me in an effort to comfort me but instead I decided to direct my hysteria at him. I wrenched around to face him and began pounding at his chest. "This is your fault! You did this on purpose! All of it! You never meant to let him have me, did you?" I just kept pounding at his chest. "Did you?" I screeched. He didn't answer, and it was probably just as well because nothing he could have said would have made me feel any differently in that moment. I blamed him for Bryn walking away from me and I wanted to hurt him like he had wounded me. I reached out and clawed my nails down his face, then his chest, and then I started ripping at his shirt as if once that was out of my way, I could rip his heart out with my bare hands like it felt like he had done to me. Khol remained still and took everything I had to give with barely a flinch . . . which only angered me more.

"P.J., stop," I heard Jenna say, but her command had little effect on me. "She's going to hurt herself," she then said to Khol.

"She'll be fine," Khol stated calmly.

"She's making you bleed," Jenna argued.

"I will heal."

"I hate you!" I seethed, directing all of my anger from everything at Khol. I just kept scratching and tearing at him until I lost all sense of everything and eventually collapsed in his arms. I vaguely remember him carrying my limp body over to my bed and depositing me there before I lost the battle of consciousness to my exhaustion.

2

I had no home. I belonged nowhere. I was a single leaf, separated from my tree of life and set adrift into a sea of nothingness. By walking away from me, Bryn had painted my world the deepest black. There was no point in going on anymore. I wouldn't take my own life; I had only tried that once in order to spare Bryn a life of torment, but I could simply stop living . . . cease to exist. Maybe if I just laid here long enough I would simply disappear into the nothingness that I felt had already swallowed me.

"Peej." The heartbreakingly familiar voice rasped just as the bed angled down from the weight applied to it. "You can't keep doing this to yourself." A large warm hand attempted to run through my ratty, tangled hair. It'd been days since I'd washed it, let alone brushed it. *So good luck with that . . . asshole.*

A flash pan of rage quickly flared through my system. How dare he break my heart into a million pieces and then seek to comfort me! He told me he would always love me . . . always fight for me . . . lies . . . all lies. "Don't touch me!" I croaked, even as my body craved nothing but more of his touches. "You don't get to comfort me when I'm this way because of you."

"Peej," Bryn whispered, as if it pained him to say my name. "It's what's best for you. We were kidding ourselves before to think we could truly be together."

I sat up and whirled around to face him, my dragon fire magic rousing just under the surface, luckily I was too weak to actually access it. "And who said you get to decide what's best for me? You don't get—" My anger fizzled out as I took in his dejected face and slumped shoulders. "I love you, Bryn. How can I live without you?" I said as I reached out to touch him. He snagged my fingers with his large hand and met my gaze. His eyes seemed to be a much darker blue than normal, as if the light from the room couldn't be reflected in them, as if he had lost a little bit of his life essence somehow.

"You won't have to live without me, Peej." His eyes moved over me and came to rest somewhere over my right shoulder. "I'm still your best friend. And that's never going to change."

A weird strangled noise escaped from the back of my throat that I seemingly had no control over. "*Best friends*? Can you actually look at me now and tell me that you truly believe there was ever a time when that's all we were?" Of course, he technically wasn't, in fact looking at me at the moment. *Coward.*

Bryn remained silent as the seconds ticked by, probably trying to think of something good to say in response to my question. But what could he say? No matter what words he used to try and sooth me, to try and make things easier on me, we both would know they would be a lie. "You almost died . . . again." He muttered as he turned his whole body away from me. "And I didn't have the power to save you."

"You're the one who's killing me now!" I exclaimed with anguish as I crumpled back down on the bed, darkness pushing around the edges of my vision. My breath caught in my throat the moment Bryn loomed over me and cupped the side of my face in his warm palm. I studied the familiar face of the man who I'd come to think of as home . . . a home that I had currently been dislodged from. His black eyebrows were furrowed as if in pain, and they stood out in stark contrast against his pale smooth skin. The planes of his face seemed harsher than I remembered them, as if some hardship had eroded away what was left of the carefree Bryn I used to know. He had changed so much over the last year . . . *We* had changed so much over the last year . . . and yet one thing had remained constant for me. "I won't let you walk away from me," I whispered, thinking of a time, which now seemed like an eternity ago, when I had determinedly decided that I would make him fight for me whether he wanted to or not.

"You can't stop me," he said, even as his thumb circled my cheek tenderly.

I focused on his full supple lips as I pursed mine, noticing his eyes follow the movement. With an abruptness that he hadn't been prepared for, as evidenced by the grunt that escaped him, I wound my fingers around the back of his neck and pulled him down to me. I arched my head up so that I could slant my lips over his as I aggressively slipped my tongue into his mouth. He only resisted me for a moment before I felt the stiffness in his body melt away and make room for another kind of tension between us. His hands slid down to explore my body in the heated way a lover does who knows exactly what his partner enjoys. I sucked on his tongue and drank down the flavor of him with a desperation I'd never felt before. Back when we had just crossed the line in our relationship, I wouldn't have really known what I was missing if he had walked away, but now . . . now I would mourn the loss of his touch with every breath I took for the rest of my life. I couldn't bear the thought.

"Don't leave me, Bryn," I choked out on a moan as I slid my hands under his shirt to slide over the smooth expanse of his muscled chest.

"I have to . . ." Bryn started to say as I plunged my tongue into his mouth again. I would kiss him until he had no rational thought left and he could no longer resist giving me what I wanted.

I somehow managed to maneuver Bryn onto his back so that I sat on top of him with my thighs astride his. I dipped down to continue kissing him as I worked on getting the both of us out of our clothes. He wrapped his hands around my waist, both trying to stop me from grinding against him and to press me harder into him at the same time.

It was then that my stomach decided to do a weird little flip flop and I suddenly felt like I was going to throw up. I lurched sideways so that I would miss Bryn, and proceeded to revisit the very little bit of food that I had eaten that day. When I finished, I rolled off him and groaned in utter mortification. Talk about a mood killer. It was just as well that Bryn was planning on leaving me because I doubted now if I could ever look him in the face again. I rolled onto my side facing away from him and silently pleaded for any deity that might be listening to open up the floor so it could swallow me whole.

Bryn stroked one of hands down my back in a soothing motion. "You okay?" His voice was still gruffer than normal, which made my stomach do another little flip flop but for a completely different reason this time. I guess throwing up didn't necessarily kill *my* mood anyways.

"Fine," I said in a clipped tone, not really sure how to react to Bryn in that moment.

"Hey," I heard Jeremy's familiar voice call through the slightly ajar door. "I was just coming to get you guys for a meeting. Khol wants to catch P.J. up on everything she's missed . . ."

His voice trailed off, probably because he was taking in the scene of Bryn's and my half-undressed state and the evidence of my upset stomach. "But I guess I could tell him you guys are busy right now."

"No," Bryn said, the bed moving as he got up and out of it. "Just give us a few minutes." I remained silenced by my complete and utter humiliation.

"Yeah, okay," Jeremy replied with uncertainty.

Silence enveloped the room after I heard the retreating footsteps of Jeremy. For a few moments I actually wondered if Bryn had gone too and I just hadn't heard him. "Do you need anything?" His voice cut through the silence and let me know that he hadn't left after all.

You, my mind supplied without thinking, but I kept that thought to myself. "No," I whispered.

"It's for the best, you know?" I fought the urge to stick my fingers in my ears to keep from hearing what else he had to say to me. Mature, I know. "We need to both try and move on."

The pain of his words sliced into my heart like an arrow hitting its mark, but from that pain stemmed fresh anger intermingled with jealously. Was there someone that he planned on moving on with? Was that what this was all about, and he was just trying to cushion the blow for me? I whipped my head around to face him, sure that my green eyes were glowing with rage, my embarrassment burned away by my hostility directed at him. "Who do you want to move on with, Bryn?" I hissed sounding somewhat less than human. "Has that buyer's remorse finally set in? Or did you figure out when you were away that there were better options out there?" Bryn's face showed surprise at my reaction, but my doubt at the authenticity of it spurred me on. Although I had no doubt that Bryn loved me . . . maybe he wanted someone else more. *More* . . . God I was really starting to hate that word. "Nala,"

I ground out her name. "You've decided to choose her over me, and this whole situation is a lucky coincidence for you, isn't it?" Nala . . . the stupid Black Dragon bitch that wanted Bryn for herself. I hated her.

"No," he said as his jaw turned to stone. "It's not like that. I don't want her. You know you're the only one for me." He locked gazes with me and I felt my anger fold up into itself. Maybe I just wanted an explanation that I could get angry at, and a reason to hate Bryn for leaving me, because surely he couldn't just walk away if he still felt the same way as he did before about me.

"Then, why?" I asked while searching his face. "No one ever said it would be easy, no one ever said—"

"No one ever said it would kill you."

I crawled toward him on my knees across the bed, stopping just short of touching him. "None of that is your fault, but if you leave me"—I reached up and caressed his face; his eyes slid shut on contact—"that will be your fault. And that will be what kills me."

I felt his jaw tick with tension under my palm just before he pulled away; leaving me to feel the cold emptiness, the loss of his skin from under my hand offered me. "I've made up my mind and nothing you can do or say will change it." He turned and walked toward the door, pausing to look at me over his shoulder. His eyes seemed to hold the weight of the world in them and for the first time ever I found myself wondering if the events of the last year had buried the Bryn from my childhood for good. "A world without you in it isn't worth living in." His voice cracked and broke an octave lower. "But a world with you alive and well, even if I can't have you, is a world worth fighting for."

My mouth opened and shut a few times, like a fish trying to breathe out of water, but by the time I found my voice, he was already gone. I sank back down on the bed in total shock, the numbness I had been feeling before Bryn had sought me out returning with full force. How could I go on without him? For me, a world where I didn't get to have him wasn't worth anything.

"Hey, you need any help getting to the meeting?" I looked up to meet Jeremy's soulful brown eyes that were currently filled with concern for me.

"I thought you left," I mumbled as my response.

After only a moment's pause Jeremy made his way farther into my room. "I did, but I came back to check on you. I was worried."

I chuckled darkly. "Or you saw an opportunity to swoop in and get me on the rebound from Bryn you mean."

He frowned and shook his head. "No, it's not like that anymore. I—well, I finally came to terms that you and me weren't ever going to happen and I've moved on. You were right, maybe I never really loved you . . . just thought I did . . . but—" He looked away and flushed. "I have feelings for someone else now. And I think this is the real thing." He looked back and gave me a tentative smile. "I'm ready to accept that offer of friendship you offered me before . . . for real this time. Or maybe I should say I can handle being a friend to you now."

I gave him a smile that threatened to crack my face. "I guess I can't keep anyone's interest, can I?" I tried to make a joke but it came out sounding dark and bitter. I gulped, trying to swallow down the sour taste in my mouth. "That's not what I meant, what I meant was that—" Much to my shame, I burst into tears before I could string together a sentence to salvage what I was really trying to say.

"Whoa, whoa, whoa, don't cry! I know this is tough right now—with everything. I understood what you meant." He encircled me with his arms and I let him so that I could cry on his shoulder . . . literally. As I sobbed into the soft cotton of his worn t-shirt I heard Jeremy clear his throat as if he wanted to say something to me and felt his muscles move restlessly against my cheek.

I pulled back enough to look at him and sniffled unabashed as his gold-flecked eyes bore into mine. "We should probably get going. I'm sure everyone's waiting on us by now."

I used the back of my hand to wipe at the tears on my face and nodded once in affirmation. In the past, I would have wanted a few minutes to try to make myself look somewhat presentable, but not anymore. I felt like crap and didn't care if the whole world knew I felt that way by way of my appearance. I did stop to pick up one of Bryn's oversized hoodie sweatshirts off the floor and pulled it over my head. I inhaled deeply and luxuriated in the small comfort his scent offered me. "I guess I'm ready to go," I mumbled more to myself than Jeremy.

He put his arm around my shoulder and guided me along as I stumbled blindly beside him. We eventually reached our destination . . . the common room . . . and I let Jeremy guide me to a chair and sit me down like I was some kind of invalid, and I guess I kind of was, emotionally speaking, that is. I was vaguely aware of the feeling that all eyes were on me, but I kept mine averted and to the ground for fear of seeing the one pair I couldn't handle seeing again so soon after their owner had just ripped my heart out . . . again.

"He's not here," I heard Khol's deep voice rumble, breaking the silence in the room. I lifted my head and met his penetrating green gaze with question. "Bryn. I think he's trying to give you some space."

My heart twisted inside my chest—that was the last thing I wanted from Bryn—and I hated the fact that Khol still seemed to be able to read my emotions after all this time. "Oh," was what I managed to choke out as a response. I let my eyes slide back down to the table despite the lack of Bryn's presence.

"There's a lot that you missed while you were . . . recovering," Khol said tactfully. "You need to be informed of the state of things."

I lifted my shoulders and shrugged. "Sure."

"We found out why the Riders are trying to kill off animals," Jenna piped up helpfully. "It was so obvious I can't believe I didn't see it right away. It's because animals can see what people have inside of them. We can use the animals to help us identify the Riders without having to use just you, P.J." She paused for dramatic effect. "And that's exactly what we've been doing."

At that I did raise my head to scan the room—not only were Jenna, Khol and Jeremy there, but also Macon, Drake, and a few dragons that I didn't recognize. Two males with silver hair, and two males with gold hair . . . representatives of the Silver and Gold Dragon factions, I realized. Before I had fallen into the coma, we had received news of each of the factions wishing to enter into talks about the alien Riders, but to see them actually being here was . . . well, kind of shocking. I did note that the Black faction was not being represented, although I saw no real purpose for any of them being present for my so-called catching up meeting. Surprisingly, for the first time since I'd awakened from my coma, I wondered about the circumstances of my shooting. "Who attacked us exactly? I mean I assume it was the Riders but—how did they find us . . . me?"

I could almost hear Khol's teeth grinding together from across the room. "We don't know how they found us, or how they managed to get past our security to hunt you down so quickly, but I can assure you nothing like that will be happening again."

"Someone ratted us out!" Jenna exclaimed in a manner that let me know this wasn't the first time she was making this particular accusation.

"No, there must be some other explanation," Khol stated flatly. "None of our kind, no matter their situation, wishes to see this world destroyed by those things."

"My lord," Macon chimed in. "I mean no disrespect in disagreeing with you, but I as well can't seem to come up with any other explanation besides betrayal of the most egregious kind."

"What a surprise that you seem to share the opinion of the tiny Speaker who you're currently bedding," Drake said with a wry smile. "Your opinion means nothing because it is not of your own making."

"And you never have a thought that goes against our lord's," Macon growled. "He'd do better with a second who could think for himself."

"Enough," Khol bellowed. "There are many other issues to discuss besides things that we don't have the answers to."

I angled my gaze suspiciously around at the strange faces in the room, and some of the ones I did know. A shudder raced up my spine to think that maybe someone in this very room could have been responsible for me nearly dying and slipping into a coma. I shifted uneasily and pulled up the hood on Bryn's sweatshirt feeling a little like a child who thought that hiding under the covers was some kind of protection from the boogey man. Silly but effective, because once cloaked in the shadow of the much too large hood, I heaved a sigh of relief as Bryn's scent swirled around me in a comforting embrace.

"Fine. Let's get on with it then," one of the Silver Dragons said with annoyance.

"As Jenna was saying," Khol started in while he searched for my eyes that were hiding in the protection of Bryn's hoodie, "we've begun using the animals as our aids in order to track down the Riders. We haven't figured out how to remove them from their hosts yet, at least not without killing them, but we'll find the answer eventually."

I inhaled sharply. "So, you're just killing them?"

"What choice do we have?" Jeremy said from beside me.

"But they're in so many people. Do you all even comprehend how many of those things came through the Gates?" I swung my head around to look at Khol, even though from the expression on his face I could tell he still couldn't see mine in the hoodie. He frowned at me though, probably picking up on my tumultuous emotions. "We can't just kill all of those people." My stomach clenched at the thought and I doubled over to dry heave, luckily there was nothing left for me to throw up. Suddenly I was surrounded by Khol, Jeremy, and Jenna, all of them vying for my attention so they could help make me feel better. Yeah, that was going to work.

"P.J., you need to take care of yourself, girl. This all can wait," Jenna said as she pushed back my hoodie and gathered up my hair like any dutiful friend would.

"I'll help you back to your room," Jeremy said at the same time as Jenna.

And Khol's deep voice interwove amongst the chatter my friends were throwing my way. "I'll take her to her room and make sure she gets what she needs . . . food, water, and maybe more healing."

"Stop!" I said with annoyance. I was feeling too boxed in by my friends. They needed to back off and leave me alone. "I'm fine. Can we just get this damn meeting over with, please?" I sat back up as the wave of nausea passed and looked at each of my friends with a determined expression in turn.

"Very well." Khol was the one who finally made the decision and everyone else slowly settled back into their seats for what would turn out to be a very long meeting indeed.

3

I had missed a lot while I slumbered away a month of my life in a coma. Truthfully, it felt like I'd missed a much bigger chunk of time because the alien Riders had really been making good use of it. Maybe they knew somehow that I was temporarily out of commission and they were trying to take advantage of our side's lack of my visions. Although, I bet they hadn't counted on Jenna and her furry little squad of spies/assassins. I suppose humans, dragons, and aliens alike all underestimate the true threat a Speaker represents . . . especially a pissed off one with a taste for revenge.

Our little band of misfits—not so little anymore with the addition of the Silver, Black, and Gold factions of dragons to our cause—had really been putting a major hurting on the Riders. Of course, as far as the media was concerned, there was some kind of crazed cult out there committing political assassinations. The Riders were starting to become desperate from what it seemed, tightening their grip on the government and any other place of power they could manage. There was a threat of martial law in the United States, and the equivalent in Europe, along with radical new laws being pushed through that severely limited the rights of the world's citizens. In a nutshell . . . things had reached DEFCON 1 at warp speed.

I stood leaning against the wall of the shower, letting the hot water beat down on my sore body. I was struggling to fully wrap my mind around everything I'd been told in the meeting, along with the fact that I would have to be facing all of it without Bryn. I mean it wasn't like he wouldn't be there fighting for our cause, but he wouldn't be *with* me, and therefore it wouldn't be the same. Nothing would be the same ever again.

With a heavy sigh I reached out and turned off the water to the shower and grabbed a towel to wrap around my middle. I wiped the steam away from the mirror and studied myself. The black dye that I had applied to my hair was completely washed away, along with any remnants of the henna I used to use, which left me with a shoulder length bob of bright strawberry blonde hair. Not only was it a horrendous shade of red, but it practically screamed baby dragon to anyone in the know. I wrapped a second towel around my offensive hair and left the bathroom, trudging slowly back to my room—the room Bryn and I used to share. He'd gathered up most of his things when I was in the meeting and moved to his own room across the compound. The better to avoid me with, apparently.

I was about two steps from my door when I felt the familiar tug of a vision overtake me, lifting me up and out of my body. I struggled to keep myself from collapsing in the hallway and attempted to make it to my room even as I felt the ground come up to meet me.

I stood in the same room I had when I was having my coma induced dream/vision, although this time around I knew with certainty that I was having a vision and not a dream. I still wasn't sure whether it was from the past, present, or future though . . . Where were some ghosts to fill me in when I needed them? Maybe they only come out to play around Christmas time?

I focused in on the woman dragon with long shining white hair; she was sitting rigidly on the edge of the bed staring blankly into the fire burning nearby her. I got the sense she was waiting for someone, so I waited with her, so to speak. Not much time passed before directly in front of her appeared the same man as I had seen her talking with before in my last vision. I noted in the back of my mind that I still hadn't actually seen his face.

He dropped down in front of her, his head bowed as if in shame, and his voice came out low and hoarse. "It is done. I have fulfilled the task you sent me to complete." She remained rigid as if the man wasn't even present in the room. He reached out to touch her, tilting his head up just enough so he could look up at her, but before he could make contact, she shirked away. The man made a strangled cry in the back of his throat. "Please . . . my love . . . Mori . . . don't punish me for something you commanded me to do."

Her face crumpled up briefly as if she would cry before smoothing out again completely. "My love," she whispered while still staring into the flames of the fire, "I don't wish to punish you, but"—a single tear slid down her cheek—"I seem to be unable to control the feelings that twist inside of me when I think of the two of you together in bed."

"I begged for you to send another," the man rasped as if in physical pain.

"And you know I could not," she replied in a chilling tone. "My visions are never wrong, you know that."

"So you will banish me from your touch, for doing something that you commanded . . . *My Queen?*" The man spat out the last part with complete and utter disgust. A second later his tone changed. "Please," he begged, "don't do this. I was never unfaithful to you in my heart. Thinking of being in your arms again was the only thing that got me through the task."

"Did you whisper words of endearment to her? Did you tell her that you loved her?" Mori asked hollowly.

"It was the only way that I could convince her to give me—*us*—what we wanted. It's what you asked of me—"

"And yet I find myself hating you for doing what I asked of you." Mori's voice cracked. "I wish to welcome you back into my bed and my heart—but I fear the latter has been crushed by your actions—no matter that I set them into motion."

"No." The man inhaled sharply. "Please don't turn away from me." He rose up and went to her in a blur of speed, covering her with his large body. I heard her gasp in surprise as she accepted his embrace with fervor . . . but only for a moment before she pushed at his chest and broke off his demanding kiss. "Mori, please . . ." the man rumbled as he desperately tried to hold on to her.

"Oh, Dragos," she murmured with tenderness even as she slid out from under him. "I fear that you will be the death of me . . ."

I didn't hear the rest of what she said to him, nor did I hear what he said in turn, because a buzzing sound had begun in both of my ears. I stumbled back in shock . . . I knew that name . . . Red hair . . . Red Dragon . . . *Dragos* . . . The man standing before me was none other than my biological father. *Holy shit!*

The vision began to fade out and I felt myself being pulled back toward my body but not before I heard Mori's voice as if it were in my head, "Paige Joplin Stone . . . you must come to me."

"Why? Who are you? Where are you?" I asked the woman who apparently my biological father was in love with, but I got no answer as everything went dark.

"Wake up, my little Seer." Khol's voice pushed at my pounding head.

Still in utter shock from what my vision had shown me, I blinked open my eyes to meet Khol's illuminated green ones. "My father . . ." I started, unsure of what else to say. I never really had a desire to meet or find out more about my biological father; he had abandoned my mom when she found out she was pregnant with me, and my dad, the only father I had ever known my entire life, had swooped in to take care of us. But then again, maybe I wouldn't have to say all that much, since Khol had probably viewed my vision right along with me through our link. I hated that I didn't mind the link when it was convenient for me. It made me feel very hypocritical—probably because I was.

Khol sat down beside me and pushed my damp hair out of my face that had obviously fallen out of my towel. "Yes, I did share the vision along with you." He studied my face as if searching for something. "Are you over being angry with me? Or do you still incorrectly blame me for what happened with Bryn?"

"I haven't decided yet," I stated as I raised my chin obstinantly at him.

Khol's lips quirked up slightly at the corners, his eyes sparkling with amusement. I had forgotten how attractive he actually is since most of the time I only have eyes for Bryn. Or maybe since I was no longer even partially bonded to Bryn, I was right back to where I started with my body craving Khol's again, just like when I had first met him. I found myself, much to my chagrin, suddenly very aware that I was wearing a towel . . . and nothing more. "Well until you do," he said with a slight chuckle, "we will still need to work together on the task at hand."

"Which one?" After all, there were so many with the Riders working overtime to take over our world.

"The task you have been charged with from your vision, of course," he stated matter of factly.

"Oh, so what . . . I'm supposed to just find this Mori? Why is she so important?" Besides the fact that she seemed to have some kind of tumultuous relationship with my biological father. Hmmm . . . those must run in the family.

Khol's face turned serious, his eyes blazing brighter. "This Mori is the queen to us all, and she has been lost to us for many years now. No one is exactly sure what happened to her. Some say she slumbers, some say she journeyed to another world . . . and some say she was killed by Dragos in a fit of jealous rage."

"My father . . . I mean my biological father, could have killed the friggin' Dragon Queen?" I felt all the color drain from my face. "But I thought there weren't any dragon kings or queens? And if she's dead, then how the hell am I supposed to find her?" I remembered asking Khol once why he thought I should be impressed that he was a Dragon Lord because a king would be better. He had then promptly informed me that there were no dragon kings. Didn't it stand to reason that meant there weren't any queens either?

Picking up on my emotions, or maybe my thoughts, because sometimes I still wondered if he could actually read my mind and he just wasn't telling me, Khol answered, "There has ever only been one queen, and she ruled us all . . . the Red . . . the Black, the Gold, and the Silver. She was all seeing and all knowing, at least that's what we all believed." He turned away from me and bowed his head as if in mourning.

My gut twisted. "Did—did you love her?" Because he could have—if she had died, that would have freed him to love another one day—me.

"We all did in a sense, we all worshipped her," Khol murmured. He turned back to face me and ran one of his long heated fingers down the side of my neck, eliciting a shiver from me. "But I've never loved another like I love you." Flames erupted in the depths of his irises. “I never knew it was even possible to love someone the way that I do you.”

“Oh,” I whispered as his hand pushed up under my head to support my neck. A feeling of liquid desire ignited in my middle, and I found myself wondering what if would be like if I let him kiss me again after all this time. So much had happened since the last time his lips had touched mine—and we’d already slept together once. It could be nice . . . *more than nice* . . . to give myself over to Khol and the feelings of lust he was currently igniting inside me. I didn’t resist him when he brought his lips down to mine and swept his tongue in to take full possession of my mouth. I even wound my hands around the back of his neck to helpfully pull him closer to me.

Wait—what was I thinking? Or maybe that was the problem . . . I wasn’t thinking. The one time I had slept with him . . . or, more aptly, let him have sex with me to save Bryn’s life, I had felt like my heart had frozen inside of my chest. Even though my body seemed to be all right with being a free agent again, my heart would always belong to Bryn. *But what if he never wants you again?* my mind whispered. *Khol would never walk away from you the way Bryn did.* No . . . I couldn’t let Bryn’s temporary rejection spur me on to do something stupid and rash. Because when Bryn changed his mind—emphasis on the *when* and not *if*—I couldn’t have done something irreparable . . . like have sex with Khol and end up mated with him. *Damn these dragon hormones!* Now that I had fully tasted all the intimacies of being part of a mated dragon pair, the craving to have that again was almost irresistible. My body craved . . . and I wanted . . . but I couldn’t let myself give into it.

“No, stop,” I gasped into Khol’s mouth as I struggled to push him away.

He pulled away from me but only briefly so that he shifted and wrapped his arms around me, pressing his face into my hair. "But you're right, my little Seer," his breath tickled my neck and I yearned to tangle my hands in his hair to pull him closer, but I remained perfectly still instead. "A dragon's love is eternal, and I would never—*could* never walk away from you—because I already would have by now. Maybe Bryn is too human to love you the way you desire . . . the way you deserve."

"But what if I am dragon enough to love Bryn forever?" I hadn't thought about that before. What if Bryn wasn't dragon enough to love me forever? And what if I am? Was I doomed to love Bryn for the rest of my life and to maybe have him move on to love someone else? Maybe more than one someone else?

"I've explained this before," Khol massaged my back slowly, which felt much more sensual than relaxing, but maybe that's what he was going for. "It's different for female dragons, that part of you isn't triggered until you've mated."

"But I *was* mated!" I exclaimed.

"To both myself *and* Bryn. Even if some part of your prior matings linger . . . it still . . ." His voice trailed off as he pulled away far enough to look into my eyes again from mere inches away. I gulped nervously at the intensity in his green depths. "It still means *I* have a chance with you too. And I'm not going to miss any opportunity I might be presented by Bryn's stupidity." He brought his lips back down to mine and kissed away any retort I may have had at the time. I moaned into his mouth as he pressed himself down into me on the bed. I felt him tugging at the towel that offered me little protection from his roving hands. I had absolutely no idea what to do. Thoughts of doubt about Bryn kept circling in my head, and yet they looped back around to the fact that I couldn't give myself to Khol for fear of losing Bryn forever . . . But what if I already had?

A sharp intake of breath acted as a small dose of sanity for me and I pushed Khol away—only to meet the dark blue eyes of none other than Bryn. It was as if my thoughts alone had conjured him up to witness my betrayal of him. *You can't betray someone if they left you at the curb like yesterday's trash,* my mind offered in my defense. A split second before Bryn's face clouded over into an unreadable mask, I saw the hurt that my actions had placed in his eyes. "Bryn!" I gasped. Khol stood and walked out of the room without another word, but I didn't miss the smug look on his face, and I'm sure Bryn didn't either.

Bryn's cool assessing gaze met mine, and my face heated with shame as he spoke. "I see that it's not going to take you long before you're mated with him then. Good."

He might as well have slapped me. "*Good?* You can't mean that!" I struggled to breathe. "*He* kissed *me*, I want you—I love you! You know that! Bryn please!" I began to feel lightheaded from lack of oxygen, if only I could manage a couple normal deep breaths.

"We're not going to have this discussion. I want you to move on, just like I'm going to . . . with Nala."

I opened and closed my mouth, unable to find my voice, the shock of what he was saying almost too much for me to handle. "Bryn, no," I rasped when I finally found my voice. "Don't do this. I've known you since we were both five years old. I know you think by pushing my buttons, by using Nala, I'll get angry and mate with Khol . . . Just please . . . stop."

"So maybe I don't have any real feelings for her, and maybe what I said to you before was true." When he finally met my eyes again, there were so many dark emotions swimming in his sea storm eyes that I couldn't see the old Bryn—*my* Bryn—in them at all. "But I want you to mate with him, and if giving myself to Nala is the only way I can make that happen"—he bared his teeth at me in a mock smile—"then I'll do it. Make no mistake about that."

"Bryn." His name rolled over my tongue and out of my mouth in a hushed whisper, carrying with it a silent plea that I could somehow make him see what a huge mistake he was making.

"I was born to be your Guardian, and I swore to myself once that I would do whatever it took to protect you, even if it meant protecting you from myself." He turned and took a step toward the door. "I'm just not strong enough—not powerful enough—not good enough to be with you. I just wish I had accepted that from day one. It would have saved us both a lot of pain." Khol chose that moment to return and he stepped into my room, pausing near Bryn. The two of them shared a very male look before Bryn left without so much as another word to me. I stared after him, hating Khol freshly in that moment.

"We must make plans for your journey," he said coolly, in an all business tone. He was a very wise dragon to not push me any more in that moment. He knew I'd talk to him about the task I was assigned by the missing Dragon Queen from my vision, but little else.

"And where exactly am I going?" I grated.

"She will let us know where and when it's time."

"What's that supposed to mean?" I asked with a sinking feeling in my stomach.

"It means we have a lot to talk about," Khol said as he closed my bedroom door behind him.

4

Knock, knock," Jenna said as she walked right into my room and flopped onto my bed.

"You know saying *knock, knock* and then walking right into someone's room is not the same thing as *actually* knocking and waiting for a reply." I feigned annoyance at her, even though the truth was I missed her . . . a lot. It felt like we hadn't had any real girl time in a long while and I had a feeling that wasn't going to change anytime soon.

"Your door was open," she retorted.

"No," I said as I stuffed the last of my clean laundry into my dresser, "It just wasn't locked."

"Same thing."

"Not really," I grumbled.

"So . . . you and Bryn are really over, huh?" I froze with my back to her, my heart tripling in time.

"Why, what do you know?" Had Bryn already mated with Nala? Wouldn't I somehow just *know*? It couldn't all be over like that . . . could it?

"Well, he did move out of your room, didn't he? And I've seen him skulking around all moody and broody. So—yeah—I connected the dots. You're not the only one that's known him forever."

My knees buckled with relief, and I slid to the ground. He hadn't mated with Nala, at least not yet. "Oh thank God," I gasped on a sharp intake of breath. Until he did, I still had a chance, and I wouldn't believe otherwise. I scooted around so I could face Jenna, my back resting against my dresser. "Have you seen him hanging around with any female dragons . . . like Nala maybe?" I couldn't seem to control my morbid curiosity.

Jenna's laugh came out sounding like a sharp bark, and she eyed me with amusement from under her black fringe of bangs. "No, he's been avoiding all female dragons like the plague. Especially Nala. Is that what he told you? That he was going to mate with someone else?"

I averted my eyes sheepishly. "Yeah, that's exactly what he told me. Right after he told me that he *wanted* me to mate with Khol."

Jenna groaned and slapped her hand against her forehead. "Men, I swear. If they weren't so useful in the bedroom, I don't think we would keep them around at all."

I couldn't help the smile that cracked my face. "Yeah, I guess." In an effort to think about something else—anything else—I was about to do the unthinkable: I was actually about to ask Jenna about her sex life. "How are you and Macon doing?" And that was all it took to send Jenna off on a male bashing tirade. She went on and on for no less than fifteen minutes . . . For most of it I tuned her out until the end, when something caught my attention.

"And you know male dragons aren't any different than any other males out there. They get all weird and possessive, and they freak out if you even talk to a friend that happens to be a guy." She sighed loudly. "I just don't know what to do."

I felt my lips turn up in a wry smile. "Yeah, uh-huh . . . so who is he?" Jenna batted her dark eyelashes over her large brown eyes that appeared to be limpid pools of innocence. I knew better. "Don't give me that face. Just spill it."

She rolled onto her back and heaved another loud sigh. "I don't know what you're talking about."

"Reeeally? Are you actually going to try and pull that crap with me? I may not be a Speaker, but I know *you*."

Jenna rolled over again onto her stomach so that she was facing me and perched her face on her hands. "I like Macon and all, maybe even more than *like* him, but we can never really be together. He's a dragon and well . . . I'm not. He can't mate with me."

"So? It's not like you can mate with anyone else either—you're human," I said as I rolled my eyes at her. This whole dragon mating thing may have seemed like an awesome thing in the beginning but now . . . not so much.

"So? Let me explain this to you P.J.—*he can*. He can mate with someone. How do you think I would feel if he felt the pull of some female dragon's powers and because he can't mate with me went off and hooked up with her? That could happen, and no one can tell me otherwise."

"Yeah, okay, point taken. So this other guy isn't a dragon . . ." My mind started shuffling through the very few possibilities that could fit that bill at the moment. And then it hit me. *Holy Crap!* "Jeremy. It's Jeremy, isn't it?" Wow. I most definitely did not see that one coming.

"No!" Jenna snapped back much too quickly. She began studying my bedspread very intently. "And even if it was . . . I can't let Macon know until I've broken things off with him . . . He would kill . . . whoever."

Whoever my ass! I internally huffed. Jenna was always getting so indignant when I didn't spill all my inner most secrets to her, and yet she wouldn't even come out and tell me that some kind of secret relationship was blooming between her and Jeremy. "Fine, whatever. But I don't wanna hear another word . . . ever . . . about me keeping things from you." I stood and stalked over to my closet. I felt a small pang in my chest when I looked at the empty left side where Bryn's clothes used to hang. Why had I come over here again?

"Don't be mad. I can't help it," Jenna groused.

My attention was suddenly diverted to a delicious mouth-watering aroma that was currently wafting through the air. "What is that smell?" I lifted my head and sniffed, following the scent like one of those cartoon characters led by their noses. It didn't take me long to find the source of the delectable aroma—it was coming from a plate that Jeremy was carrying past my room with a steak and some other sides on it. I snatched the plate from him and attacked it like a wild animal. I noted his surprised face in the back of my mind as I gobbled down the entire meal, with my bare hands, in less than five minutes. When I was all finished, as I licked at my bloodied fingers, I looked up to see Jenna and Jeremy both staring at me with worry on their faces.

It was Jeremy that spoke first. "Does Bryn know?"

"Know what?" I asked as my stomach clenched unpleasantly. I rubbed my belly and frowned as a sudden wave of nausea hit me. "Oh my God, I think I'm going to be sick again." I scrambled to make it to the bathroom, and luckily made it just in time to throw up the entire meal I had just eaten into the sink. I was going for the toilet . . . but oh well . . . at least it wasn't on the floor.

Both Jenna and Jeremy crowded into the bathroom seconds behind me and Jenna gathered up my hair, but it seemed like my feelings of nausea had passed just as quickly as they had hit. I rinsed my mouth out with some mouthwash and turned to face my friends with embarrassment. I really hated getting sick in front of people. "Sorry guys. I think I must be coming down with something, or maybe it's left over ickiness from the coma."

Jeremy studied my face for a minute with furrowed brows. He finally seemed to come to some conclusion and shock washed across his face. "You don't know, do you?"

"Know what?" Both Jenna and I asked at the same time.

"That you're . . ." He paused to look around and pushed the bathroom door shut behind us, which clicked closed ominously. "That you're pregnant," he whispered.

"I'm not pregnant!" I squeaked as I felt all of the color drain from my face.

"Of course you're not," Jenna said reassuringly, while she shot Jeremy a nasty glare. "Why would you upset her by saying something like that?"

"Because it's true," Jeremy said as he eyed us both warily like we might attack him at any moment.

"And you would know that becau—?" Jenna clamped her mouth shut mid sentence and turned to deliver me a stricken look.

"What?" I squeaked, a feeling of complete and utter dread settling over me.

"Jenna just remembered how I could know. I even knew when you were a virgin, P.J., remember? Just from reading your energies." His eyes darted around the room and he cleared his throat. "That's how I know you're pregnant."

"No, that's not possible . . ." My voice trailed off as something very pertinent occurred to me. In all of the madness that had happened before with Khol claiming me, me trying to take my own life, me mating with Bryn . . . I might have missed a few of my birth control pills. And then something else occurred to me. "What if it's not Bryn's?"

Khol and I had been together once, but that's all it takes sometimes.

"You're not far enough along," Jeremy replied. "It's definitely Bryn's."

Oh God . . . I was pregnant with Bryn's child and he had just broken things off with me. What was I going to do? "Don't tell him," I croaked. "Don't tell anyone."

"He deserves to know," Jeremy stated firmly.

"No he doesn't," I said between clenched teeth as I gripped the sides of the sink and met my own eyes in the reflection of the mirror. "He walked away from me, and I'm not going to be one of those pathetic girls who uses a pregnancy to force her ex to get back with her." I flicked my gaze to both Jenna and Jeremy's in the mirror. "He either wants me or he doesn't." Silence enveloped the bathroom and I gulped down the bile that rose up in my throat. "Promise me," I whispered. "Just promise me," I said again with a little bit more force.

"I promise," Jenna immediately responded, but Jeremy remained silent.

"Jeremy, please. Be my friend like you said you were going to be." I turned to look him directly in the eyes but he turned his head. "Please," I rasped.

"Jeremy, just promise her," Jenna growled.

"I can't," he mumbled. "I just can't. He has the right to know."

Desperate for a way to at least stall him from telling Bryn, I grasped at straws. "At least wait. Give me some time. Let what's going to play out, play out."

"But it could make a difference in what he decides."

"Exactly!" I exclaimed with exasperation. "And I don't want it to! I need for him to decide about me without this influencing him!"

"So you would risk him and you mating to other dragons when you could prevent it—"

"It's not that simple," I interjected before he could finish. "I want him to be with me for me and no other reason. I love him too much for anything less. I would always wonder if he was only with me because of the child." Most girls if faced with my situation would use the pregnancy to win Bryn back, but not me. I'd never been normal. Besides what if finding out I was pregnant with his child had the opposite effect? He was already willing to let me mate with Khol because he thought he wasn't strong enough to protect me, how would he feel if he knew it wouldn't just be me he was protecting anymore?

Jeremy shifted uncomfortably under my and Jenna's stares. "Fine." He finally caved. "I won't go and just tell him, but if he asks—"

"Why would he ask?" Jenna snapped. "Now you're just being ridiculous."

"I'll take it," I said on an exhale of relief. It may not have been exactly what I wanted, but it was close enough, at least for the time being. Besides Jenna was right, I doubted Bryn would ever ask anyone in passing if I was pregnant, especially Jeremy. "Now"—I turned toward the door on shaky legs—"I need to go lay down for awhile or something. This is all just—too much."

"We'll help you," Jenna said with a false cheer to her voice. I could tell she was just as much in shock as I was. I was the responsible one after all. Well, at least I used to be. I always thought that if one of us got pregnant, it would be her.

I opened the door to find Khol standing on the other side with a wild look in his eyes. He reached out and snatched me up into his arms before I could even blink and the next thing I knew we were in another room . . . not mine . . . but his. "I guess you know?" I mumbled, already knowing the answer. Of course he would have picked up the information through our connection. *Duh.*

He set me down on his bed gingerly as if I might break. "It could be mine."

I rolled my eyes. *Men.* "No, it can't. Jeremy, who happens to be an energy reader extraordinaire, says that I'm not far enough along for it to possibly be yours."

"The gestation period of a dragon is different than a human's."

I squeezed my eyes together tightly. "Of course it is." And of course, Jeremy wouldn't know that, just like I wouldn't.

"You being half dragon, and me being full-blooded, if it was mine, the pregnancy would progress more slowly despite you being part human because the child would be mostly dragon. I would imagine if it were Bryn's, then the pregnancy would happen more along the human time line."

"So what you're telling me," I said with my eyes still closed, "is that the child I'm carrying could be either of yours?"

"Yes," Khol grunted. I could tell he wasn't any more pleased with the situation than I was.

"Maybe I just shouldn't have it," I whispered more to myself than him.

He responded with a low growl that bounced off the walls and made me cringe away from him as I squinched my eyes closed even tighter. "You will not end your pregnancy no matter who the father is."

My eyes snapped open as anger began to boil my blood. Who was he to tell me what to do with *my* body? "Why not?" I glared into his angry glowing eyes that burned brighter than any high beams I'd ever seen. "It's *my* body and *my* choice."

He leaned into me and took me by the shoulders, another growl erupting from his chest. "It could be *my* child, and therefore *I* have a say."

"No—you don't. Especially if it's yours. What happened between us, even though I technically accepted it . . . it was about as close to rape without actually being rape as it could be." It was a tad more complicated than that, but I wanted to hurt him, and that was a sure fire way to do it.

"Please," his face softened to show the pain that was really fueling his anger. "I will take care of you . . . and the child . . . no matter who the father is. I will love you and the baby until the end of time." I'd never seen Khol look so vulnerable before. I could see in his face exactly how much he wanted me . . . and my child for his own. I knew in that moment that he would do exactly what he promised . . . unlike Bryn . . . and he would never walk away from me. Maybe the best choice for me, and my child, would be mating with Khol. He would be strong enough to protect us, to keep us completely safe. *Wait* . . . what was I thinking? Were my hormones already making me lose control of my sanity? *Maybe that's what happened before too?*

"Your dragon instincts are taking over in order to protect your child. That part of you knows what would be best for you . . ." Khol reached out his large warm hand and placed it on my stomach. "And for the child."

I brought my much smaller hand up to rest on top of his. "Khol—thank you. I don't know what else to say. But I'm not that girl. A part of me wants to be—but I would end up hating myself if I made my decision based solely on what's easier for me." I paused to try and gather my thoughts better; everything was happening so fast, as per usual in my world. "I thought everything was settled. We've been down this road before . . . kind of . . . with the whole you and me and Bryn thing. It actually feels a little déjà vu-ish. I can't keep going in circles." But how would I stop? Maybe . . . I don't know . . . Maybe it was time to let fate decide once and for all. A plan slowly started to form in my mind, and honestly I didn't see any other option that I could live with. "I'm going to let fate decide." I lifted my face up so I could meet Khol's eyes. "Whoever's child I'm carrying . . . I'll mate with him."

Khol's jaw ticked with tension. "And if Bryn has already mated with another, or refuses you because of his stubbornness?"

Would he? Would Bryn refuse his child and me if that ended up being the case? I just couldn't imagine him doing that to me, but then again I had never imagined him actually walking away from me either. "I'll cross that bridge when I get to it." I grimaced. *Almost nineteen and pregnant . . . Way to go, P.J.!* "Is there a way to tell this early?" I was sadly uneducated when it came to paternity stuff. Of course never in a million years did I ever think I'd end up having a "*who's your daddy?*" moment.

"No, not without risking the health of the child." He cupped my face in his hand tenderly, his illuminated green eyes glowing with hope. "But does that mean that you've decided to keep it?"

I bit my lip as I looked at him. "Yeah, I guess it does." *Huh.* I was going to be a mom. I—P.J. Stone was—going to be . . . a mom. *I'm going to be a mommy.* I knew it would happen eventually, but the feelings of a panic attack began in my chest and starting worming its way through my nervous system. "I can't be a mom," I choked out as I gasped for air. Why was it suddenly so hot in here? And why did it feel like I had an elephant sitting on my chest? I reached out and dug my nails into Khol's arm. "I can't—" But I couldn't finish the sentence, my lungs wouldn't let me.

He laid me back down on his bed and pushed my now sweaty hair out of my face as I continued to struggle for oxygen. "Shhh . . . my little Seer. I will take care of you." He dipped his head down to brush his lips against mine and it was as if they contained the oxygen my body was craving. I took in a shaky deep breath as my eyes fluttered shut. "That's right," I heard Khol murmur in a cajoling tone. "Rest. You need to rest."

"But what about our plans to find the dragon Queen. What about . . .?"

Khol's lips brushed against my forehead this time, and his sweet caress made me feel all warm and safe inside, quieting my worries. "You rest now, and afterwards we can go to our Queen." *We*—he wasn't planning on going with me before, but I guess he'd changed his mind, or me being knocked up had changed his mind for him. "No matter what, I'll be by your side; you won't go through this alone." It was the last thing I heard before I fell into a fitful sleep.

I woke up alone in Khol's bed. I lay there a few minutes trying to wrap my mind around the fact that I was actually pregnant. My hand slid down to touch my belly; it was as flat as ever. Did that mean the gestation period was moving slower like a dragon's because Khol was the father or had the child just been conceived more recently? How long would I have to wait to find out who my baby's daddy was? Maybe I should go on *Maury Povich* to find out.

I rolled out of bed and lumbered over to the door, wanting nothing more than a nice hot shower and some breakfast. Pancakes—no waffles—no scrambled eggs and bacon—wait—I don't even like scrambled eggs and bacon, or maybe I did now. Or maybe the baby did? It certainly seemed to have a predilection for meat. Did that mean it was mostly dragon? I was so caught up in thoughts about breakfast and the baby that I ran head first into Bryn's chest. "Oh . . ." His delectable scent stole the rest of the words from my mouth. His eyes then flashed an intense dragon blue as they skimmed down to briefly rest upon my stomach before they made their way back up to my face. My head swam at the realization. *He knew.* He knew that I was pregnant.

"Peej," he said gruffly. "I was just on my way to see you. Why are you out of bed?" He lifted his hand up to touch me but then stopped short as if he suddenly thought better of it.

I tried to control my voice. "Who told you?" But it came out shaky anyways.

"Khol."

I slid my eyes shut unable to look at him. "Of course he did." I never thought to tell Khol not to inform Bryn of my circumstances; I'd been too upset and focused on other things.

"So you really were planning on not telling me?" His voice broke an octave lower than normal and I cringed at the accusation, especially because it was true.

I slowly opened my eyes but I still couldn't manage to meet his, so I let my gaze settle on the floor in between us. "I didn't want it to affect your decision about me—about us."

"Whether you like it or not, it makes a difference if you're carrying my child," Bryn ground out.

Sudden tears splashed down my face and my lower lip began to tremble uncontrollably. "I just wanted you to pick me for me—not because I might be pregnant with your child."

Bryn tilted my chin up toward him with his index finger and the minute my eyes met his, I wanted nothing more than to throw myself into his arms. But I fought the urge and remained where I was. "Peej, I never stopped wanting you, and I never will. All those things I've said to you about loving you—I will—always. But that's not what all of this is about. I just wanna protect you—make sure you're safe. Khol is your best option for that, but if you are carrying my kid"—he ground his teeth together—"then he's not raising *my* kid."

I slid my gaze away from him again, even though his finger still rested under my chin. "And if it's not yours?"

Bryn's hand dropped away from me. "Then it's obvious. You mate with Khol."

Had Khol told him about my plan too? "So you're going to go along with me mating with whoever's child this is?" I brought my hand up to rub my stomach.

Bryn was silent for a few moments and I could have counted the seconds by my heartbeats, but I had nothing else to say so I waited anxiously for what his response would be. "Yes," he finally said. "Khol and I have already discussed the arrangements. We're both going to take care of you until the day we all get our answer and then—"

"And then I'll mate with one of you."

Bryn nodded once in affirmation. He swallowed a few times, his Adam's apple dancing up and down in his throat nervously. "I don't want this to be weird. I'm sorry about what I did before; you have to know that. You have to know I love you, Peej. Nothing could ever change that."

"Bryn," I interrupted and he let me. "I've known you almost all of my life. I know you better than I think I even know myself sometimes and yet . . ." My face crumpled up but I continued on. "I never thought you'd walk away from me the way you did. If—if it turns out to be yours . . ." I rubbed my belly again. "How do I know you won't walk away again at some point because you're feeling insecure or something?"

He stared at me in shock, his dark blue eyes muting out almost all of the reflected light in them. "You think I would leave you and my kid?" I let him see all the hurt in my eyes that he had placed there, and as his face clouded over . . . that's when I knew he finally understood what he had truly done to me . . . to us. He'd broken us in some way and taken away the only thing that I'd been sure about since this whole mess started . . . him. "Peej—" he started.

I shook my head. "No, now isn't the time. I have to get ready to search for—"

"The dragon Queen, yeah, I know. Khol filled me in on that part too. We're both going with you now." My mouth dropped open ready to catch any nearby flies. "Like I said, we're both going to take care of you until we all get our answer."

"Oh," was all I could manage. Well, wasn't this new development a nice little plot twist in the story of my life? Me going on a quest, of sorts, with both of the guys who could be the father of my child. Fabulous . . . *absolutely fabulous.*

5

It's one thing to want someone, to desire to be with them, but it's an entirely different thing to actually *need* them. I never wanted to need anyone ever again. I had a desire to be a stronger version of myself so I could be ready for whatever my new life could throw at me, and truth be told, I had been deluding myself. I thought I had become tougher, stronger, but in actuality I had just been leaning on Bryn more and more. And when he decided to walk away from me, I broke into a million pieces. I had to learn how to rely on myself, and only myself, if I had any hope of truly becoming the person I strived to be. I needed to grow up and to stop clinging to the insecure habits of a child, because . . . well . . . I was going to have a child, so I couldn't be one anymore. It was time to get off the carousel from hell that I'd been circling on and to develop myself into an actual functioning adult. If Bryn and Khol thought that I was going to make 'taking care of me' a piece of cake, then they had another thing coming, because I would no longer lean on the shoulder of any man for support. What was that saying? Oh yeah . . . I am woman hear me roar! *Rowr!* I chuckled to myself as I roared like a lioness in my head. Hmmm . . . maybe the pregnancy hormones are making me a little *off.*

"What's so amusing?" Khol's voice cut into my inner musings.

I couldn't help the smile that spread across my face. "Nothing that you would appreciate." Nope, he definitely wouldn't be appreciating any time soon what had just been tickling my funny bone.

"Why don't you try me?" Khol said with a glint of amusement in his eyes.

I eyed him suspiciously. Sometimes I swore that he could read my mind and he just wasn't telling me. But then again, what would he find amusing about what I had just been thinking? Unless he was under the testosterone driven impression I was deluding myself and that I needed him and Bryn. Or did he find me amusing like you find your new kitten when she tries to puff up and act all intimidating but all she manages to be is super cute? "No, I don't think I will," I snapped with annoyance.

Khol's glint of amusement spread into a full smile that threatened to blind me. "Have it your way, kitten."

Ugh . . . how was he getting under my skin so easily? Did he just read my mind, or did he just get the kitten thing from my emotions? I narrowed my eyes at him. "Why don't you just leave me alone?" I ground out through clenched teeth.

Khol's face drew into serious lines, signaling the subject was closed as far as he was concerned. "It's time."

"Oh." My mind was reeling. "What should I bring with me? Anything specific? Why didn't I think to ask you before?" A jolt of adrenaline coursing through my system made me start to pace the small space in my room.

"You have nothing to worry about, my little Seer. We shouldn't be gone long." Khol took my hand in his and tugged me toward the door. The fact that he was taking every opportunity to touch me since the bond with Bryn had been broken wasn't going unnoticed. I hated that his touches comforted and excited me, making me crave more from him. *More* . . . that word had come back to haunt me tenfold in the past year. But I wouldn't cave, and I wouldn't let myself *need* a man's touch ever again. And yet . . . *damn* I certainly *wanted* it right now.

I trudged along after Khol, mentally chastising myself the entire way until I found us standing in a clearing out in the woods where Bryn, Jeremy, Jenna, and Macon stood waiting for us. I drank in the sight of Bryn greedily, and noticed his eyes flare dragon blue when his gaze snagged on Khol's and my intertwined hands. I automatically tried to tug my hand free, but Khol tightened his grip possessively. It was then the two of them locked eyes in a very male way. So that was going to be the way of it? So much for their agreed truce until we found out who the father of my child was. Or maybe the truce was keeping them from actual physical blows like it had come down to in the past. But I wasn't going to let myself get caught up in any of it again. I would stick to my plan and let fate decide my course of action. Until then it was hands off for both of them.

"You're not all going with us now, are you?" I asked as I finally freed my hand from Khol's grasp, causing his lips to turn down slightly at the corners, and Bryn's to tip up. *Ugh . . . men.*

"No." Jenna's lip stuck out in a demonstrative pout. "Khol says it might draw too much attention to you if we all go. As if the two of them aren't going to draw plenty of stares." She waved her hands first in Bryn's direction and then Khol's.

I laughed. She kind of had a point. Both Bryn and Khol, even if they looked nothing alike, shared the drop dead gorgeous gene. "So why are you all here then?"

Jeremy cleared his throat. "I need to open the Gate for you guys."

My eyebrows shot up in surprise at his words. I hadn't been aware that we were going to be doing any traveling of that kind. Khol had simply explained to me that the Queen would let us know through some kind of sign when we would begin our journey. Khol had also informed me that I needed to be ready to go at anytime, to which I hadn't been as evidenced by my lack of being packed status. He said that in the old days, the days when the Dragon Queen had reined supreme, that was how it had been done. If she wished to see me then it only made sense that we would follow suit because that's what she would be expecting. I had been under the impression we would receive the sign, or rather, Khol would since he knew what to look for, and we'd simply travel to wherever she had deigned it appropriate for us to meet with her. Although Khol had alluded to the possibility it could be a bit more complicated than that, I had chosen to oversimplify the situation, it seemed. Maybe we would be *searching* for her after all. My stomach dropped into my feet. Why did this whole thing suddenly have the feel of some kind of quest from the days of yore? I just wasn't the quest kind of girl. I had a feeling it would be bad for my complexion.

"So where are you opening the Gate to?" I asked hesitantly, not sure if I really wanted to know. As if I wouldn't know shortly anyways.

"Well, I'm just kind of opening it," Jeremy said with a note of confusion in his voice.

Khol stepped forward and captured my gaze with his. "She will bring us to where we are supposed to be. We must trust in her . . . in the dragon ways."

"You've got to be kidding me!" Jenna exclaimed. "You guys can't just step into a Gate without any sense of where you're going! You guys could—"

"Get lost," I finished her sentence for her and gulped while still maintaining eye contact with Khol. His green eyes were imploring me to trust him, but that wasn't the problem; I did trust him, just not some Dragon Queen who I had never met. "I know. But I trust Khol. He wouldn't let anything happen to me or . . ." My voice trailed off as I raised my hand to my stomach. "Or my baby." I finished up knowing that I didn't exactly sound as confident as I had hoped I would.

"P.J., you can't go." Jenna stared at me with an intensity that seemed to say she was under the impression she had suddenly become a *Jedi* and could will me not to go with her mind alone.

I thought about refusing to go, but I had too many questions and the Queen seemed to hold all the answers. "I have to." I had no other choice, just like with a lot of other things in my life.

Khol took my left hand in his and stepped forward with me in tow, while Bryn grasped my right hand tightly in his and followed along with us. I suddenly felt overheated touching both Khol and Bryn at the same time, and my overly hormonal addled brain conjured up images of the three of us together in a much different scene. One that I pushed away as quickly as it sprang to life because it wasn't actually something I would ever consider in reality. But the effects of my momentary fantasy still had me wishing for a cold shower and a little bit of space from the two men at my side. How was I ever going to get through this with them?

"Begin," Khol commanded to Jeremy in a tone that was meant to halt any more protests from Jenna. Too bad Jenna didn't get the memo.

"Jeremy, don't," Jenna snapped, before whipping her head around to plead with Macon next. "Macon, please, don't let him take her into the Gate like that."

Macon smiled tightly at her and then glanced up at a very annoyed looking Khol. "It's the way of the dragon," he said flatly. "Something that I don't expect you to understand." His tone held an undercurrent of emotion that pointed at a double meaning to his words. Uh-oh, had Jenna been voicing her discontent about the mating situation to him like she had been with me earlier this week?

Jenna's face flushed with anger. Not a good sign. "Not everything is about the way of the dragon. Everything can't be explained away using that stupid excuse."

Macon's eyes grew brighter with his own escalating anger. "It's not an excuse, it's just the way things are."

They squared off with each other in silent battle, none of us privy to what was really going on between them. It was Jenna who spoke first. "It's over." Her voice was ragged. "I can't deal with all of this dragon bullshit anymore."

"Your best friends are both half dragon, do you plan on turning your back on them too?" Macon snarled, but there was no mistaking the pain in his eyes.

"I'm not sleeping with them! And besides look at the mess being part dragon got them into! I don't wanna end up like them!" *Ouch.* How about telling us what you really think?

"Do you think you're fooling me? I know you have an interest in someone else. Don't hide behind the dragon excuse," Macon growled.

"You don't know anything! You—"

"Enough!" Khol hissed, his hand gripping mine tighter. "This isn't the time or place for the two of you to air out your problems." He turned back to Jeremy, his jaw twitching in renewed annoyance. "Begin. Now."

Jeremy nodded nervously, his wide brown eyes averted away from Jenna and Macon. I almost wanted to laugh if he thought that was going to keep him out of the argument.

Macon seemed to already have a clue about what was going on with Jenna, and if he hadn't figured it out already, it wouldn't take him long to find out Jenna's new object of affection was Jeremy.

A sudden crackling of energy drew my attention to Jeremy and what he was doing and kept it riveted there. I'd never actually seen a Gatekeeper open a Gate before. Sure I'd been taught what to expect but nothing compared to actually seeing it with your own eyes. Jeremy's hands moved in quick sweeping motions, and he moved back and forth and side to side as if doing some kind of weird dance steps, but he did them with such confidence and grace that I sat back in utter awe of him. Slowly the Gate appeared before us, much like I'd seen in my visions, it looked as if a piece of sky had been ripped into the side of the forest. Different shades of purple and blue with flecks of night shown in a pulsating, changing state. I gasped at its beauty, unable to put into words the true nature of what I was seeing.

Jeremy stepped aside and Khol tugged me forward, and I pulled Bryn with me. I had an errant thought about why the Queen would require us to make this kind of travel when Khol couldn't open the Gate. In fact, as far as I knew, no dragon could travel the way we were about to, so how could it be tradition? Fear spiked through me. What if we were making a huge mistake? But I had no time to follow my thought thread any farther before I found myself stepping into the Gate and a feeling of ice raced along my skin. I inhaled the cold crisp air sharply and tried to focus my eyes on what I was seeing . . . or rather not seeing. The colors from the outside of the Gate had given way to complete and utter darkness. If not for still being able to feel Khol and Bryn's hands clutched in each of mine, I would have panicked.

"Keep going," Khol's voice sounded in my head. "Let her guide us to where we need to be."

So I did the only thing I could think of to do . . . I focused my thoughts on the image of the dragon Queen and began repeating her name in my head over and over again.

Mori . . . Mori . . . Mori . . . Mori . . . Mori . . .

The last thing I remembered was . . . "Damn it!" I sat up with a start. "Why do I keep passing out, or getting knocked out or whatever? I swear I've spent more time unconscious in the last year than not!"

"Where are we?" I heard Bryn's groggy voice rumble in response to my rant.

I blinked the fuzz from my eyes and focused in on Bryn's prone figure lying next to me in an unfamiliar bed. I won't lie . . . It kind of made me feel slightly better to know that I wasn't the only one who'd been knocked out this round. "We're in the Smokey Mountains," Khol said, sounding not at all like he'd lost the battle with consciousness anytime recently, much to my dismay.

I turned toward his voice and saw that his massive back was angled toward us as he stared out a ginormous window that took up almost the whole wall of the room we were in. "How do you know?" I asked.

"I, as I'm sure you've already figured out, did not succumb to the magic inside the Gates and remained awake where as the two of you didn't."

I glared at his back, which seemed to mock me, I swear, or maybe that was just Khol's tone. "How long have we been out?" I asked choosing to ignore my feelings of annoyance.

"Just a few hours." He finally turned so that I could see his face and he regarded me as if his mind was still partially somewhere else. I was just about to ask him if he'd seen the Queen or knew where we needed to go when he dipped down on one knee beside the bed and offered me a letter. "This is for you."

I suspiciously regarded the letter resting in his outstretched palm for a moment before taking it. The plain white envelope with my entire name printed on it in elegant script was kind of giving me the creeps for some reason. After a few more seconds of staring at it, I finally decided I was being ridiculous and I just needed to open it. With short jerky motions I tore into the envelope to produce a single piece of white paper about the size of an index card. In the same handwriting as was found on the front of the envelope were two lines of text . . .

Let him go. Don't leave the cabin for any reason.

"What does it say?" Khol asked. Like he couldn't just pull it out of my mind somehow, or at least get the gist of it. He was so patronizing sometimes.

I responded while still staring at the note. "Where did you get this?"

"So, I'm guessing you saved her . . . again." Bryn's irritated voice caused me to whip around just in time to see him pull himself out of bed and stagger a bit before righting himself.

"I'm stronger than you are . . . older," Khol stated with irritation of his own. And I guess I couldn't really blame him, we'd been down this road one too many times lately.

Bryn's face darkened as he gazed at me. "Maybe we should skip this whole waiting to see who the father is and you should just go ahead and mate with him." He punched the wall in frustration. "Who was I kidding, anyways? He'd keep the both of you safer even if it is mine."

"Bryn—" I started, but he was already stalking toward the door. His moodiness and childishness directed at Khol had gone way beyond ridiculous. I was tired of having to worry about how he would react to everything. Anger short-circuited my brain and I yelled at him without thinking. "Fine, just walk away! If you were half as good at the dragon stuff as you are at doing that then you'd be the most powerful dragon of all time!" Bryn stopped where he was without turning toward me and I could see that every muscle in his body had gone rigid. I should have stopped there, but I couldn't seem to help myself. "I hope it's not yours!" As soon as the words were out of my mouth, I wished that I could stuff them back in somehow. I didn't mean it; in fact, I wanted nothing more than for Bryn to be the father of my child. Having a child with Khol and therefore being mated to him would seem just too wrong for words. No matter how upset at Bryn I got, I knew he was truly the only one for me. He was my home, and I wanted my baby to belong there too.

Bryn made some kind of indecipherable noise that didn't even sound human before continuing on his way. I jumped to my feet to give him chase, but then Khol grabbed my arm, stopping me short. "Let him go."

I tried frantically to free myself from Khol's iron grip but to no avail. "You have no right to tell me what to do," I snarled at him.

"Not me, it's what the note told you to do."

I dropped my tear filled eyes down to the tiny piece of white paper that I was still clutching in my hand and sucked in a shaky breath. "That's not possible." How the hell had someone known to leave a note for me about something that hadn't even happened yet?

"You're not thinking clearly. You of all people know how possible such a thing is . . . you being a Seer." Khol dropped his voice to a low cajoling tone as if not to spook me.

Right. I wasn't thinking clearly. The whole pregnancy thing coupled with Bryn being an utter idiot had fried my brain. *Of course* I knew the dragon Queen was some kind of Seer, otherwise I wouldn't be here. "But I can't just let him go. Who knows what he'll do when he's like this." I bit my lip and unleashed my imploring eyes on Khol. "Will you—"

"No. I won't—" he started, already knowing what I was going to ask.

"Please." I whispered as I let my tears finally spill down my cheeks, leaving salty trails in their wake. "Please go talk to him."

Khol reached out to cup my face tenderly, even as he gritted his teeth in aggravation. "Your tears are my biggest weakness." He said gruffly before he turned to seek out Bryn.

Satisfied in knowing that Khol would bring Bryn back to me, in a manner of speaking, I sunk back down on the bed and studied the note that had to be from the dragon Queen. The first part of *let him go* had already come to pass, but what about the second part? How long would I have to remain in this cabin? I had a sinking feeling I wasn't going to like the answer.

And what about the whole Bryn and Khol situation? By letting fate decide the outcome of who I would mate with, was I really being cruel to both of them? I was determined not to need either one of them, but I was kidding myself if I thought I wouldn't *want* either one of them.

I sat on the bed and stared out the window until the sun dipped below the horizon and the stars crested the night sky. Where the hell were Bryn and Khol?

6

"Paige Joplin Stone, awake now . . . for we have much to talk about and a very short time to do it in."

"Huh?" I mumbled as I reached up to groggily rub my eyes with the backs of my hands. Then realization hit me. "The Queen!" I blurted as I tumbled out of bed focusing in on her. But there was something not quite right. She stood before me, exactly as she had looked in my visions, except she seemed almost transparent.

"Be careful. You wouldn't want to injure the little one growing inside of you," she said with tenderness in her voice.

"What's wrong with you?" I asked without thinking, and then flushed with embarrassment. One simply shouldn't ask a queen what was wrong with her, at least I would imagine because I'd never met one before, human or otherwise. "I'm sorry. I—"

She brushed my comment aside with a wave of her dainty, yet almost transparent hand. "Surprisingly, you remind me much of myself at your age. Or rather I should say it might surprise you, because of course it's no surprise to me." She smiled at me and I found myself studying her more closely. It was the first time I'd seen her smile, and there was something very familiar about it. If only I could put my finger on what it was. She stepped toward me, distracting me from my current train of thought, and focused down on my stomach. Her gaze glazed over for a moment before she looked back up to meet my eyes. "He will be beautiful."

My heart skipped a beat. "You can see him? Can you also see who the father is?" If she could tell me—

"Yes, I can see who the father is, but I won't tell you."

"Why not?" I demanded in a shrill voice. "If you know—"

"Because it will change the path for all of you and I cannot let that happen. Too much is at risk already. Just know he will be perfectly healthy."

Then her words truly sunk in. *A boy.* I was having a boy. An image of Bryn when he was a child flashed in my mind, his black hair tousled and hanging in his bright blue eyes that always seemed to glitter with mischief, his patented smile complete with dimples inviting me to join in on the fun. My heart clenched. I wanted it to be his so desperately. "Why am I here?" I asked trying to dislodge the image of the Bryn that had first captured my attention when I was still a child myself.

"First I will answer your question of what is wrong with me." Amusement twinkled in her eyes. "I'm not really here. At least my body isn't. This is the only way I could come to you."

"But if you could leave your body, then why make me travel to you? Why not come to me if it's so important?" I was about to bombard her with more questions but then I stopped myself. She was the friggin' dragon Queen after all, not just some random dragon. I could at least *try* to show her some respect.

"I want you to be at ease with me," she said in a very Khol-like manner, in which I mean it was as if she had plucked the thoughts right out of my mind and answered them. But then again if Khol could do it, then I'm sure the dragon Queen could do it as well. I exhaled a huge breath as she continued on. "I'm very near death—I have been for some time now, and I only linger to finish the tasks I have set into motion." I nodded my head unable to find a response. She was dying, or near death . . . the same thing in my book. What is someone supposed to say to that? "My body is near here, protected by Dragos, who awaits my death to follow me into the afterlife."

That got a response out of me. "My biological father is near here? Does he want to meet me?" The real question was . . . did I want to meet him? And what did she mean by follow her into the afterlife?

The Queen's face tensed and she turned away from me so I couldn't see her eyes. "No, he has no interest in meeting you. Although he would never harm you—he blames you for the deterioration of our relationship and ultimately my death, and therefore his death as well."

After seeing what I had in my visions I could understand why he blamed me for the deterioration of their relationship, I suppose, but her death? And his? "I don't understand."

"Dragos knows the outcome of my visit here, but not the reasons. As for his death . . . he is my mate and he does not wish to go on without me. It's even doubtful if he could. Mates such as us sometimes follow each other into death because our bond is so tight." I inhaled sharply at her words. Was she implying something that would happen today—with me—would ultimately cause her to meet her demise? And my biological father too? He was my birth father and even though I was unsure about my feelings for him, I didn't want him to die. "I couldn't let him know the truth. It would have ruined everything." She began pacing the small area in front of the huge window. "There were so many pieces and one wrong step could have meant the end of this world. It still can. I looked at it from every angle, fought to find another way . . . There just wasn't . . . isn't. I sacrificed so much, letting him be with another, it ruined us despite our love, and I still have one thing left to do." She brought her illuminated golden eyes up to mine abruptly. "I must give my powers, and therefore my life, to you . . . my daughter."

"What?" I backed up until my knees caught the edge of the bed and I tumbled back onto it before sitting up so I could look at her again. "You're not my mother." But her smile, her face . . . "Everyone always said how much I looked like my mom," I whispered.

"That's why she was chosen."

"What? No." My mind was reeling. And yet her words, deep down, felt right to me somehow.

"Dragos impregnated who you thought was your mother so that the switch would be believable. No one, not even him, knew what I planned to do. He still believes you to be his half-human daughter—if he knew . . ." She shook her head as if trying to dislodge some thought from her mind before continuing on. "He must never be allowed to know differently. Not that he has much time left, but I foresaw that my child . . . you . . . if I kept you . . . you would have been killed in your tiny crib when you were only five days old. Instead, the other child was, and you were left to grow up untargeted by those who wished to strip the dragons of their future queen." I felt all the blood drain from my face. I had just learned that I had a half sister and she had been murdered in my place, and that I was apparently the future dragon Queen. Can you say brain overload? "I gave you up so I could protect you."

Tears had begun to track down my face and I sucked in one shaky breath after another. "Why are you telling all of this to me now?" I managed to choke out.

"Did you really think that you could be so strong as a half breed? Your powers took longer to develop as a dragon, that's why you received your first vision so late. It's also why your powers call so strongly to ones such as Khol. He only believes you to be half human because of your emotions, he does not understand that being raised by humans, even a full-blooded dragon would not see the world as most dragons do. The way we are is more nurture than nature, but he does not believe that. Most dragons don't. You've only just begun to experience what you can do. You need to know these things because it is time."

"And Bryn? How is it that another dragon grew up so close to me?"

"I made sure he was there. He needed to be. I can't tell you anymore about him without risking a change in the future."

"But if I'm full-blooded dragon then why can't Bryn and I mate bond completely? And—" *Holy Shit!* "And does that mean I'll be able to shift into a dragon?" The thought actually scared me to death. I had been relieved back when Khol had explained to me that half-breeds couldn't take on the second form of a dragon. In fact, it hadn't gone unnoticed by me that Khol and the others had never shown me their other form. Khol must have picked up on my fear of seeing it. Maybe I was afraid because deep down I had known what I really was and didn't want to accept it.

"You're not strong enough to mate bond with someone like Bryn yet."

"*Yet*—that means one day I could. That means one day I could fully be mated with Bryn." My heart leapt in my chest with joy. There had always been the question about if Bryn and I would ever be able to fully bond with each other, even after we'd both come into our full set of powers. Now the question was answered, and it felt like I had just won the lottery.

"If he's the father of your child, you mean," the Queen stated matter of factly. "Because isn't that what you decided?"

I dropped my head to study my feet. *Huh. I kind of need a pedicure.* "Yeah, it is." But could I really go through with mating with Khol when I could truly and completely bond with Bryn? Maybe I would never have to answer that.

"With my powers added to yours, you will be the ultimate weapon to extinguish those dirty little creatures that have been threatening our world." She hissed with disdain. "I'm just sorry I never got to know you, my daughter . . . or my future grandson. And I'm sorry that so much will rest on your shoulders alone. Things will get worse before they get better."

It suddenly occurred to me. "If I'm full-blooded dragon, then the child could possibly be full-blooded as well—if Khol is the father."

"Yes, but that information still won't reveal the father to you any sooner than it's meant to be revealed." Her face hardened into stone. "Now focus, daughter. Khol and Bryn will be back soon and there are still a few things left we need to deal with."

"Okay," I squeaked, hating how young I sounded.

"You must know that these creatures can only get a hold in people that already have a darkness in them. There are very few that are pure enough to fight them off. Once inside, after a time, they bond so completely with the human that the human no longer remembers it being any other way. They don't know the alien is in them, but the alien has full awareness. The human rationalizes the actions the alien forces it to make. I tell you this because there is a way to remove the aliens from the humans, but they will still target you when they are gone, the fake motives for their actions will still be firmly planted in their minds. You'll never be able to go back to your normal life if that's the course of action you wish to take. Or . . ." She paused and began to study my face intently. "You could just continue to kill them like your friends have been doing."

"No," I gasped. "Killing them isn't an option at least as far as I'm concerned."

A slight smile tugged at her lips and she nodded once with approval. Apparently I had passed the test. "Good. Then there is only one thing left for me to do." She strode over to stand in front of me and then pushed her palms against my temples. A sudden burning heat began to spread through me.

"Wait!" I cried out. "I still have so many questions. You can't do this yet!"

"The answers will be shown to you when the time is right. You will have the guidance to take control of all of your powers new and old when you need to." I began to feel light headed as the heat emanating from her palms began coursing through my body. "I am sorry about your hair," I bewilderingly heard her say. "Of course I am partial to the new color, but I know how much you'll hate it."

"What are you talking about?" I mumbled with distress. "What about my hair?"

But then a bright warm light engulfed me and I suddenly felt like a nice nap was in order as I felt my eyes flutter shut.

So many questions . . . I had so many questions. They were all swirling around in my mind as I regained consciousness. Was I really a full-blooded dragon? Then why couldn't I do the whole disappearing act that even Bryn had already managed to master? How could I have grown up with the people I thought were my parents, and never known I wasn't human? Why when I had been behind the boundaries of Khol's lair had I not been able to have visions? We'd thought it was because my Seer magic was blocked and my dragon magic had taken control . . . but if I was truly full-blooded dragon that would mean my visions came from my dragon magic. So why had I been effected the same way that Bryn had? Maybe the magic my people possessed and the dragons possessed weren't as different as we had all originally thought. But I guess I couldn't really say they were my people anymore. My people . . . or species to be more specific . . . was dragon. How was I supposed to ever get used to that—to knowing I wasn't even human? I certainly still *felt* human.

"Peej!" I heard Bryn's voice call out with alarm. "What the hell happened to her?" I felt warm strong arms scoop me up and press me into a rock hard chest . . . Bryn's chest. His enticing scent washed over me and I snuggled into him and inhaled with delight. I was home . . . finally.

"Amazing," I heard Khol murmur. "I didn't know. She hid it from all of us." It was in that moment I knew Khol understood it all . . . who I was . . . what had happened . . . all of it.

"Don't just stand there, heal her. That's what you're good for after all," Bryn growled, ignoring Khol's words.

"She doesn't need healing. She's perfect," Khol said with reverence.

"Peej? Can you hear me? Peej?"

I was completely conscious and fully capable of responding to Bryn, but I didn't want to open my eyes and deal with reality just yet. I simply wanted to remain burrowed in his arms, where I felt so safe and content. There, pressed up against him, I could pretend that nothing had changed between us. I didn't want to open my eyes and face the very real reality that I could still lose him forever.

"There's no reason to keep clutching her to you like a rag doll," Khol ground out. "Place her back down on the bed. She's fine." Uh-oh . . . the jig was up, Khol must have sensed

I just wanted Bryn to hold me and obviously he wasn't a fan of my plan.

"Bryn?" I murmured, pretending that I was just waking up.

"But then again, maybe I should give her some of my healing energy, just to be on the safe side," Khol spoke up, not letting Bryn get a chance to respond to me. "Give her to me," Khol ordered, and surprisingly Bryn obeyed.

I opened my eyes just in time to meet Khol's deep green gaze instead of the sea storm eyes I'd been hoping for. "What are you doing?" I hissed between clenched teeth.

Khol's eyes twinkled. "Why, healing you, of course, since you didn't seem able to regain consciousness quickly enough, pointing at the fact that you might indeed be injured."

I glared up at him angrily, but his face told me if I called him out, then he'd do the same in return. Ugh. I hated how he seemed to know every thought in my mind! "Stop it," I grated.

"Stop what? I only seek to make you comfortable, my little Queen." His hot, fevered lips met mine in a crushing blow, pushing all thoughts except for his caress instantaneously from my mind. His magic rolled over me like a tidal wave threatening to drown me. It was so strong; I'd never felt anything like it before. Held in his arms, basking in his power, with his kiss promising things that I couldn't quite fathom, I found myself wondering, again, what it would be like to give myself to Khol completely.

"That's enough!" Bryn's angry voice broke through my reverie, and caused my entire body to flush with embarrassment, or maybe it was something else.

I made sure to not look at either of them when Khol put me back down on the bed. I cleared my throat and swallowed in an effort to combat my nerves. "I'm feeling much better now. Thank you Khol." And that's when I swore I heard Jenna's voice in my mind. *"I know something he could do for you that would make you feel* much *better.*" *Shut up! Shut up! Shut up!* I thought vehemently at the imaginary Jenna voice. I couldn't even seem to find peace in my own head anymore.

Feeling angry, mostly at myself, I stood and stalked over to the bathroom, intent on seeing why the Queen had apologized about my hair. I wouldn't allow myself to think about the fact that me having her powers, even though I didn't feel any different, probably meant that both she and Dragos were already dead. And I most certainly wouldn't allow myself to think about the fact that I had been lucky enough to have two sets of parents in my lifetime and now they were both dead. I flicked on the lights attached to the mirror in the bathroom and gasped in horror at what was reflected back at me. "Oh. My. God." I reached up to touch the white glossy hair that was now in place of the strawberry blonde that had once adorned my head. Who would have thought that I would ever want that god-awful shade back? That's when I noticed that the eyes that were studying my new ghastly shade of hair were no longer green, but the same gold the Queen's had been . . . and they were glowing. My mouth fell open as I stared stricken at the stranger in the mirror who seemed to match me in mood and horror. "I need—" My voice came out shaky and high-pitched. "I need—" I tried again.

Khol appeared behind me and met my glowing eyes with his own illuminated pair. "What do you need, my little Queen?"

Not once, but twice he'd now referred to me as *my little Queen* instead of *my little Seer*, which had been his term of endearment prior to our little jaunt to the mountains. And I didn't want to be anyone's queen, let alone deal with the intimacy his nickname pointed at. Had Khol and I become closer than I'd realized over the last couple of months because I felt so comfortable around him? I hated to admit that there was no one I trusted more than him at the moment, not even

Bryn after he'd broken my trust by walking away from our relationship. But I wasn't a queen, not really, and . . . "Don't call me that!" I erupted. "And I need some hair dye, damn it! I can't go around in public like this! It looks ridiculous!"

"You can't dye it," Khol stated a little too calmly for my taste.

"Don't tell me that I can't dye it! It's my hair and I'll do whatever the hell I want with it!" Where did he get off thinking he could tell me first what to do about the baby who was growing in *my* body, and then tell me about *my* hair? I had to draw the line somewhere.

Khol's face contorted into the familiar look of aggravation mixed with wariness that he seemed to reserve specifically for me. "No, I mean, you can't . . . literally. It's the magic that has changed the color, and it's the magic that will prevent any hair dye from taking root."

"Bullshit!" I hissed. "Just watch me!"

"It's a waste of your time," Khol retorted in a monotone voice. I don't know if he was trying to be calm to talk me off the ledge, so to speak, but it in fact was having the opposite effect.

"Bryn!" I yelled, whirling around to take in his bulky form hunched over on the bed with his face in his hands, making me stop short. "What's wrong?" I made my way swiftly to his side and dropped down on my knees beside him so I could look up into his face. Well, I would once I got his hands out of the way. After a few short tugs, his hands fell from his face and he looked at me with tears glistening in his eyes. "Bryn?" I asked on shaky breath. What could possibly cause him to tear up, because Bryn wasn't exactly the type of guy who welled up easily? In fact, I don't think I'd ever seen him look so remorseful.

He reached out and wrapped a piece of my hair around his index finger. Slowly, while still staring at me, he brought his other hand to gently cup my cheek with his thumb resting near my left eye. "It doesn't feel like you anymore. It's as if my Peej is gone."

"Don't be ridiculous." I tried to smile but my face felt too tight. "I dyed my hair before and you were okay with it; this won't be any different."

His sea storm eyes sparked with dragon blue, making them appear fathomless. "It's not because of your hair . . ." He circled his thumb by my left eye causing my lashes to flutter involuntarily. ". . . Or even your eyes." His grip tightened in my hair and on my face, but not enough to hurt. "It's just all of it—when I look at you—you're not the Peej I grew up with anymore."

"Of course I am. I'll always be her." But was I really? Was I ever her to begin with? Or was she just an illusion I created for myself out of the information I thought to be true about me?

"No." He shook his head slowly while still staring at me. "She was lost to me before I ever really had her."

"What are you saying?" Was he trying to tell me that he didn't love me anymore? That too much had changed? My heart picked up speed as I waited for him to respond.

"I'm saying that if I thought you were too good for me before well . . ." His voice broke off and he stood abruptly. "I don't know if I can stick with what we agreed to anymore."

"You have to," I whispered. "You just have to." It was the only chance I had to truly be with him and he couldn't take that away from me. I wouldn't let him. "I'll order you. I'm Queen now, and you're half dragon. I'll order you to stick to the plan." I wasn't sure if I could do that, but being queen had to come with some kind of perks.

I expected a fight, the usual Bryn pigheaded stubbornness, but what I got was worse. I got acquiescence. "If that's what you want." He then turned to stare out the window, his next words a low rumble. "I am your willing servant."

"*Servant*? What? No! That's not what I want. Bryn, don't do this to me!" My voice was starting to climb octaves and I felt a wave of unfamiliar power wash over me. The heat coursing through my veins fueled my anger. But Bryn didn't respond, and he just kept staring out the cabin window like I hadn't even said anything. "Don't do this to me!" I screeched a second time.

Finally Bryn spoke. "I'll meet you guys back at the compound." And just like that he was gone.

Khol had remained circumspectly quiet up until now, but when Bryn disappeared, he apparently decided he needed to intervene. He grabbed both of my shoulders and shook me enough to get my attention, but not enough to cause me alarm. His green eyes flashed with anger as he looked down at me. "I've let this go on for long enough; it's time for you to grow up. Not only are you going to be a mother, but also you're going to be only the second ever dragon Queen. It's time for you to start thinking about something other than Bryn. You're not a child in high school anymore. You're a woman, fully grown. And he's behaving every bit the baby dragon I've accused him of being. He doesn't deserve you if he isn't even willing to attempt to fight for you." His nostrils flared in and out as his chest heaved with emotion. "I'm right here. I'll never leave you. I'll never walk away. And my words are more than just words, haven't I shown you that time and time again?"

What I wanted to say was that I didn't care—that I loved Bryn and always would no matter the consequences but—but I knew I would only prove his point right about me needing to grow up. Which would mean maybe the rest of what he said was right too. And the truth was, somewhere along the line I had started caring about what Khol thought of me. "We're sticking to the plan," I croaked. "So there's no point in talking about it anymore."

Khol's jaw ticked with tension before the planes in his face hardened out, his eyes cooling to reflect no emotion. "You will have to lead our people. It's the legacy that Mori, your true mother, left for you."

My lower lip trembled as I stared into his aloof eyes. "I can't. I don't have it in me to be a queen of anything. I'm not strong enough. I wish I was, but I'm not . . . clearly."

He wrapped his arms around me, surrounding me in his heat, a comfort that I allowed myself to accept, although reluctantly. "She wouldn't have given you the crown if she didn't know you were capable. You might not feel strong now, but I'll help you . . . I'll be your strength until you can find it in yourself to stand on your own."

"Why?" I asked, my voice muffled by his embrace. "Why are you always helping me when . . . ?" I didn't want to say the rest, but I didn't have to because I knew Khol would understand. He always understood. Why was he always helping me when I was in love with Bryn? Why was he always what I needed most, when I needed it, despite the fact that I so rarely showed him the gratitude that he deserved?

"Because a dragon's love is eternal . . . and unconditional. Denying you what you need when I know I can provide it would be like denying myself the air I need to breathe."

"But I don't wanna need anyone ever again." I mouthed the sentiments that I had been thinking barely a day ago.

"A noble notion indeed, but an unrealistic one. We all need others for something, whether it be the food we eat, or the shelter we dwell in. We—"

"You don't need anyone." I blurted out, interrupting him. "You could probably do everything for yourself, if you wanted."

Khol exhaled a long breath ending on a sigh. His arms tightened around me. "I need you."

"Me?"

"Yes. I need you to give me a reason to keep on going. I've already been alive much longer than you can currently comprehend, and that is why I grew weary. That is why I slept. That is why I withdrew from this world, taking my people with me." He began running his hands through my hair, his power tickling my senses, and I relaxed into him even more. "But from the first moment I felt your power calling to me . . . I awoke with a purpose . . . a purpose that morphed into a labor of love. Everything I do, everything I am is for you. If not for you, this world could have been destroyed and it would have passed beyond my notice. You brought me back to life, my little Queen."

Khol was everything a girl like me could ask for . . . caring, strong, smart, handsome, and even funny sometimes. And he was head over heels in love with me. More than that, he loved me probably deeper than even I could comprehend. I pulled away from him just far enough so that I could gaze up into his eyes. They were no longer cool and aloof, but filled with the vulnerability that a man wears after confessing the true depth of his emotions to the woman he loves. And that woman was me. "Khol—" I started but my throat closed up. I bit my lip, hating the fact that I was wondering what it would be like to let him claim me. Being mated to a man like Khol would definitely not be the worst thing in the world. Maybe I would even grow to love him back in the way that he wanted one day. After all, being a dragon put time firmly on our side. I then began to wonder what would happen if I gave him a willing kiss? Just one. And what would happen if that kiss led to more? Would I eventually forget what it was like to feel Bryn's body holding mine, and only crave Khol's? Could I abandon Bryn the way he seemingly abandoned me?

I stood on my tiptoes and reached for Khol's lips with mine, and when they met, he pulled me to him as if he might never let go. I let my tongue explore his mouth, the taste and feel of him unfamiliar, and yet not unpleasant, just different than Bryn. Khol let me control the pace of our kiss, even though I could feel the tension in his body urging him to take control. After a few moments, a wave of lust washed over me, blanking my mind. It was completely unpreventable from my current position of being pressed so tightly against Khol, and as all coherent thoughts were carried away, I deepened our kiss. Khol's answering growl of approval only seemed to spur my body's desirers on further, and with my true loss of control, Khol's tenuous grip on his snapped. We fell back onto the bed, which was conveniently close, and he covered my body with his.

"Let me make love to you," Khol growled against the bare skin of my chest.

When had that happened? I wondered.

"Let me erase the bad memory of the first time we were together"—his voice cracked as his warm hands deftly dipped below the waistband of my jeans—"and what followed . . . with me worshipping your body and laying claim to you the way I should have from the beginning."

I'm sure Khol didn't mean to stir up bad memories, but the mere mention of our first time made me remember the feeling of my heart turning to ice in my chest even as he delivered me physical pleasure. He hadn't raped me, but he had blackmailed his way into my bed by threatening Bryn's life. Shortly afterward I had tried to end my own life in order to save Bryn's. Khol had caused all of that to happen and yet . . . I had forgiven him . . . truly. Or maybe I saw the Khol that was currently trying to push his long fingers past the barrier of my panties, as a different man than the one who had done those things to me. And maybe he well and truly was, just like Bryn had accused me of not being the same P.J. he had once known, maybe Khol wasn't the same either. Maybe none of us were the same.

But I wasn't ready to let Bryn go, and I wasn't ready to pull away from Khol's touch either. I had absolutely no idea what to do. "Khol—" His name turned into a moan as his fingers finally accomplished their goal. "Khol . . . wait."

"Just let me do this just for you. Let me take away some of your pain." Khol's gruff voice seemed to tickle things on the inside of me and I shuddered. "Your hormones are out of control, I can feel it, let me take some of the edge off."

I couldn't deny the extreme lusty feelings that my pregnancy hormones seemed to constantly stoke. And no longer having a regular sex partner really seemed to be doing a number on my brain, and by number I mean turning it to mush. A thought dawned on me. "You made it so my morning sickness is gone." Funny, how I hadn't really thought about its absence until now.

He tugged at my pants and soon I lay before him with only one small scrap of silk keeping me from being naked. "Yes, and I could do so much more for you if you just let me."

I bit my lip and met his fire backlit eyes with uncertainty. "But you won't try to take it farther than I want? You won't try to claim me when I can't think straight?" Which I was dangerously close to already. "I don't trust myself with you." It had to be said, even if I hated admitting it to him and myself.

A small smile tipped up the corners of his supple mouth. "Then trust in me, my little Queen. My pants will stay on; I swear it. I will only touch and kiss you, nothing else. I will never claim you again unless you beg me for it."

What the hell was I doing? But I wanted it, so badly. I swore I would never make fun of Jenna again for being a slave to her hormones. "Okay," I murmured knowing I most certainly would come to regret the decision that my pregnant brain coupled with Bryn's fresh rejection was making for me. Khol was offering me both pleasure and acceptance, the two things that I needed more than anything in that moment.

The word had barely escaped my lips when Khol ripped my panties from my body. I shivered under his rapt gaze and fought to keep from blushing as his rough palms skimmed down my body only to push up underneath me to lift my core up toward him. "What are you doing?" My voice shook with nerves as he dipped his head to hover where his fingers had been minutes before. "You said touching and kissing only."

His eyes, completely filled with flames now, met mine as they looked up the line of my body. "I didn't say *where* I would kiss you."

Understanding skittered through my mind, pushing past the shock his words caused. I hadn't even considered . . . I just assumed he would continue to use his fingers. "Oh God!" I screamed as he kissed me long and deep in a way that I'd never experienced before. Bryn had wanted to do this for me, but I had been shy, despite everything else we'd done. And boy was that a mistake . . . I never knew what I was missing.

Khol's dark auburn hair moving between my legs was erotic in a way I never would have imagined. His shoulder length hair had fallen out of the gumband securing it at the nape of his neck, and the silky strands tickled my thighs while he focused on giving me pleasure. The man definitely knew what he was doing, of course he'd had plenty of time to perfect his technique on who knew how many partners, a fact I really didn't want to contemplate at the moment. I clutched at the bed sheets, finding that not enough, I arched up and dug my nails into Khol's shoulders, which caused him to practically purr like a cat—after all, he was treating me like a saucer of milk. I fell back onto the bed, my muscles coiling tight, my heels digging into his back, and then I felt his power push its way into me to heighten everything I was feeling times twenty. It was too much, all just too much, and I erupted into a million pieces of pleasure all the while screaming Khol's name until my voice gave out, followed by my body. I swear I didn't see anything for a few seconds after my collapse.

"That was—" I started, after managing to find my voice.

"I'm not done yet." Khol growled before starting back in on me.

"No!" I screamed in alarm, meaning it and yet not. Could somebody die from pleasure? I was pretty sure I was going to find out very soon.

Was it possible to love more than one person at the same time? I had always thought it just kind of a convenient notion that authors of novels and screen plays used to amp up intrigue in their stories. I could remember more than a few times while reading a book or watching a movie, I had laughed and rolled my eyes at the heroine for finding herself in such a situation. And yet . . . here I was . . . in love with both Bryn and Khol . . . at the same time.

I couldn't pretend anymore that when Bryn and I were semi-mated, my feelings for Khol hadn't changed. Under those circumstances, those emotions had been allowed to bloom without me feeling threatened by the very man that cultivated them. I hadn't even realized it was happening until the bond between Bryn and I had been severed completely. Then my attraction to Khol could no longer be overlooked because those feelings ran so much deeper than the superficial ones they had been when we first met. Khol wasn't a cruel, conniving dragon like I had originally thought, but just a man who hadn't known how to love me because he'd never loved anyone before. He'd been driven by his dragon instincts on how to claim me, but when push came to shove, he had sacrificed his happiness for mine. He wasn't stupid. Now that there was another chance to be with me, unlike Bryn, Khol was doing everything in his power to capture my heart . . . and it was beginning to work. I never would have let him touch me the way he just had if things were the same between us.

"Khol?" I whispered. He pushed my still sweaty hair out of my face as I curled into his side. He still wore his pants, as promised, and I still wore nothing, but at the moment I was too languid to care.

"Yes, my little Queen?" He couldn't hide the smile in his voice, and I for once wouldn't begrudge him his arrogance. The man deserved every little bit that he felt about himself.

"I just wanted to tell you . . . that . . . well . . ." Should I tell him how I felt? Could I? The nature of our relationship had suddenly shifted and I didn't quite know how to handle it.

"Shhh . . . my little Queen . . . as per usual . . . I already know what you're feeling. Don't trouble yourself in order to tell me." Yep, he was definitely feeling very pleased with himself.

"Oh, well then you know that this doesn't really change anything. I still love Bryn . . . too." I hated having to talk about it, but it was only fair. Although I knew this talk would be much easier than the one I would have to have with Bryn. Or did I have to tell Bryn at all?

I felt Khol's body tense against mine. "Yes, I don't need to be reminded of your feelings for him now though. Soon enough we will all have to return to reality."

I sat up and scowled down at him, my cheeks flushing when I met his eyes. They held secrets now, ones that only lovers truly shared. "I'm sorry. It's just that I feel so—so confused. About all of this."

Khol's gaze flicked away from me. "Will you tell him then? In the sense of fairness, about the intimacies we shared?"

Had he picked up on the fact that I was thinking about not telling Bryn?

"No," I blurted out, deciding on the spot. "I'm not going to tell him, just like I never told you about the things that Bryn and I did together behind closed doors."

His glowing green eyes flicked back to me with anger. "But I *knew*. Of course I knew. With me being so closely connected to your emotions, how could I not?" He sat up and threaded his fingers into my hair at the base of my neck. "So I ask you again, will *you* tell him, or will *I* have to?"

"Why would you do that?" I asked in horror. "What purpose would it serve?"

Khol bared his teeth at me in a mock smile, a growl erupting from his chest. "It would serve the purpose of you being able to see if he'll pull away from you even more. If the fact that I am your lover now too scares him away, then his love isn't pure . . . not like mine."

"No sane guy would be happy to find out what happened between us! Of course it's going to bother him! You can't tell me it doesn't bother you to know what Bryn and I've done together!"

"Yes, it *bothers* me," he hissed. "And it should bother him if he truly loves you, which he does, in his own way, but it shouldn't run him off. When a dragon loves, he loves unconditionally, and if you came to me after being with a thousand men, I would love you just the same. My love for you will never change, fade, or die."

"He's not fully dragon!" I screeched with frustration.

Khol tugged me closer to him with the hand that was still threaded in my hair. "But you and I are. And someone like you—a full-blooded dragon—will never be satisfied unless you are loved completely. The way you deserve. I had my doubts before, even when I thought you were half human. You will crave *more* than he can give you." *Yes . . . more*. My body seemed to call out, and fresh feelings of lust ignited in me, my eyes dropping to his lush lips on their own accord. What would happen if I initiated a kiss for the second time this evening? I hadn't exactly minded the results the first kiss had yielded. But Khol pushed me away and stood before I could make my move. "Put your clothes back on . . . what's left of them. It's time for us to return."

"But the note said—"

"That time has passed."

"How do you know?" I asked.

"I just do."

I hastened to pull my clothes back on, eager to get back to the compound and away from our fight. No good could come from it, either we'd end up saying things we didn't mean, or I would end up letting him claim me despite my determination to stick to my plan. But I couldn't help but wonder . . . Was Khol right? Did it matter that I was a dragon and Bryn wasn't? Maybe I wanted things from Bryn that his genetic makeup made impossible for him to give me. I'd always thought that love conquered all. And I believed that was still true. But maybe the question wasn't *would* love conquer all, but rather *whose*?

7

My liege," The short, stocky balding man said as he hunched over into a bow in front of his master. "I have news."

"Well," his master snapped, "stop sniveling on the ground in front of me and spit it out."

The man shakily pulled himself up to his full height of about 5'5" and attempted to meet his master's eyes. "There are whispers . . ."

"Spit it out," his master interjected with anger. "Whispers of what?"

"Whispers that their queen has risen."

"No!" His master bellowed, slamming his meaty fist into his desk. "Their queen has been gone for decades, presumed dead." A hush fell over the large room that seemed to tick on for hours; finally the master spoke again. "What of our contact?"

The short man started shaking uncontrollable at the question. "D-dead," he stammered. "The dragon sent only his head back, apparently—apparently—"

"Apparently what?"

"Apparently he felt very put out about the fact the girl was injured. The boy was to be our only target."

"The girl must die," his master growled, his human façade threatening to slip. "Find another way."

"Yes, my liege." The man made a hasty retreat toward the door.

"And Terrance," his master called. "No more excuses. I've grown to like this planet and all it has to offer. I'm not about to let the dragons and one silly little Seer put a stop to my plans."

The man nodded as he left, not wanting to linger for fear of having to bear the brunt of his master's anger. He'd gotten off light this time, but he had no misgivings about what would happen if he failed a second time. The girl had to die at any cost.

8

Khol ushered me back to the compound and deposited me in his room with the order to stay put until he came to get me. He muttered something about announcing me to the dragons, which I could only take one way . . . that he wanted to declare me their queen. I wasn't really sure how I felt about that, being that I was a little wrapped up in the current deteriorating state of my love life.

As my mind wandered, I couldn't help but wonder if the haphazard writing on my locker last year that had declared me to be a *slut* hadn't been a portent of the future, instead of just the words of some mean spirited student. Was I now in fact a slut? When the number of guys I'd had sex with had gone from one to two, because it hadn't exactly been my idea, it didn't feel as wrong as it did to have let Khol give me his intimate kiss when I was still involved with Bryn. The fact was my body craved both of them, and my heart loved both of them, but that didn't mean that gave me the right to have loose morals. I'd never thought myself the type of girl who would treat such intimacies with such a cavalier attitude. If not for the fact that it would have caused me to be mated to Khol, I probably would have begged him to make love to me earlier. Maybe I shouldn't have been so hard on Jenna all these years.

A knock preceded Khol's door swinging open and I looked up from my pensive perch on the edge of his bed to see Jeremy striding into the room. He smiled, a look of relief washing over his face. "Hey, Khol told me you were back. I'm beyond relieved everything turned out okay."

I harrumphed. "*Okay.* Yeah, whatever." If okay meant that my whole world had been turned upside down in a matter of minutes by my dear old Queen Mummy, then yeah, everything was okay.

His smile faltered as he studied me. "What happened?"

"Where's Jenna?" I grumbled. "I really think she's the one I need to talk to right about now."

He scowled and clenched his jaw. "She's with Macon, fighting."

"But I thought she broke it off with him? I mean that's the way it seemed to me."

"He doesn't want to let her go." Jeremy started pacing. "And I can't really blame him."

"Oh, I see." Although I didn't. Well, not really. I mean if Jenna didn't want to be with Macon anymore, he should just let her go, you can't make someone stay with you. *Shit.* Wasn't that exactly what I was doing with Bryn? I shook my head with uncertainty. No, it was different with Bryn and me because Bryn actually loved me. Jenna wanted someone else. *Totally different. End of story.* "Does he know about you two yet?"

Jeremy stopped his pacing and came to sit beside me on the bed. "No, there isn't any *us* yet. Not really." He then flopped back on the bed with a huge sigh. "I think she still wants to be with him."

"Don't be ridiculous. Besides him being a dragon and her being human puts a lot of obstacles between them. Obstacles that Jenna doesn't seem very inclined to wanna deal with."

Jeremy's eyes slid shut and he spoke through clenched teeth. "I don't wanna be her second choice just because it's too hard to be with him. You of all people should understand that."

"Yeah, I do." My thoughts turned to my baby and how I hadn't wanted Bryn to know that I was pregnant so it wouldn't affect his choices regarding our relationship. But Khol had let that cat out of the bag, and now everything was so tangled up that I was beginning to wonder if I'd ever get things unknotted. My hand rose involuntarily to my stomach. The motion comforted me for some reason. "Maybe she's just a little confused right now, but that doesn't mean you're her second choice. It is possible to have strong feelings for more than one person at the same time, maybe even love two people at the same time."

"Speaking from experience?" Jeremy asked a little too casually. I turned to look at him and I realized he was now staring at me with question in his eyes. I looked away quickly and bit my lip. Why did I feel like such a horrible person for loving both Bryn and Khol? "You can talk to me. We're supposed to be friends now, remember?"

I gnawed on my lower lip for a few seconds before exhaling a huge breath. I began to speak while studying the far wall, unable to meet Jeremy's eyes for fear of breaking down if I allowed myself to see pity or some other soft emotion in him. "Does that make me a horrible person?" Tears began to gather in the corners of my eyes despite my best efforts to stave them off. "I'm pregnant, and I don't know which one of them is the father. I love them both, despite everything that's happened, I do, I really do. And I don't know how to handle it." I paused and swallowed a few times trying to combat the sudden dryness in my throat. "Do you think I'm a slut, Jeremy?"

As soon as I let myself utter the words out loud, it was like I'd opened the flood gate and rivers of salt water began to track down my cheeks.

"What? You can't be serious," Jeremy exclaimed in utter disbelief.

It was then that Jenna decided to make her entrance, and a dramatic one it was indeed. She flung Khol's door open with such force it slammed against the wall behind it and swung back to hit her in the shoulder. She staggered more from the surprise of it but toppled over none the less and landed on her ass with a look of shock intermingled with anger etched across her face. She looked over at me and blew her bangs out of her face with a puff of exasperated breath. "What'd I miss?"

Jeremy left my side and hurried over to help Jenna to her feet. As soon as they touched, a huge smile spread across her face that left him seeming a bit dazed. I had the sudden urge to look away like I was witnessing something I had no right to, as if the look they shared was meant to be kept behind closed doors. *No us yet*, my ass Jeremy. I'd never seen Jenna look at a guy with the true look of adoration that she was currently giving him, lust yes, but this was definitely more than that. And like a light switched off, Jenna turned her focus from Jeremy to me and narrowed her eyes. "That's not really a good look for you, you know? I mean if you were going to do something drastic with your hair I would have thought you'd have the sense to consult with me first." How could I have almost forgotten? Of course my new aversion to mirrors probably helped, not to mention that Jeremy hadn't said anything. "And what's up with your eyes?" Jenna's face pinched together as if my appearance physically pained her, and who knew maybe it did. Although it was probably more likely she was just pained by the fact that she thought I went and had a major makeover without her help.

I raised my hand up to touch my hair self-consciously and fresh tears spilled down my face. "I know it's awful," I hiccupped.

Jenna came to stand in front of me and began to study me with her self-proclaimed discerning eyes. "This is why you should have come to me, grasshopper." Her lips twitched up into a smile. "But no worries, your sensei is here now."

"You don't understand. I didn't do this to myself." I motioned frantically at my white hair. "She did—the Queen."

"Huh. Well, she might be a queen of something but it's definitely not of colorists." Ugh. What did I have to do to get her to understand?

Thankfully Jeremy seemed to be quicker on the uptake at the moment. "It's not dyed, Jenna." His eyes widened almost imperceptibly as he began studying me as well. "Her energy is different . . . way different. I can almost see the traces of the magic that did it. It's permanent."

"That bitch!" Jenna hissed. "She magically fried your hair? What the hell happened when you met with her?" And as if the words took a minute to seep into her consciousness, she whipped her head around to look at Jeremy. "What do you mean it's permanent? Like P.J.'s hair is like this forever?"

"That's usually what permanent means," Jeremy retorted dryly.

Her face scrunched up into a look of pity as she turned back toward me again. "Oh, well, that's okay. The bright side is that you can pick any color you want to dye it. You'll have to do it more often to avoid getting white roots, but old people do it all the time so—"

"No!" I exclaimed in frustration. "It's un-dyable! I'm stuck being a white haired freak for the rest of my very long dragon life!"

"At least you're only half dragon so you won't—"

A strangled sound escaped from me as I flung myself face down on Khol's bed. "Just stop Jenna! Stop!" I screamed into the comforter. "Next maybe you'd like to bring up the fact that I don't know who the father of my baby is!"

I felt the bed shift, a signal that Jenna had taken up residence next to me and then a moment later more movement meant Jeremy had joined her. "What happened when you met with her?" Jenna exclaimed as if I was the one antagonizing her. *Typical.*

"I'll tell you what happened," I grumbled as I rolled on my side away from her. "She turned my already screwed up life on its head. I don't even know where to begin."

"How about with why the hell did she fry your hair?"

I had to talk about all the things that had been going on with me and I didn't even care what Jeremy heard, because I knew once I started talking it was all coming out. "I'm one hundred percent dragon. That's the first thing." The silence that clung to our little group told me I'd actually managed to shock both Jenna and Jeremy . . . a feat not to be taken lightly. "The second is that the Queen is—was actually my biological mother. She passed on her magic to me, which did this to my hair." I tugged angrily on a few affronting white strands. "And this to my eyes." I waved my hand in front of my face demonstratively. "By passing on her magic to me, I'm to be the next dragon Queen, but it also killed her and my father, even longer story, because of what she did. Bryn now has high tailed it for the hills because he thinks he's *especially* not good enough for me now, and I hooked up with Khol because I realized I love him too. But I still love Bryn and so I've discovered that not only am I pregnant with a child who I don't know who the father is, but I'm the future, or current dragon Queen, I'm really not sure, who is in love with two men at the same time, and—and—apparently I'm a slut now too!" I gasped for air having spit out everything without stopping to breathe or pause once, but it was all out there now.

"You are not a slut," Jenna stated firmly. "Who said you were? If anyone is in this room, it's me."

"Jenna—" Jeremy started, but Jenna cut him off.

"Please, Jeremy, don't try to argue that I'm not. I know what I am. And so do you. Just because . . . things are developing between us . . . well, it doesn't change my past."

"But—"

"No buts about it. We're going to have to agree to disagree then. Although, I'm sure we can both say that P.J. is not a slut. Who the hell told you that anyways?" Jenna asked me again.

"Me. I told me that I'm a slut. I hooked up with Khol and I'm still involved with Bryn. I just—"

"Oh for Christ's sake. It has to be the pregnancy hormones that are making you act all crazy. You were a virgin until after you turned eighteen years old. You've been with two guys. *Two guys.* Two guys doesn't make you a slut, P.J." She paused and chuckled to herself. "Unless, if you were with both of them at once, then maybe I'd be willing to reconsider calling you a slut."

"Jenna! Of course I wasn't with both of them at once! You know I'd never do something like that!" Which made me wonder if Jenna had ever been with more than one guy at the same time. Something I so didn't want to think about.

Her voice took on a far away dreamy tone. "Can you imagine being with Bryn and Khol at the same time?"

"No!" Jeremy and I exclaimed at the same time.

"Talk about ecstasy overload," Jenna finished up as if Jeremy and I hadn't just screamed at her to stop. "Anyways . . ." She seemed to internally shake herself. And it was a good thing too, because I couldn't help but feel just a tad violent toward her for mentally imagining a threesome on herself with the two men *I* was in love with. "You're not a slut, P.J. Case closed." She blinked at me a few times, and then another smile crept onto her face. "Wait. When you say *hooked* up with Khol, I'm assuming we're talking about more than kissing or you wouldn't be feeling so guilty. So . . . spill it. What happened?" She leaned toward me with an eager expression on her face, which caused me to stuff my face back down into Khol's comforter.

"I don't wanna talk about it," I said.

"Oh, but you're going to." Jenna's voice had taken on a hard edge. "I'm not leaving until you do." And I knew she wasn't bluffing. I knew she'd sit there and pester me until I told her exactly what happened between Khol and me.

My face heated as memories of his intimate kiss skittered across my mind. "Maybe it's genetic," I mumbled to myself.

"What is?" Jenna asked.

"Me and my slut like behavior."

"For the last time . . . you are not a slut," Jenna practically growled. "You're just trying to avoid talking about what happened between you and Khol. You're not fooling me."

I sighed. "Maybe I am, but that doesn't change the truth. Khol told me once that dragon females were nearly insatiable when it comes to . . . well, you know. So maybe I just can't help it."

"Or you just happen to want Khol and Bryn. If you were a genetic slut then you would have been putting out years ago. And again I will say . . . being with two guys doesn't make you a slut. Now . . . time to spill what happened between you and Khol. No more subject changes." Jenna resumed her eager stare.

"Fine," I grated. "Khol and I . . . well I let Khol . . . he—"

"Just say it!" Jenna demanded. "What? What? What? He what?"

"Well he . . ." I wasn't sure if I could actually say it out loud. "He . . . kissed me—"

"And!" Jenna leaned forward on the bed, reminding me very much of a vulture waiting to scavenge a body.

"It wasn't a regular kiss . . ." My whole body flushed, and my heart began to race as I again thought of what I'd let Khol do to me.

"Oh my God! Just spit it out already!"

I squeezed my eyes shut. "He kissed me . . . well . . ." I pointed down toward the general vicinity of my middle, opening my eyes to meet Jenna's confused brown pools. "Down there," I hissed, looking at her with meaning. *Come on Speaker—get there faster.*

I saw comprehension wash over her as a grin spread across her face. "Holy shit! You let Khol go down on you?" She started bouncing up and down on the bed and I resumed my ostrich head in the sand position . . . a.k.a. my face stuffed into Khol's comforter.

"You did!" Jenna exclaimed with excitement. "Did you like it? I mean was it good? I need details!"

"I think I'm gonna head out now," I heard Jeremy mumble. "I got some—stuff to do. I'll see you guys later." He scuffled out of the room, his face flushed with embarrassment.

Neither Jenna or I acknowledged Jeremy's leaving, but as soon as the door clicked shut signaling he was gone, Jenna exploded into girly excitement. "Details! I need details! EEEEEE! I can't believe you let him do that to you! I'm so proud! Oh wait . . . did you reciprocate? Come on P.J. . . . I need details!"

I rolled onto my back and stared at the ceiling. "Yeah, it was good. Beyond good, I've never felt anything like it. Plus, with his magic . . . yeah . . . like I said, I've never felt anything like it." I worried my bottom lip between my teeth. "And no, I didn't reciprocate."

"Let me get this straight." Jenna's eyes had widened to resemble tiny saucers. "He went down on you, and he didn't even expect you to do it back?"

"He said he just wanted to help me take the edge off . . . You know, because of the extra hormones I've got going on with my pregnancy."

Jenna flopped back onto the bed beside me with a huge sigh. "He's got it bad for you. No joke. If that isn't love then I don't know what is. Plus, all the other stuff he's always doing for you, but he's still a guy, you know. You're so lucky." She exhaled a loud demonstrative sigh.

"Macon loves you, and so does Jeremy."

"Yeah well, Macon acts like reciprocation is his God given right. I used to think it was kind of hot how he took all the control and everything, but now I mostly think it's annoying."

"Jeremy wouldn't do that." I'd always liked Jeremy and I couldn't pass up the opportunity to put in a good word for him. "Jeremy really cares about you, you know."

"Yeah, yeah, yeah." Jenna waved her hand in the air. "I don't wanna talk about it. I wanna talk about what you're gonna do about everything that's going on with you."

I scowled in her direction. Typical Jenna. She didn't want to talk about stuff she wasn't ready to, but she was always forcing me to divulge information before I was ready. "I don't know what I'm gonna do." I crossed my arms over my chest.

"Well, I'll tell you one thing you need to do . . . Pick some new colors for your wardrobe because what you've got now is so going to clash with your new hair." She paused as if thinking. "And you're going to need some new eye makeup. Hey, if Storm from X-Men can look hot with white hair, then you can too. We'll make it work."

I started to giggle as I mentally pictured Jenna trying to dress me up in various superhero type costumes. "I'm not a superhero, Jenna. Just—"

She rolled to face me at the same time I rolled to face her. "A queen." We both burst into laughter.

"Who would have ever thought our lives would have gotten so complicated?" I said, grasping at my side because I was laughing so hard. It was all so funny because it all . . . wasn't.

"Certainly not me," she barked out. "I used to be worried we'd miss out on all the adventures. And"—she clutched at her side too—"I used to worry you'd die a virgin. Ha! Look at you now!"

"Hey! Not funny!" But I couldn't help but laugh harder. It felt good to just let go of some of the tension with Jenna. It made me feel like some of the weight had been lifted off of my shoulders . . . even if it was only temporary.

A prickling of power slid across my skin causing goose bumps to erupt all over my body. I sucked in a ragged breath a split second before Khol appeared a few feet in front of the bed. "That's new," I muttered as I locked eyes with him.

"Oh hey, Khol," Jenna said. "We were just talking about you." She giggled. "All good stuff, I promise. But I have a few questions for you . . ."

"Jenna, stop!" God only knew what kind of questions she had for Khol.

She turned to me with an over exaggerated pout. "Fine, then." Her eyes sparkled with mischief. "I'll just leave you two alone. Just one question first . . ."

"Get out Jenna!" I yelled. "I'll talk to you later." I gave her my best stern face, which actually seemed to work.

"Alright," she said in a singsong voice. "I'll see you two later." She practically skipped from the room with delight.

I turned to address Khol, my face heating with embarrassment. "Sorry about that. I—"

Khol stole the words from my mouth with a blinding smile. "It makes me happy to see you smiling again, my little Queen." He dropped down on his knees in front of me. "I only wish that I had been the one to lighten your mood." He cupped my face in his large warm hands, his eyes flaring brighter.

The vision slammed into me, forcing the air from my lungs as I gasped to breathe. Unlike some of the visions I've had in the past, it was almost as if I was watching two TV screens at the same time. I could still see Khol as clear as day in front of me, but I also saw a second scene unfolding in front of me that dragged my attention toward it.

"Fight for her if you love her," Khol growled as he stepped into the space directly in front of Bryn.

"I thought you'd be happy if I walked away," Bryn slumped into himself, a look of defeat etched into every plane on his face. "You're the better man . . . or rather dragon . . . You win."

Khol grabbed Bryn by the front of his shirt, his eyes erupting into flames. "I will win this battle fair and square, not because you simply gave up," Khol spat the last words with distain, as if giving up were the worst thing anyone could ever do.

"We'll wait to see who the father is, like we agreed. That's all I can promise." Bryn wasn't even struggling against Khol; he seemed utterly and totally broken.

"You and I both know she won't be able to stick to that, she always has and always will follow her heart. She'll try, but she is after all a female dragon." Khol's lips turned up at the corners in a cruel smile. "She's already wavering in her decision. I plan to take advantage of any opportunity she'll give me. I'll claim her before the child is born, if her will slips for even a moment, I'll claim her."

"Why are you telling me this?" Bryn whispered, his eyes flaring dragon blue for the briefest of moments.

"Because I love her, and I know she would never forgive me a second time if I tried to rip you away from her. I need to make sure she feels you had a fair chance. But I can't fight my instincts. I will claim her."

"I know you love her, maybe even as much as I do. But that's why I'm walking away, because I can't protect her. I love her too much to see her suffer because of my selfishness."

"This will be the only warning you get," Khol stated with force. "Do not upset her needlessly when it's too late for the two of you. There's no going back this time, once she's mine . . . she's mine."

Bryn pulled free of Khol's grasp and bared his teeth at him. "Message received and noted. Now leave me the hell alone."

The vision faded away slowly and I found myself staring into Khol's eyes. "What did you see, my little Queen?"

"You don't know?" I breathed.

"No. The vision was closed to me for some reason. Tell me what you saw."

"It was just Bryn and you talking . . . about me. You told him to fight for me—you told him—"

"The Queen's powers are beginning to show themselves in you. I know of which conversation you're referring to because it only just occurred, before I came to see you here." Khol pushed the hair on the left side of my face behind my ear. "But it was not meant for you to witness."

"Yeah, I kind of got that," I said dryly. "So you plan on seducing me away from Bryn to break our bargain?"

Khol hesitated for a moment before responding. "Yes. I've made no secret about my desire to claim you . . . the right way this time."

I tried to be mad at Khol as I stared into his strong chiseled face, meeting his fire-consumed eyes. I tried to be mad at him as I ran my fingertips over his high cheekbones and brought the fingers of one of my hands to caress his firm and yet supple lips. I tried to be mad at him as he gripped my hair at the base of my neck and tugged gently as he sucked one of my fingers into his mouth, reminding me of other things his oh so talented mouth could do. And I tried to be mad at him as his free hand slipped up to pull me closer to him, eliciting a moan from me. "I can't trust you not to cheat," I murmured.

"No, you can't." He nibbled on my fingertips before letting my hand drop away so he could claim my lips. I clutched at him, unsure of whether to push him away or pull him closer, my body craving his touch, and yet my mind screaming at me to punish him for his actions.

"Let's end this now." He began kissing a heated path down the side of my neck and I finally decided that pulling him closer was the best course of action to take at the moment. "Let me claim you so that none of us suffer any longer. You saw for yourself, he won't fight for you."

"It could be Bryn's child," I said, trying not to lose control under Khol's heated lips.

"He still doesn't want to fight for you, and I don't care who the father is. I will love it like it is mine . . . either way."

"I know," was all I could manage to say; my brain was short-circuiting on lust. Khol continued his way down my body, nibbling, kissing and suckling. He paused to tug at my pants and alarm bells began sounding in my head. I knew he was intending to wear me down slowly, another few rounds of what he'd done to me before and I'd be begging for him to make love to me, consequences be damned. So I decided to do whatever I could to prevent that scenario from happening. "Wait . . . stop!" I said with desperation. "Let me—" Let me what? Then my thoughts went to what Jenna had asked earlier. "Let me . . . reciprocate." Khol stopped short, his heated gaze resting heavily upon me. "Please, I want to." I pushed up from my prone position and dipped down on my knees in front of him. As I unzipped his pants, I felt Khol's body thrum with tension. He seemed almost reluctant to let me repay his favor from earlier, or maybe he saw my aversion tactic for what it was.

Khol caught my head in both of his hands and he forced me to look up at him. "Are you sure you want to do this?" His voice came out sounding strained, and broke an octave lower about halfway through.

I searched my feelings, asking myself if I really wanted to do for Khol, something that I'd only ever done for Bryn, and only a handful of times at that. But the answering clench of my stomach followed by a rush of heat to my middle let me know that I did indeed want to give Khol this particular gift. "I'm sure," I rasped. I was surprised at my feelings, but I didn't doubt them. The more I thought about it, the more I liked the idea of me taking control of Khol, of me having power over him in that kind of intimate way. "Now just sit back and relax," I commanded.

And Khol obeyed.

9

"No. Just stop. I let you curl my hair but you're not attacking me with hairspray again. The last time I let you at me with that stuff I had to deep condition . . . twice . . . before I could even get a brush through it." I scowled at Jenna, who was currently brandishing the biggest can of hairspray I'd ever seen.

Her brows furrowed together with annoyance. "Just a little bit, or your hair's gonna fall."

I stood abruptly and scrambled away from her, waving my hands around my head to keep her from spraying at me on the run. "I said no!"

"Come on, P.J., I don't see what the big deal is!" She vaulted after me and pushed down the aerosol button on the top of the can and let loose a stream of spray in my direction.

"The big deal is that my hair is already white, if you spray it until it could withstand a tsunami then I'm going to look like a little old lady!" I crouched as Jenna shot another stream of hairspray at me.

"Don't be ridiculous, you're almost nineteen not ninety, and without make-up you still look like you're twelve, so just let me make you look pretty for this stupid announcement thing!"

"No means no Jenna!" I screeched as I whirled around and grabbed the can from her, but still managed to get shot in the face. "Oh come on!" I coughed.

A prickling of power across my skin signaling Khol's emanate arrival made me stop and straighten up. I still hadn't figured out what was going on with me being able to sense Khol's arrival before he actually appeared, or how I could tell it was him, but I had a feeling it had something to do with my still new to me powers. I hadn't had the opportunity to test out if I could sense it with anybody but him yet, but I was sure I wouldn't have to wait long.

"Khol," I breathed as he appeared a few feet in front of me. The smile he gave me made me weak in the knees, and I knew the answering one I wore probably made me look like I was a little drunk. And maybe in some ways I was. "I'm not ready yet," I murmured trying to ignore the little flip-flop that my stomach did as memories of what we'd done together, of how he had let me explore him with my mouth with leisure, and of just how he tasted, rose unbidden to my mind.

"My little Queen," he practically purred, and I had to fight the urge to fan myself.

"Jenna, hey . . . um . . . can you give us a couple minutes?" I said without breaking eye contact with Khol. I wanted a few minutes alone with him after what happened between us. We hadn't really gotten a chance to talk; in fact, right after I'd finished . . . my job . . . Drake had called him away on some sort of dragon business. At the time I was kind of relieved because I was pretty sure I was about five seconds away from doing something stupid with him, but now I was regretting the lost intimacy that being with him afterwards would have surely offered me.

"Yeah, I guess," Jenna pouted. "But don't do anything to mess up your hair." She left the room grumbling under her breath about not being appreciated enough.

"I brought you something," Khol said with a twinkle in his eyes. He then produced a small rectangular shaped box from behind him.

"What is it?" I asked.

"You'll just have to open it to find out."

"Yeah, okay." I made my way over to him and hesitantly took the box from his outstretched hand. I wasn't used to getting gifts from men, especially men who'd seen me naked. *Except for Bryn*, my mind protested, but I quickly pushed the thought aside, and ignored the weird pressure in my earlobes from the small sapphire studs that Bryn had given me for my birthday almost a year ago. The black velvet box creaked its protest as I opened it, and I inhaled sharply at what was inside. Nestled on more black velvet was an enormous red stone surrounded by a dragon with outstretched wings. The dragon itself was intricately made, every small detail etched into the shiny silver metal with care. It was a pendant that I'd never seen the like of, and I was pretty sure I never would again. *Fire and Water*, I thought numbly, *ruby and sapphire*. Khol was a Fire dragon, and Bryn a Water dragon. The symbolism was too obvious to be ignored, but I decided to do just that. "That isn't real, is it?"

Khol snorted. "As if I would gift you with a fake ruby. And that's not silver, but white gold." I didn't miss the pride in Khol's voice as he informed me of the very expensive gift I was clutching in my hands. "I thought the Queen of us all should have some suitable jewelry to adorn herself with. You will wear it, won't you?"

"Of course I will." I usually wasn't much of a jewelry girl, but for some reason the necklace just seemed to call to me, and the thought of not wearing such a beautiful thing suddenly seemed ridiculous.

"Then let me put it on you." Khol took the necklace from my hands and stood behind me. I lifted my hair so he could have better access, and he placed the cool metal against my skin and fastened it. He then kissed the back of my neck before I dropped my hair back into place. I shivered belatedly from the combination.

I reached up to caress the pendant that was already heating from the contact with my skin. "Thank you," I whispered.

"My father gave it to me." I sucked in a breath as his words tickled my bare shoulder. "He told me to give it one day to the one I love . . . my *Anam Cara*."

"Oh. Khol, no—"

"I know you're not my *Anam Cara* . . . but no matter what happens, you will always be the one that I love." His voice had grown ragged and he pulled me back into him, wrapping his arms around me. "Wear it for me . . . please."

What could I say to that, really? "Okay."

His hand skimmed up the side of my body and came to rest over the pendant, which was resting conveniently close to my cleavage. "I have more gifts for you, my little Queen." His voice dipped to a low intimate growl. I merely nodded as my eyes slid shut and his enticing scent spiraled around me. It wasn't as familiar and comforting as Bryn's had become to me, but it was on the fast track to being its rival. "Drake," Khol called, and a feeling of power, definitely with a different feel than Khol's, ran over my skin. Drake appeared a moment later in front of us holding a large clothing box and a smaller shoebox.

Khol took the boxes from Drake, who shot me a smug smile before dipping down in a low bow before me. "My Queen. It warms the cockles of my heart to see you have decided to cast the baby dragon aside to be with my lord. A wise decision indeed."

I opened my mouth to protest but Khol beat me to the punchline. "That's enough Drake. No one asked for your commentary. Leave us."

Drake dipped lower, his voice almost a whisper, "My apologies, my lord, it won't happen again." And with that he took his leave.

Khol met my eyes and held them with his intense gaze. "Don't read too much into what Drake says, he of course sees things the way he wants them to be."

I bit my lip and swallowed down the angry words I was about to say. "Yeah, I know. Just as long as all of us are on the same page." But I wasn't really sure *any* of us were on the same page.

"Now open your gifts," Khol said as he set them on the bed.

I obligingly took the lid off the clothing box first and gasped my surprise. "It's beautiful." I giggled with delight. Inside was the most amazing crimson silk dress I'd ever seen. It matched the ruby in my new necklace perfectly. I didn't bother asking Khol if he'd planned it that way because I knew he did. I pulled the dress out and ran my hands over the luxurious material. "I guess this is for tonight too?"

"Yes. I wanted you to look your new role, and you deserve to be dressed in nothing less than the best silks and jewelry in the world, whether you were a queen or not. Try it on, I want to make sure it fits."

"Okay," I said with excitement. I knew it was kind of shallow, especially with everything else that was going on, but I'd never owned such a beautiful dress. Maybe I could blame it on the dragon acquisitiveness that had to be part of my nature since I was in fact one hundred percent dragon. "You're really putting the hardcore press on me, aren't you?" I asked with a touch of humor.

But Khol's eyes were completely serious when he answered, "Yes. I've made no secret about the fact that I want you for my own. Now that I know you're fully dragon, I also know what buttons to push to help grow your affections toward me. My tactics were different when I thought you to be half human."

Choosing to ignore his mini confession session, I simply wanted to put the dress on so I could feel the soft material against my skin. "Turn around," I commanded. "So I can—"

"But I have already seen you naked," Khol protested.

My voice went up an octave. "That's different. You're a guy—you don't understand. Just turn around." He grumbled under his breath but did what I asked of him. As soon as I double-checked to make sure he wasn't peaking, I slipped out of my jeans and sweater and into the crimson dream. I realized that it wasn't the type of dress that I could wear a bra with, or my normal boy cut panties, so I made quick work of removing those garments as well. If the skirt on the dress hadn't have been so long and flowy I might have felt odd, but in the dress with nothing underneath I felt like some siren from the 40s or 50s. All I needed was one of those long cigarette holders . . . or was that the 20s?

"You look absolutely stunning," Khol's voice was warm and seductive. I couldn't even be bothered by the fact that I hadn't told him he could turn around yet.

I walked over to the bed to open what I was already sure were a matching pair of shoes, and I wasn't disappointed. They were a low-heeled set of elegant slippers that actually appeared to exude comfort. I slipped them on and turned to deliver Khol a dazzling smile. "Thank you. It's all so amazing." Nothing like a little retail pick-me-up to brighten a girl's mood.

Khol came to me in a blur of speed, wrapping his arms around me and tipping my face up toward his. "Believe me, the pleasure is all mine." He brushed his lips against mine at first softly before he deepened our kiss, and I was suddenly *very* aware that I had nothing on underneath my dress.

"You're just lucky I didn't do her make-up yet," Jenna's petulant voice cut into my Khol induced fog.

He reluctantly pulled away from me, but his heated gaze caused me to flush under its intensity. "I'll leave the two of you, for now. Call for me when you're ready." The question was would I ever be ready? For Khol that is? I was so out of my league with him, and he was playing by a set of rules that I'd barely been introduced to.

"Wow," Jenna said as she surveyed my new look, compliments of Khol. "Who would have thought any straight man could dress a woman so well." She nodded her head in approval. "The man knows what he's doing." A wicked grin spread across her face. "In more ways than one."

"Shut up and finish helping me get ready. I don't need your running commentary," I said with a small smile threatening to outbreak on my face, I was feeling more than giddy. Khol had really stepped up his game lately, in and out of the bedroom. I went to stand in front of the bathroom mirror again and was surprised by the image that was reflected back at me. I hardly recognized myself. The red of the dress combined with my white hair, and large dragon pendant, made me look completely non-human, but then again I guess I wasn't . . . human that is. My hair had mostly grown out of the long angled bob it had been cut into and it hung in loose curls just past my shoulders. The gold of my eyes picked up the red of my dress and made them seem more of an amber shade. I would definitely be believable as a dragon Queen if I did say so myself, and the new look was even starting to grow on me . . . a little.

"That's one hell of a rock. I'm guessing it's real?" Jenna eyed the ruby centerpiece of my dragon pendant. "Does it mean something special? I mean is it like royal jewelry or something?"

I ran my hand over the necklace idly as Jenna began applying my make-up. "No, it's just a gift from Khol. But I do think it's appropriate, with the dragon and all."

"*Just* a gift." She snorted. "I wish someone would give me something like that. But yeah, it seems to fit you perfectly."

Her words suddenly made me want to tear the pendant from my neck. Everything about it seemed to declare me changed and different, because the fact that it fit me perfectly now . . . well I knew something like it would never have been me before. I inhaled and exhaled a few times to keep me from doing something stupid. *I was different.* No point in trying to deny that anymore, it was time I just accepted that fact and stopped fighting it. "You almost done?" I asked, fidgeting impatiently.

"Almost, now keep still before I poke you in the eye or something."

After a few more applications of this and that, Jenna announced my transformation complete. As I stood I caught the hem of my dress on the heel of my shoe and to keep myself from falling, I grabbed Jenna's wrist . . . and was rewarded with being thrown into another vision.

"Hey Khol," Jenna said as she sashayed through the open door of his bedroom. In the back of my mind I noted that Jenna's hair was rainbow colored, so this had to be another vision from the past. And from the look of Khol's bedroom, it seemed like this vision took place when we had been in the dragon realm in Khol's lair.

"What is it that you require, little Speaker?" Khol didn't even turn to look at her as she walked further into the room.

"Well, it's not really just what I require, but maybe what you require too." She ran her fingertips down his back and around him, then down his chest when she came to stand in front of him. There was no question what she wanted. She stood on

her tiptoes and attempted to wrap her arms around his neck, but Khol was too tall for her, so she settled her hands back on his chest. "So what do you say?" She batted her eyelashes up at him and smiled.

"I'm in love with another, which you already know." Khol locked her wrists in his hands and took a step back from her.

Jenna rolled her eyes. "Who is currently doing the nasty with her new mate, and that isn't you in case you haven't noticed." She wriggled one hand free from him and ran it down his front. "I just thought I could comfort you is all."

A low growl escaped from Khol's throat. "I will never seek comfort from you."

Jenna frowned and dropped her hand away from him. "It's not like she's going to care. She's with Bryn. She loves Bryn. In fact, she tried to off herself after you were with her. I'm thinking that pretty much means you don't have a shot in hell with her."

"Get out," Khol's voice sounded barely human. "Get out before I throw you out!"

Alarm registered across Jenna's face and she scurried for the door, shutting it quickly behind her. As soon as she was gone, Khol started pacing back and forth, a wild look in his eyes. He then stalked into the bathroom, halting in front of the very same bathtub where I had attempted to end my life. The tub looked clean, no trace of my blood anywhere to be seen. Khol stared at the empty tub for a few more minutes before he dropped to his knees clutching at the sides. An inhuman roar wretched from his chest just as he ripped the tub from the ground and threw it against the large mirror on the opposite wall, the sound of shattering glass echoed in my ears. He then continued his rampage, obliterating almost every square inch of the bathroom.

When he was finished, he stood surveying his work, his breathing ragged. "Drake," he called out hoarsely.

The large dragon appeared a second later and dropped down into a deep bow. "My lord."

"Take care of this," Khol said with no emotion. "And speak of it to no one."

"That, of course, is a given, my lord," Drake responded in the same emotionless tone. He then shifted and stood facing Khol with question and worry intermingled on his face. "If I may be so bold to ask . . . why did you not merely kill him?"

Khol picked up a piece of the broken tub and studied it for a moment before answering. "She would never have forgiven me. I know that now."

"But she would be yours."

"Not completely. Not in the way that I truly desire her to be." Khol's face contorted into a mask of pain for the briefest of moments before becoming emotionless again.

"I do not understand, my lord. It is the way of the dragon."

"But it is not the way of love." Khol clenched and unclenched his fists. "And I fear love makes me grow weak." He whirled around and disappeared.

Drake remained motionless staring at the spot where Khol had just been. "I fear that too, my lord," he whispered to himself.

I looked up at Jenna and let go of her wrist. So many emotions were swirling around in me at once. The first was my shock at seeing a side of Khol that he'd never let me see before, a side of him that made me love him just a little bit more than I had a few moments ago. And the second was an irrational anger at Jenna for her attempt at trying to seduce him. I knew logically that I'd been with Bryn, and that Jenna would have seen nothing wrong by going after Khol who I had no real claims on . . . but the dragon in me roared at the horrible offense.

"You tried to seduce Khol," I growled at her. "And you never even said anything."

"Uhh . . . duh! Why wouldn't I try to seduce him? He's smoking hot, and I wasn't serious with Macon yet, and—besides you were with Bryn!" She cried out the last part with outrage. "I didn't do anything wrong!"

"If you didn't think you did anything wrong, then why did you never say anything?" I could feel my dragon fire magic rising up from underneath the surface and I fought to keep it under control. My mind conjured up an image of what Khol and I had done together, but with Jenna in my place. I think my blood actually began to boil. "Why didn't you tell me?" I screeched.

"You were with Bryn!" Jenna screeched back, as she moved toward the door.

Khol appeared just in the nick of time as flames shot out of my palms in the general direction of Jenna. Khol grabbed my hands and began siphoning off my energy, but I still heard Jenna scream even though I knew the flames hadn't touched her.

I heard Macon's voice as he entered the fray. "What the hell is going on?"

"She tried to burn me!" I heard Jenna cry out.

"That's because you're a slut who tried to screw Khol!" I growled between clenched teeth.

"You were with Bryn!" she screeched back at me.

"My lord?" Macon's shaky voice said with question.

"Nothing happened," he responded in a flat tone. "Take her out of here." He paused and seemed to think better of what he said. "Do not punish her, it was before the two of you were seriously involved."

"Don't punish her my ass!" I hissed as I struggled inside the iron bars that were Khol's arms. "If you don't I will!" But Macon and Jenna were already gone, and the adrenaline rush that had been fueling me suddenly dissipated into wave of dizziness.

"Hush," Khol crooned as he kissed the top of my head. "You must learn to keep your dragon temper under control. You may end up hurting someone you do not wish to one day."

"But she tried to seduce you," was my lame attempt at an excuse even though the rational side of me was already beginning to chastise my behavior toward Jenna. She was right; I had no right to be angry with her for what she did. I had been with Bryn at the time and had no claims on Khol. So why did I still feel so betrayed by her? "You don't seem all that upset," I groused at Khol. Yes, he had advised me that I would regret hurting Jenna, but he didn't seem angry at all by my outburst . . . not really.

"I'm sure I don't have to explain to you why." I could hear the smile in his voice.

No, he didn't have to explain why he was so pleased, not really. He was completely digging the fact that I had gotten all crazy jealous over him. "Why didn't you hook up with her? It's not like you didn't know I was with Bryn."

Khol turned me in his arms and brushed his warm lips over mine. "Let's not talk about it."

"But I wanna know." I fought the feelings of lust that his soft kisses where inflaming in me. He didn't answer and pulled me closer to him in his arms. "I said I wanna know." And just like that another vision slammed into me.

Khol was sprawled out on his bed, a tortured pensive expression on his face when a soft knock on his door caught his attention. "Yes," he growled.

The door opened slowly and a tall beautiful woman, with long curly red hair stepped through the door hesitantly. I'd never laid eyes on her, but the minute she spoke, I knew who she was. "My lord." She curtsied low. "Drake has sent me to you." It was Shannon—the female dragon that Khol had once used to try and forget me. The memory of him kicking her out of his room so he could heal me played across my mind briefly.

Khol stood and glowered at her. "I didn't ask for him to send you."

She smiled at him in a flirtatious way. "But maybe you should give me a chance before sending me away."

"I don't want what you're offering me . . . at least not from you." Khol's green illuminated eyes sparked with anger.

Shannon approached him with more confidence. "No, but I can help ease your pain. Help you forget her, for I am dragon after all." She came to stand in front of him and dropped the dress that she had been wearing, showing that she had nothing on underneath. When Khol didn't say anything, she obviously took it as a step in the right direction, so she sat on the edge of the bed and leaned back in a blatant offering.

In a blur of motion, Khol snatched her up by the arms and pinned her to the wall. "Not on the bed," he commanded, his voice dipping to sound inhuman. She stood up on her tiptoes and tried to kiss him, his response was to flip her around and push her face first into the wall.

"Yes, you don't have to be gentle with me—"

"Don't speak," Khol snarled. He unbuckled his pants with one hand while still holding Shannon up against the wall with the other. He closed his eyes and slid into her. She moaned her delight, which only seemed to annoy Khol more. "I said not to speak—not even a sound." I was completely and utterly taken aback. I'd known the aftermath of Shannon and Khol's coupling, but I'd at least thought he'd been somewhat decent to her while they were together. Boy was I wrong. With his eyes firmly shut he moved in and out of her sensually. He even let go of her wrists to wrap her hair around his fist. Things from that point on seemed to go pretty smoothly until Khol broke his silence with a moaned profession of love . . . for me.

I was suddenly staring into Khol's illuminated green eyes, the live version, the vision fading as fast as it had come. My heart clenched at the realization of what I had just witnessed. I'd asked to know why Khol hadn't hooked up with Jenna, and my new powers, in a roundabout way, had shown me. He had used Shannon, and apparently even pretended she was me, or at least tried. He didn't want to do that to Jenna, my friend.

"Khol—" I started.

"I wish you wouldn't have seen that," Khol's voice was somber. "I was not at my best then . . . right after it happened."

"I had no idea." Apparently about a lot of things. One of which was how deeply Khol had loved me even then. Would it have made a difference then? No. But now was a whole different story. I reached around him and pulled at the gumband that was holding his hair back and then entangled my hands in his long auburn hair that spilled around his shoulders. I studied him as he studied me. He was so otherworldly in his dragon beauty. He could have been the inspiration for romance novel covers everywhere, but he was the real thing . . . and mine . . . if I really wanted him for keeps. He'd never forsaken me, not truly, not even when he thought I was mated to Bryn for good. "I love you," I said just before I brought my lips up to take control of his. I thought about giving myself to him right then and there, to ending the dilemma of who I would be mated to once and for all, but then uncertainty began to snake its way up my spine and into my system. I loved Bryn too. He'd been the most important person in my life since the age of five. Was I really willing to throw that all away for someone I hadn't even known for an entire year yet? *Bryn threw you away, not the other way around.* A very helpful, or not so helpful voice, depending on how I looked at it, whispered in my head.

Khol broke our kiss and pulled away. "Not now—not like this—not until you're sure."

"But I thought you told Bryn you would take advantage if my will slipped, even for a second. *It's slipping.*" I looked at him with meaning, partly wondering if the dropping my dress trick that Shannon had employed would work for me.

"I meant it when I said it." He placed his hands on the straps of my dress, obviously guessing what I was thinking. "But now that I might actually be able to have you the way I want you, with no doubts"—he cupped my face in both of his large warm hands and stared into my eyes with flames igniting in his irises—"I want that. More than you can imagine." I just stared at him and swallowed, not knowing what to say, and trying to *not* listen to what my body was telling me to do. Which pretty much entailed destroying all clothes that were keeping us apart at the moment. "I'll let Drake know you're ready for the announcement to be made. Do any last minute things . . . You have five minutes." And then he pulled a Khol and popped out of existence.

Great. Things just kept getting more and more complicated. What other kinds of drama would my new powers bring to me? It was probably better not to ask.

10

I shifted nervously as I stood next to Khol waiting to be announced. We had traveled to his lair, a place we hadn't been to for some time, because apparently we didn't have any rooms that were big enough or appropriate for the proclamation that I was the next dragon Queen back at the compound. Of course, the actual journey had been almost instantaneous since Khol had just transported me there with his dragon powers. Again I found myself wondering why I didn't seem to have the ability to transport myself. I thought it was the coolest dragon power I'd seen so far and I wanted it, damn it! I made a mental note to ask Khol about it later.

"Is this all really necessary?" I whispered to Khol. "It all feels beyond ridiculous."

He delivered me a patronizing smile that made me want to swipe it off his face. "Yes, it's important to make yourself known. To gain the loyalty of all the factions. This is the easiest way to go about it."

"But who says they're all just going to bow down to me? Not much has changed except for my hair and eye color. And the last time I checked, I wasn't getting much respect around here."

"Your hair and eye color is undeniable proof of your powers, none can dispute them. And with your powers comes the mantel of Queen." He took my hand and laced it with his. "I know you don't feel it yet, but you will one day be what your true mother was to all of us before, and you will be adored beyond all measure."

"Yeah, you're right. I don't feel very all knowing and adored beyond measure right now," I grumbled.

Khol dipped his head to skim his soft supple lips against my temple. "I already adore you beyond all measure." His voice broke an octave lower and my stomach did a little flip flop. I was going to have to have a chat with my traitorous body a little bit later.

Khol suddenly straightened up and placed my hand over his arm and began to move toward the huge oak door in front of us. "It's time," he said.

"But I didn't hear anything. How do you know?" In fact, it had just occurred to me that I hadn't heard anything, not even people, or I guess dragons talking.

"There's a sound proofing spell on this room. Drake informed me through telepathy that it was time," Khol stated matter-of-factly, as he continued moving me forward.

"Oh," I mumbled as my witty response.

I gripped his arm tighter and followed close beside him, my nerves beginning to ratchet up. At least I didn't have to worry about my morning sickness deciding to make an appearance, so I could also announce that I was pregnant in front of a bunch of dragons I didn't know. Khol paused and looked down at me, his eyes trying to assure me that everything would be okay, and then he pulled the door open. The noise of the room hit me like a physical force and I had to concentrate not to stagger back. Khol wasn't kidding about the soundproofing spell. But as soon as I stepped into the room with Khol, all talking and noise abruptly stopped, as if the spell had fallen back around everyone again. I swear if someone had dropped a pin I would have heard it. I kept my eyes straightforward and tried not to look at anyone because I had the distinct feeling everyone in the room was staring. I could feel their eyes burning into me.

"Look at her hair!" some unknown voice called out. And then the room erupted into chaos.

"I thought you said I was gonna be announced," I grated through clenched teeth at Khol.

"And you are." He led me up to the front of the room where I was then forced to face the crowd. I dug my nails into Khol's arm, pretty sure I was going to draw blood, but he didn't make any protests. There were so many dragons in the room, more than I thought still existed by the way Khol had talked in the past. And all the factions were represented . . . Red, Black, Silver, and Gold. "Behold . . . our new queen," Khol's voice washed over the crowd and one by one, they began to drop down on their knees to show deference to me. Once it seemed like everyone had taken the plunge, even Khol himself dropped to one knee in front of me, clasping my hand to his forehead. I began to tremble, not knowing what to do. My eyes skimmed over the crowd—most of the dragons' eyes were facing the floor, but I immediately caught the gaze of one dragon in particular who was not studying the marble, or maybe I should say half dragon . . . Bryn. He was staring at me, a look of anguish swirling in his sea storm eyes. When he realized I was looking back, he flicked his eyes to the floor as well. My chest constricted, and I fought to keep my composure. It shouldn't be this way, Bryn should be standing beside me, like he always has, not kneeling down before me like everyone else in the crowd. And Jenna? Where was Jenna? I didn't see her anywhere. I know we'd had a little bit of a falling out, but I wanted her beside me too. It suddenly felt like I was losing everyone I held dear to me.

"Tell them they can rise," Khol whispered under his breath.

"Oh," I said. "Right." I was in so over my head. "You may all rise." Everyone began slowly lumbering to their feet and Khol repositioned himself beside me and intertwined my fingers with his again. I tightened my grip on his hand as if he were my only lifeline. And maybe he was. "What should I do now?" I whispered to Khol under my breath, while still staring straight ahead.

"If you wish, I will speak for you. It is not unheard of to have a trusted advisor to do so," he whispered back.

"Yeah, do that." I sighed with relief.

Khol stepped forward and dropped my hand and I had to fight the urge to reach for it. *Ugh. Pathetic.* "Our queen wishes me to speak on her behalf." Khol delivered the crowd a charming smile. "She is a little overwhelmed by all of this. As I'm sure you all can understand." A few chuckles were heard in response and a low buzz of conversation resumed in the room. I took that as a good sign. "I'm sure all of you are wondering how this all came about, and I will tell you . . ."

A little while later I found myself back in my own room, much to Khol's dismay, and sprawled out on my bed. I couldn't help but feel small in it since it still hadn't been that long since I had shared it with Bryn. Here I was . . . a friggin' Dragon Queen . . . and I'd never felt so tiny and alone in all of my life. But I didn't want to begin relying on Khol the way that I had relied on Bryn. I would take a mate, and in him I wanted a partner, not someone that had to constantly take care of me. Why did it always seem like the men in my life wanted to take care of me? Or maybe because they were both at least part dragon, it was in their nature? And if that were the case, then would I constantly have to fight my own nature to not let them?

A knock on my door made me scramble up into a sitting position. "Come in," I called, hoping it was either Khol or Bryn. Or maybe even Jenna. I really needed to fix things with her. I just didn't have the energy to make the first move at the moment. I heaved a sigh of disappointment when a small female dragon with short-cropped silver hair stepped into view. I inclined my head inquisitively at her and she bowed down in front of me, which was pretty low because I was sitting.

"My queen," she greeted.

I studied the top of her head for a moment, and jealously that she got to have silver hair, which was so pretty, while I got stuck with white, spiked through my system. Why the hell did I have to be stuck with white hair? "Yes," I responded, not outwardly showing any of my inner angst. *Go me!*

She raised her face to look at me with violet eyes. *And she gets violet eyes*? I inwardly groaned. *So not fair!* "My name is Tatiana, my queen, and I belong to the Silver Dragon faction."

"Yeah, I kind of figured that," I said with annoyance as I motioned to her hair.

Her lips turned up in a slight smile. "Yes, well I know you are relatively new to our world. I just wanted to clarify."

"Look, I don't mean to be rude or anything, but could you please get to the point?" I was doing my best not to sound like a petulant child. I didn't think it was working out for me too well.

"No need to apologize, my queen, you are still young, patience will come to you in time."

I barked a harsh laugh at her. "Doubtful, but please continue."

She produced a white envelope about the size and shape as the one I had received from the old queen, my biological mother, when I had been in the Smokey Mountains. A feeling of foreboding washed over me. "My clan has been holding onto this for a very long time. Our instructions were to give it to you today, after the announcement."

"How long have you been holding on to this?" I whispered.

"Since before your birth," Tatiana responded.

"Oh. Well then, I already know who it's from. Thank you." I reached out and took the envelope from her and stared down at it wishing it would simply disappear.

"It was our pleasure to serve both the old and new queen," she said as she rose and headed for the door.

"Thank you again," I said without looking up at her. My attention was riveted on the small white envelope resting in the palm of my hand. I had no doubt who it was from. Guess my birth mother thought she could still shake up my life even from beyond the grave. I tore the envelope open, kind of wondering in the back of my mind, how the Silver Dragon faction had resisted the temptation to open it themselves. I personally would never have been able to withstand the temptation. Inside was a letter written in the same scrawling handwriting that had adorned my previous message from my birth mother.

My Dear Child,

It is imperative that you understand that what I am about to ask of you, if you deviate from it and think that you can find a better way, it will result in your death. And therefore also the deaths of the ones you love. I have foreseen it. Please trust in my powers, which are now your own, for one day you will need to rely on them. But for now they are still growing and changing within you. You, for the moment, lack the skill to control them the way that's it's taken me many decades to learn how to do so myself.

This evening there will be an attempt on your life by someone you thought you could trust. She has let a Rider slip into her, for all humans carry some darkness in them, and it will convince her you have caused all of her problems. She will try to end your life by poisoning you, so do not accept any nourishment from anyone this evening. It will save your life. But do not fear; eventually, if you follow the path I have laid out for you, you will be able to save her. That should offer you some small comfort.

Once the commotion steals everyone's attention, you are to strike out on your own; I've had a trusted subject place a care package hidden in the back of your closet behind a loose panel with everything that you will need, including a way to keep Khol from tracking you. You must do this on your own, and I'm sorry for that my daughter. But I will help you whenever I can. Find the strength that already exists in you.

~M

My hands were shaking as I struggled to process what I had just read in the letter. Jenna was going to try and kill me; there were no other female humans that I trusted—it had to be her. But I could save her if I followed the path my birth mother had laid out for me . . . That was indeed a comfort. And it looked like it was time for me to stand on my own, something that I had been wanting for awhile, so why did it suddenly have the feel of "be careful what you wish for"?

"I hope you have good news for me this time," his master snapped as Terrance entered the room.

"Yes. One of our most trusted is in place. The girl will be dead by week's end, as promised."

A smile slowly spread across his master's face. "Excellent. Most excellent indeed. Let me know when it is done." He flicked his hand in a dismissive motion. "You may go now."

Terrance breathed a sigh of relief as he exited his master's office. By the end of the week the girl would be dead and all would be well once more.

I found the care package hidden in the back of my closet, although I wish my birth mother would have had the forethought to warn me about the huge icky spider that had been laying in wait for me. I almost knocked myself unconscious when it crawled over my hand, and I slammed the side of my head into the closet door in an attempt to escape my creepy tormentor. But besides that, everything else had gone smoothly. My birth mother had thought of everything . . . wigs, colored contacts, fake ID, credit cards . . . and even some sort of magic bracelet to dampen Khol's connection to me. She left more instructions, which informed me I was not to put it on until after, when Khol was distracted, or he would notice something was wrong before I could make a break for it. The plan was for me to enroll myself under the false name she had given me at a specific high school to which I had been given directions. She said from there I would figure out what to do. She had even left a letter for Khol, which I was not to open, that had directions inside for him to follow. I won't lie; the not opening the letter to Khol was proving to be the most difficult part of the plan. I sighed and pushed my duffle bag full of everything I was taking with me into the back of my closet. I didn't want to risk anyone seeing it and therefore cause them to ask questions. At this point, questions were bad. The fact was, it seemed like I was running away, and in some ways that felt easier than anything I'd done in a long time. I just hoped I wasn't in high school too long because my baby bump would eventually show up. The thought made me bring my hand up to my stomach protectively. My birth mother wouldn't put my baby in danger, would she? I doubted it, but I couldn't seem to push the worry aside completely.

"Hey," Jeremy's voice made me jump about a mile and I looked up to see him carrying a tray with milk and cookies on it.

"God, you scared me." I chuckled nervously at him.

"Sorry. But the good news is that I bring a peace offering from Jenna. She wanted me to drop these off on my way to workout. She even made me promise not to steal any for myself." He smiled at me and set the tray on my nightstand. "I'll come by on my way back, okay? To talk"

"Yeah, okay," I interjected before he could finish. I was letting my nerves get the best of me and it was probably better if he just went to go workout so he wasn't in danger himself.

Jeremy eyed me curiously, probably picking up on my nervous energy. "She also said to tell you she'd be down to check on you in a bit, and if you wanted to talk, then she'd be ready."

Yeah, I bet she'd be down to check on me—to make sure I was dead. I had to fight back the laughter that bubbled up in my chest. "Yep, I'll be here . . . ready to talk."

Jeremy gave me one last curious glance before ducking out of my room. "Okay, I'll see you in a bit."

I didn't know what was weirder . . . the fact that Jeremy seemed so cavalier about how I had tried to fry his lady love earlier, like we'd had a normal girl fight, or that my best girlfriend was trying to kill me. Or maybe the weirdest thing of all was how I was now taking all of these things in stride, like they were totally normal. Oh yeah, my life was definitely not turning out the way I had thought it would, not by a long shot.

"Khol," I called out on shaky breath. "I need you."

Khol appeared almost before the last syllable of my request had left my mouth, and he rushed to me with worry etched into the furrows of his face. "What is it? What's wrong?"

I looked up at him and tried to mentally record every last detail about him, from his long auburn hair, to his high strong cheekbones that flowed up to his dragon green eyes. When I was with Khol I always felt so tiny in comparison to his large proportions, something that I'd always liked. He made me feel safe and protected, like I was the most precious thing in the world to him. I was going to miss him . . . more than I wanted to admit to myself. Khol had become a constant in my life from the first day he had literally popped into it. I loved Bryn too, but the fact was Bryn had been ripped away from me when I had needed him the most. I knew it wasn't his fault, and I never blamed him, but he didn't have an excuse now for walking away from me. Because he had done just that . . . walked away from me. His intentions might be sincere, and he might be doing it out of love for me, but that still didn't change the fact that I felt like he had abandoned me and that I couldn't trust him to always be there for me. I knew emphatically that Khol would never ever walk away from me, no matter what. He'd proved it time and time again, and truth be told, that was very important to me, especially with me having a baby on the way. I wish I wasn't going to have to leave him behind soon. It wasn't like I had a choice if I wanted to live, according to my birth mother, but it still didn't make me feel any better about the situation. How would he react when I was gone and he couldn't find me? My chest tightened as I thought about what he might do. I shook myself internally. I had to deal with the task at hand. "Jenna is trying to kill me. I mean not Jenna really . . . but a Rider got into her."

Khol studied me with sharp eyes. "Are you sure?"

I swallowed the lump in my throat. "Yes, my birth mother left me a letter. She told me a Rider had slipped into her and she was going to try and poison me and not to accept anything to eat or drink from anyone tonight." My lower lip began to tremble. "And sure enough Jenna sent Jeremy down with milk and cookies for me. She had to send him because . . ." Tears began to track down my cheeks much to my chagrin. I had told myself that I wouldn't get emotional over this. It wasn't Jenna, not really, and I would find a way to save her just like my birth mother said I could.

"Because if you saw her you would see the Rider in her," Khol completed my sentence for me.

"Yeah," I whispered.

"Then I must—"

"Don't hurt her!" I said in a rush. "I mean I know you're going to have to lock her up or something but don't hurt her—please! Promise me you won't! I can save her! I know I can! Just not now!"

Khol came to me and wrapped his comforting frame around me. "I know what she means to you. I promise not to hurt her."

"Thank you," I croaked.

"Drake," Khol called with his arms still around me.

"Yes, my lord," I heard Drake's low voice rumble in response a moment later.

"Go to the little Speaker, escort her to a cell, a Rider has taken up residence in her, so expect a fight."

"Should I just not kill her then?" Drake asked as if he was inquiring about the weather.

"No!" I exclaimed, pulling free of Khol. "Don't hurt her!" I met Khol's sympathetic eyes. "You go—please. I trust you."

Khol nodded. "I will see to it myself then. Drake, get rid of those . . . They are poison." He motioned briefly to the plate, and then he turned back to me and brushed his lips across mine. “I will be back shortly.”

A feeling of sadness washed over me as I thought about how I wouldn’t be there when he got back. I knew he would feel my sadness, but I was hoping he thought it was connected with Jenna’s situation. Soon I wouldn’t have to worry about him reading my emotions at all, and for the first time ever that made me sad too. “Okay,” I said.

Both Khol and Drake disappeared, Drake taking the milk and cookies with him and Khol off to imprison my best female friend.

I inhaled and exhaled a few times to try and center myself. It didn’t work, and for the millionth time in my life, I wondered who that kind of crap ever actually worked for? I raced to my closet and pulled the duffle bag with my things in it out of its hiding place. It was now or never, life or death, I had to do what I needed to do in order to save my world . . . and the people I loved. I placed the letter that my birth mother had intended for Khol on my bed where I knew he would see it when he returned for me. Again my chest tightened thinking about how he would react when he discovered I was gone and realized he couldn’t track me. But there was no time for thoughts like that now.

I reached into the bag and snapped the shiny bronze bracelet onto my left wrist. It was a perfect fit . . . of course. I turned my thoughts to the task at hand, steeling myself for what needed to be done and set out on my way. It was only the fate of the world that was depending on me to be successful. *Yep . . . no pressure at all.*

11

Your transcripts have already been sent over from your previous school. I just need you to fill out a couple forms and I need to see some form of identification from you."

"Yeah, sure." I shifted nervously from foot to foot as I dug into my bag to produce my fake ID for the elderly office lady. As I handed it to her, I tried to keep my hand from shaking. My birth mom seemed to have thought of everything, but I couldn't seem to shake the feeling that at any minute someone would see me for what I really was . . . a fraud.

The office lady looked over my ID and copied down a few things before handing it back to me with a smile. "Here you go. You can sit over there and fill out these forms." She slid some papers attached to a clipboard in my direction. "And when you're done just bring them back to me and I'll give you your class schedule."

"Okay. Thanks," I said numbly as I slid the clipboard off the counter and made my way over to the greenish couch she had indicated to me. The forms were pretty standard stuff, just asking for some information that I'm pretty sure they already had, but I filled them out anyways. When I was finished, I made my way back up to the counter and slid the clipboard back across the counter to the office lady. She looked over the forms briefly and then motioned for me to wait a minute with her finger.

"Here you are," she said after digging around in a file to produce my class schedule. "If you have any problems, just let me know." And with a smile and a nod she essentially dismissed me.

Of all the things I could have been faced with, going back to high school was definitely one of the worst. Not to mention that I found myself in the unfamiliar territory of being enrolled in a high school in Spring Hill, Tennessee. I'd never been to the south, unless I counted the vision I'd had about the Rider taking over Senator Bill Wexington, which I didn't. I wasn't even sure what the plan was beyond me enrolling here and pretending to be a normal high school senior.

I snorted. Yeah . . . okay . . . I was going to blend in no problem with my white hair and rainbow colored hairpieces that I'd clipped in to try and make me less old lady and more punk rock. I was currently channeling Jenna's old look, which I was worried might be a bit much for the south, even if I didn't really have a choice. I would have donned a wig, but that probably would have made me stick out even more . . . so multicolored hair and brown contact lenses it was.

As soon as I left the office, I bee-lined it directly to the girl's room. I had already missed homeroom and part of first period, so I figured I'd just jump right into my schedule starting with my second class and to pass the time hide out in the bathroom until then. As soon as I was inside, I let my bag drop from my shoulder as I gripped the sides of a sink and glared at my own reflection. "You can do this," I told my punk rock reflection. "You don't need Bryn, or Khol, or Jenna, or even Jeremy. You got this." My eyes slid down to the chain that held the ruby dragon pendant that Khol had given me. I tugged it free from my shirt and wrapped my hand around it.

"Then let me put it on you." Khol took the necklace from my hands and walked behind me. I lifted my hair so he could have better access, and he placed the cool metal against my skin and fastened it. He then kissed the back of my neck before I dropped my hair back into place. I shivered belatedly from the combination.

I shook my head to dislodge the memory and dropped the pendant back inside my black t-shirt. I wouldn't let myself grow morose over thoughts of either Khol or Bryn. They were a different problem that I didn't have time to deal with now, and yet without thinking I brought my hand up to my stomach, the motion still comforting me for some reason. "We'll get through this," I whispered to myself and my unborn child.

"Your stomach giving you trouble?" A feminine voice drawled from behind me. Her accent wasn't quite southern but there was a definite twangy undertone.

I dropped my hand and turned toward the owner of the voice. She was about 5'1" with long blonde straight hair that hung almost to her waist. She had the glowing stereotypical tan that I usually associated with girls from the south. Even though she was a petite little thing, she had some traffic stopping curves that made my jealously spike for a brief second. She wore a light pink t-shirt over a short jean skirt and cowboy boots . . . *cowboy boots.* I didn't think people actually wore those anywhere but on a farm. *Toto, we're definitely not in Kansas anymore, or maybe I should say Pittsburgh?*

I fidgeted nervously as I saw her take in my appearance. If she represented the typical style for my new school then I had even less hope of fitting in than I had originally thought. "I guess I'm a little nervous," I muttered. "It's my first day."

"I'm Laila," she said with a smile. "You're not from around here, are you?" She then laughed. "Of course you're not, with the way you're dressed and all."

"That bad?" I said with a grimace. "I was kind of hoping to blend in."

"You'll do fine. The guys around here will probably fall all over the new Yankee girl. They get all excited when they see something new and different. The girls on the other hand might be a different story."

Figured. I needed more guy attention like I needed another hole in my head. "Yeah, well I have a boyfriend . . . from back home. I'm not currently shopping for more trouble."

Laila threw her head back and laughed. "Ain't that the truth? Boys are nothin' but trouble sometimes."

I thought about all the drama, even though I loved them both, that Khol and Bryn had caused in my life, and I gave her a wry smile. "Sometimes?"

She stepped forward and linked her arm with mine. "Oh honey, you and I are gonna get along famously." She pulled my class schedule out of my other hand and began reading it. "We have almost the exact same schedule." She started walking and tugged me along beside her. "You can start counting your blessings, cuz I got your back now, hun."

I couldn't help but smile. Laila was like a smaller, peppier, southern version of Jenna. It would be nice to feel like I had a friend while I was off on my own trying to save the world.

"I don't think I can take much more of this," I grumbled to Laila as I tried to unsuccessfully ignore all the stares I was receiving at lunch. I suddenly wasn't very hungry, and I dropped the French fry that I was about to eat back down on my tray. "This school isn't very big; you think everyone would have seen me by now so that they could all stop staring." The other thing that was bothering me, which I couldn't tell Laila, was that her school was completely infested with Riders. It had skeeved me completely out at first, but I seemed relatively safe as long as I didn't let on to them that I could see them. In that case, my first day nerves covered up my 'holy crap my lab partner has an alien parasite inside of him' nerves very nicely.

"They'll get over it in a day or two," Laila replied with cheer. "Besides gettin' stared at isn't always a bad thing."

"It is to me," I grumped. This whole situation was bringing up bad memories of my last couple of weeks at my old school where I had been shunned and persecuted for things that I hadn't even really done. The girls had hated me there too, and the guys all wanted to hook up with me. The one explained the other. But at least I'd had Jenna and Jeremy there.

"So, how attached are you to your boyfriend back home?" Laila asked with false nonchalance.

I raised my gaze to eye her sharply. "Very. Why?"

"Well I don't know, it's just that only the hottest boy in all of Spring Hill High School is on his way over here right now."

And he had a Rider inside of him. "Shit," I swore under my breath, and froze in my seat as I watched the tall slender and yet completely ripped boy walk over gracefully toward me. I tried really hard to focus on his outer features and not on the duel imagery that usually freaked me out, but I was struggling. My breathing was coming in short little erratic bursts, and by the time he slid into the seat beside me, I was on the verge of hyperventilating.

"Hey, I'm Cliff, what's your name?" Cliff and the Rider both smiled at me, or well I guess they were sort of one in the same, but either way the thing was grinning at me.

"I'm P—Paige," I stammered. And now I knew why my birth mother had used my real first name on my fake ID.

With my nerves, I had started to say P.J., and Paige was an easy save after that.

"Well, Paige," the thing said with a slight southern draw much like Laila's. "What do you think of our little school? Prolly a ton different than what you're used to, I bet." An easy grin settled onto its face as he looked at me expectantly.

I swallowed at the huge lump that had taken up residence in my throat. First, I had to stop thinking of the Rider as an *it*. I had to think of Cliff as a normal, non-alien hosting, teenage boy. I tried to meet his eyes but cringed away at the duel imagery again. I was so screwed. "I . . . umm . . ." I stammered.

"Well, look at you, Cliff. You got Paige all flustered. She's kind of shy, you know?" Laila interjected, obviously trying to save me from myself. If only she knew the real reason behind my nerves.

"No need to be shy around me," Cliff responded directly to me. He then reached out and patted my bare arm with his hand, in what he had surely meant as a reassuring gesture. But let me assure you, there was *nothing* reassuring about it.

I stood abruptly, as if a current of electricity had been shot through my body, my chair toppling noisily to the floor. I'd been in close quarters with one of the Riders before, namely the Emo boy from hell when he had tried to kill me and then bludgeoned me with the back of his shot gun, but I'd never had skin to skin contact with one before. It was wrong, so very wrong. I began to shake as a vision threatened to force its way into me. What would happen if I passed out right here and now? Would any of the Riders be suspicious of me or would they merely think I was sick or something? *Too late for the what if*, I thought numbly as I crumpled to the floor.

I focused in on Cliff, who was standing in front of a bathroom mirror wearing nothing but a towel. His dark blonde hair appeared darker from his obviously recent shower, and moisture glistened on his well toned, and tanned body. If not for the duel imagery of the alien Rider inside of him, I might have taken the time to appreciate his vast hotness. As it was, I was fighting the urge to not dry heave at the wrongness of it all. I then noticed that Cliff was staring at himself with a slight grimace etched into his chiseled features. "What's wrong with you?" he muttered to his own image. Although I was sure Cliff couldn't see the Rider that was currently residing inside his body, the Rider frowned out from inside him, obviously not liking Cliff's reaction to it. The Rider's face then contorted into what could have passed for it being in pain. "Get out of my head," Cliff grated between clenched teeth as he raised his hands to press against the side of his temples. "This isn't who you are." It was then I realized I was witnessing a battle of wills between Cliff and the Rider inside of him. Cliff began to shake, and a trickle of blood slowly slipped from one nostril and oozed down his face. "I said to get out," he whispered, his voice affected by his effort. And then something wondrous happened. The Rider just kind of poured out of him, looking like not much more than smoke, and it reformed in the shape of the alien standing just behind Cliff. Unfortunately for Cliff, that was right about the time his eyes rolled into the back of his head and he collapsed to the ground with a loud thud. The Rider looked at him with rage and let out a silent scream before he just disappeared.

I gasped as I woke up in the confines of someone's arms. Someone's arms that weren't Bryn or Khol's. "Stop," I croaked before my eyes even managed to flutter open. "Low blood sugar."

"What?" Cliff's slight southern drawl answered me in confusion.

My eyes popped open in alarm and I looked up into Cliff's face, who still had a Rider staring back at me from inside of him. It was time for me to be confused myself. I saw the Rider leave his body. I saw it disappear. What did it mean that it was back? Why was I shown the vision if it didn't mean anything?

"I have low blood sugar. I'm fine. You can put me down," I said managing to sound much more stable.

"You're not fine. You passed out cold back there. I'm taking you to the nurse. She might need to call—"

"I said to put me down!" I demanded shrilly at the same time that I attempted to extradite myself from his arms. And for my effort I ended up back on the ground, on my ass. *Lovely.* My breath left me with a soft *oof* before I scrambled to my feet. I narrowed my eyes and glared at my would-be savior, and host to the Rider, Cliff, who was staring at me with surprise.

"How did you do that? You're stronger than you look."

Shit. Not good. "Adrenaline?" I said unsurely. "Yeah, adrenaline." I repeated with more confidence. "I don't like to be carried around like that, okay?" My mind skittered through the many times that both Bryn and Khol had both carried me in such a manner over the last year. A wave of homesickness washed over me as I longed for nothing more than to be back with them . . . where I belonged. And then a wave of nausea crashed over me and stole away any sentimental feelings I had been carrying as I proceeded to throw up right on Cliff's shoes. I wiped my mouth with the back of my hand and met his blue eyes with horror. "I'm so sorry I—" I what? Apparently my morning sickness was back with a vengeance now that Khol wasn't nearby to do his magic mojo to help me out. Any hope I had at blending in lay splattered all over Cliff's ruined kicks. But surely my birth mother would have seen this and taken it into consideration. I mean . . . she'd been ready for everything else. Right?

"There you are." A vaguely familiar female voice said with saccharine sweetness. Long feminine pale fingers, and yet strangely strong in their grip, wrapped around the bicep of my left arm and tugged me to a full upright position. I whirled my head around as fast as I could and met the dark eyes of probably the last person in the world I expected to see coming to my rescue . . . Nala. My lips opened and closed like a guppy . . . and a very surprised guppy at that. Nala and I had effectively been avoiding each other since . . . well, since we first met. She wanted Bryn, and Bryn was mine. At least he used to be. And wanting the same guy didn't exactly produce warm and fuzzy friendship feelings between two people. *What the hell?*

"What are you doing here?" I said while trying to cover both my surprise and animosity toward her.

She gave me what best could be described as a patronizing older sister look. Loving, but with a touch of exasperation. "Your mom sent me over because she realized you forgot your medication. She was worried something like—well, exactly like—this would happen."

I turned my head away from Cliff, who was now shaking his feet in attempt to dislodge my less than thoughtful gift from him. "Medication?" I mouthed.

Nala gave me a sharp look that was obviously telling me to go along with her story. Normally, just because of our mutual dislike for each other in our past, I wouldn't have trusted her, but I had a sneaking suspicion because of her choice of words that my birth mother had been meddling from beyond the grave again. "Oh, right, I forgot."

"What kind of medication?" Cliff asked with concern. "I mean—"

"Oh, she'll be fine," Nala interjected. "She just has an ear infection that causes her to get dizzy and if she's not careful, well . . ." She then motioned at the second viewing of my lunch.

Ear infection. Now why hadn't I thought of that? "I'm sorry." I mumbled in Cliff's general direction not wanting to see his face, or rather the Rider that was hiding behind his face. "And I didn't mean to snap at you either."

"It's alright," Cliff reassured me. "It just means you're going to have to make it up to me."

Not a chance in hell, buddy. "Oh, um . . . sure."

"Great," he said with cheer, as if he didn't have my puke all over his shoes. "I'll be seeing you then."

"Not if I can help it," I mumbled.

"What?" he said with a hitch in his voice.

"Oh, nothing," I said louder. "I just said thanks for helping."

The brightness in his voice returned. "No problem. I hope you feel better soon, Paige." And with that the hot boy known as Cliff exited stage left with the alien that had rode in on him.

I exhaled a huge sigh of relief and refocused my attention on Nala. Her long black hair was pulled back in a loose French braid and her blue eyes met mine as a smirk began to tilt the corners of his full lips up. I really hated how pretty she was. "So, care to share with me the real reason why you're here?" A sudden excited thought made fresh adrenaline course through my system. "Bryn and Khol—"

"Aren't here."

"Oh," I said, trying not to sound too crestfallen. I just hate feeling so alone and vulnerable, I told myself. It was *not* because I needed either one of them to make me feel safe. I was an adult woman, and I could stand on my own two feet completely on my own. *Right.*

"I'll explain everything, but not here." Her bright blue eyes scanned the empty hallway as if she thought someone might jump out of a locker at any moment. And I thought I could be paranoid.

"Yeah, okay." I was pretty eager to get the hell out of this place and end my first day as a pretend student, even if it meant leaving with Nala.

Once we were safely back at my humble abode . . . a.k.a. the huge old creepy house that my birth mother had instructed me to take up residence in. Apparently staying in a place where it looked like probably multiple murders had taken place in was a lot safer than say . . . a cozy apartment or something. I hadn't slept well since I'd been staying here. I was half convinced the ghost of some victim past would attack me in my sleep. I hated to admit it but I was kind of glad to have company, even if that company was Nala. "Alright . . . we're safe from prying ears now. Care to explain why you're here?" I huffed, wondering if we were indeed safe from *all* varieties of prying ears. Well, at least any spirits that might be hanging around didn't frequent any gossip circles that might report pack to the Riders. I hoped.

"I brought you some tea, it's made up of some herbs that will help with your morning sickness," Nala said as if I hadn't said anything.

"How do I know you're not trying to poison me?"

She heaved a huge sigh and met my eyes with what reminded me a little bit of Khol's exasperated face that he reserved especially for me. "So use your powers to see where I got it from." She then lifted her arm up in an invitation for me to touch her.

I worried my bottom lip between my teeth. So far I hadn't received a vision on purpose . . . ever. Sure, I'd asked questions and gotten the answers in the form of a vision, but even then, I hadn't done anything but muse about the subject of interest. Like when I had wanted to know why Khol hadn't used Jenna to try and forget me when I had been mated to Bryn. But what would it hurt to try? Besides my fragile ego, that is. "I will then," I retorted with false bravado as I reached out and grasped her wrist. I closed my eyes tightly and silently pleaded with my powers. *Show me where Nala got these herbs for my tea from . . . please.* I felt myself sliding into a vision much more smoothly than I'd ever experienced before. It was actually working! I mentally did a happy little jig.

"You know where she went." Khol's beautifully sculpted face was twisted with a mix of anger and desperation. "Tell me," he growled low in his throat as he reached out and grabbed Nala by her shoulders. "I'll burn you to a crisp where you stand if you don't!"

Her eyes widened slightly with fear. "I was instructed not to tell anyone—you specifically. I was told that you would know why you can't know this information, that you wouldn't be happy but would understand."

Khol abruptly released his tight grip on her shoulders and turned away from her, his dragon green eyes glowing brighter. "Yes, I was . . . informed." His voice was low and inhuman. "And no, I'm not happy."

"So—" Nala started but Khol didn't let her finish.

"Drake," he bellowed. Barely a second passed before Drake appeared in a low crouch before Khol. He didn't speak and appeared to be waiting for whatever Khol would say next. "These herbs will help her?" I'm not sure if anyone else was picking up on the slight tremble in his voice, but it made me want to go to him and to take him in my arms.

"Yes, they will help her, I swear it," Drake rumbled low without lifting his face to meet Khol's penetrating gaze.

The muscles in Khol's jaw contracted as he studied the top of Drake's head for a moment before responding. "Fine then. Go, before I change my mind."

I snapped back into my body and the present where I was still gripping Nala's wrist. I felt a single tear slide down my cheek and I let go of her so I could wipe at it with the back of my hand. Just seeing Khol, even if it was in a vision, made my homesickness that much more acute. And what about Bryn? How was he handling the news of my disappearance? Another vision ripped me suddenly from my body.

Bryn lay on his back, the dark sheets that covered his bed twisted around his legs. His pale muscled chest glistened with sweat and his chest heaved in and out as he slept restlessly. "Peej—" My name slipped from his sleep-encrusted lips. He looked bad. Or what I mean is not well somehow. Even with his eyes shut, I could almost see the torment that lurked in his unseen gaze. Dark circles marred his otherwise perfect face, and his skin wasn't just pale but almost sickly looking. "Peej—" He repeated my name again as his face furrowed with worry, and then he sat up suddenly and gasped for air. He ran his hand through his sweaty black hair and blinked in confusion as he looked down at the empty spot beside him where I wasn't. I saw a moment of regret play across his face before it turned into cold hard determination. He reached over for a glass that had been resting on the table beside his bed and drank the contents before sliding back down in between his sheets. "I'll make sure you're safe Peej, no matter the cost."

"Something's wrong with Bryn!" I exclaimed as I slammed back into the present for the second time within minutes. Maybe whatever was wrong with him was making him act the way that he was toward me. What if there was more than meets the eye with him and me feeling bitter that he'd turned away from me was completely unfair. I loved both Bryn and Khol, I'd come to terms with that truth, but no matter how much I tried to deny it there was nothing Bryn could truly do to turn me away from him. He was my first love, my best friend . . . my home. What if—

"Here," Nala said interrupting my inner turmoil over Bryn and Khol. "Drink it while it's still hot so it doesn't taste as bad."

I crinkled my nose at the pungent smell that was wafting at me from the mug that Nala was pushing in my direction. "No way that stuff is going to make me *stop* throwing up."

"Just drink it already. It'll fix things."

"I'm not going to drink it if I don't want to," I groused. I knew I sounded like a petulant child but I still wasn't a Nala fan, even if she seemed to be trying to help me.

Nala heaved a huge sigh. “Look, I know you don’t like me, or trust me, and I can’t really blame you. But let me lay it out for you. You’re the queen of us all now . . . do you really think I want to make you my enemy?”

I narrowed my eyes at her. “Too late.” She wanted Bryn, and had tried to take him from me. That point fast tracked her to the top of my enemy list as far as I was concerned.

“I didn’t know you. And it’s the way of the dragon. Besides, if Bryn could have been swayed that easily, I would have been doing you a favor.”

“Are you kidding? I mean . . . are you serious right now?” I could feel my dragon magic pushing up from inside of me. If Nala weren’t careful, *I’d* end up burning her to crisp where she stood without a second thought.

She raised her hands up defensively as if she sensed the danger she was in. “Look, he doesn’t want me. He’s made that crystal clear.”

“But you still want him.” My voice came out as a low inhuman growl and I would have put money down that my eyes were glowing too.

“Yes, but it doesn’t matter. I have pride, you know. I’m not going to chase after Bryn when he’s clearly made his choice.”

My anger suddenly left me as quickly as it had come, and I felt my face crumple up involuntarily. “Yeah, he has. He thinks I should mate with Khol.” Much to my chagrin, huge fat tears began to roll down my cheeks. *Damn pregnancy hormones!*

Nala rolled her eyes. “Young male dragons are the worst. They haven’t fully come into their powers yet but they’ve already got the alpha male ego thing down pat.” She shook her head and frowned. “He doesn’t really want you to mate with Khol. He just has this idea that he should be able to protect you completely, unfortunately he doesn’t have the power yet—”

"And Khol does?" I interjected.

"Precisely." She then smiled at me. "Although fully matured male dragons are no better. I think you've learned that from Khol."

Laughter bubbled up and escaped from my chest. "Between the two of them I'm lucky I still have my sanity." I paused and looked down at my hands that glistened from the tears I'd just wiped from my face. "At least I think I do."

"I almost feel sorry for you," Nala snorted. "Almost. If not for the fact that you have two powerful, handsome male dragons fighting over you." She snorted again. "Never mind, I actually don't feel sorry for you at all."

"Bryn isn't fighting for me at all. He's given up."

Her face grew serious and she met my eyes. "He's fighting for your safety, and sacrificing himself in the process. It's not the fight you want, but it does prove how much he loves you."

I wasn't quite sure what to say. I knew on some level that she was right, and I hated it. Bryn was only trying to protect me, and seeing in my vision how much he was suffering made me feel like someone had reached inside of my chest and put my heart in a death grip. But I loved Khol now too. I inevitably would end up crushing one of them when I mated with the other. It was easier on some level to be angry with Bryn when I was with Khol. Because otherwise I'd have to admit to myself that maybe on some level I'd betrayed Bryn just as much as he'd betrayed me. I reached up and rested my hand on my abdomen. "It doesn't matter," I murmured more to myself than Nala. And it didn't. Whoever the father of my child was, he will be my mate. I'd made up my mind to let fate decide, because no matter which way I looked at it . . . fate was going to play its hand anyways.

"So you're really going to mate with whoever the father of your child is?" Nala asked.

I gave her a sad smile. "Yes." She simply grunted as her response and pushed the mug that contained the fowl smelling concoction closer to me. I stared at it for a moment, before deciding to just drink it despite the fact that Nala was the one giving it to me. I'd clearly seen she wasn't trying to poison me and cutting my nose off to spite my face would only result in more humiliation by way of puke. I picked up the mug and chugged it down as fast as I could. It burned my throat, nose and eyes and I coughed demonstratively when I'd managed to get all of it into my stomach. "Blak!" I exclaimed. "That was just as bad as I thought it would be!" A sudden wave of tiredness swept over me. "What the hell?" I slurred as I fought to keep my eyes open.

"Oh, didn't I mention that you should only take this before bed because it's supposed to really knock you out?" Nala paused and winked at me. "No? Oh my bad. Nighty night, little Queenie."

Panic rose up in me for a second before I had the chance to think about it. Nala wouldn't risk hurting me because she knew it would result in her own death, but that didn't stop her from being a bitch to me. A title that I thought she deserved to hear out loud. "Bitch," I grated just before I felt myself slump down onto the kitchen table.

I knew it was a dream right away, or a memory really.

I stood alone with Khol in his old room.

"Please," I whispered, my whole body beginning to tremble. "Don't do this to me."

"I'm sorry I don't have a choice anymore."

"It'll be rape. Are you telling me you have no choice but to rape me? I don't believe that." My words came out shaky as I tried to withhold the onslaught of tears that were pooling in my eyes.

He came to stand mere inches away from me, his voice barely a whisper. "You'll enjoy it, I promise. I know your body craves mine. That isn't rape, coercion maybe, but not rape."

He leaned forward to kiss me and I ducked down so he missed and got the side of my face. "But my heart and soul still crave Bryn. You'll deny me that for the rest of my life? Because once you claim me for your mate, I won't want him anymore, will I? At least not physically?"

"No, you won't. And it's better that way." He grabbed my wrists and pushed them up over my head, causing my heart to triple in time.

"I'll never forgive you for this," I hissed.

A sad smile turned Khol's lips up ever so slightly at the corners. "But you will because only I will be able to give you what you crave when I'm your mate. And dragon's are quite insatiable, especially the females; you haven't even begun to experience the full scope of your dragon side."

Bryn's image flooded my mind, and just like that time in the woods when I was almost raped, all I wished for was for him to come to my rescue. "Bryn!" I mentally screamed. "Please, somehow don't let this happen to me—to us!" I struggled in Khol's grasp, but he was much too strong for me. He managed to keep me pinned with just one hand holding both my wrists as he tore at my clothes. I screamed with fury. I couldn't—wouldn't let him do this. When he dipped his head to kiss me, I bit his lip, causing him to growl low in his chest, his eyes glowing brighter. I tasted the tangy copper flavor of his blood as he persisted, delving his tongue into my mouth.

"Get your hands off her. She's mine," a heartbreakingly familiar voice growled with menace from behind Khol. I had a moment of intermingled relief and joy before the smile on Khol's face set internal alarm bells going off inside of me.

And then I knew—it was a trap. "Bryn!" I screamed.

My dream then shifted to a different memory.

"I wanna be with you, Bryn. I don't wanna be with anyone else. Ever."

He stilled for a moment, breaking our kiss and pulling back just enough so he could look into my eyes. "We'll find a way. Somehow—we'll find a way." And then his lips sought mine out again. That was all I needed to hear. Bryn would fight for me. Somehow we would make it work.

We stayed like that for I'm not sure how long, just making out furiously in the woods across from my house. But before things could progress much farther, Bryn pulled away, even with my protesting lips trying to ensnare his again. "Not like this. Your first time can't be like this."

I tried to catch my breath as I gazed up into his beautiful blue eyes. My insides churned for him. "You can't take it back. You can't say we'll find a way and then take it back. That would be even worse than if you'd never said anything at all." It would kill me, but I left that part unsaid.

He cupped my face in both of his large hands and spoke inches from my face. "No. There's no going back. I want this." He shook his head slightly. "No. I need this. I need you. I can't imagine my life without you. Just being your Guardian isn't enough—it'd never be enough."

I sat up in my bed with a scream caught in my throat, and came face to face with . . . myself.

A feeling of dread snaked its way up my spine as I met the green eyes of the *me* I used to be. *This was it, the sign that I'd finally lost it. Padded room here I come.* "Don't worry, you're still dreaming," the me with enviable lush long red auburn hair said with a wry smile.

I heaved a huge sigh of relief. "Okay, so what am I trying to tell myself? The symbolism, now that I know I'm dreaming, isn't lost on me."

My old self chuckled. "No, you're not exactly being very subtle at the moment." She then looked at me again and all the amusement drained out of her face. "You're letting your fear of being alone rule your decisions."

"No I'm not. I'm here, aren't I? Facing this task . . . alone . . . without Bryn and Khol. I—"

"You know that's not what I'm talking about. You know I mean with the whole Bryn and Khol situation. When Bryn broke your heart . . . our heart . . . you ran into Khol's open arms because it was easy. How can you run to him after everything he's put you through? How can you think about choosing him after you tried to end your own life for Bryn's sake?"

"I love Khol too!" My voice went up an octave as I pleaded my defense . . . to myself. Maybe I was ready for a padded room, even if it was a dream. "Since you're a part of my subconscious, I shouldn't need to tell you that I love him too! You know I do!"

"Not like Bryn. And you know that's true. Bryn is our home. He always will be, no matter how he's hurt us. Don't let your fears rule you. You need to grow up. Your insecurities and fear of being alone have ruled you from the beginning. For all your constant declarations of love for Bryn, you didn't waste any time with Khol or with Jeremy the last time he was by your side."

"That's not fair. That's not—"

"The truth hurts sometimes. Stop with all the teenage angst and drama. You're going to have a child of your own soon. Fight for Bryn, and stop making excuses to hide behind your own insecurities, because if you're not careful, you really will end up the slut you're afraid you already are. All sluts aren't created equal you know. Some are just afraid to be alone. Some are just looking for unconditional love."

"But he doesn't want me!" I practically screeched, choosing to ignore what else I'd just said to myself. "And I wouldn't be a slut if I mated with Khol I'd—"

"Be settling and you know it." I quirked an eyebrow at myself. "And are you so sure Bryn doesn't want you? Or is something else going on?"

"What do you mean?" My mind flashed to how bad Bryn had looked in the vision I'd had just before I'd drunk the herbs Nala had given me to knock me out. "Tell me."

"Well, the problem with me being you is that I only know what you know. But we both know that something isn't right. Bryn would never walk away from you the way that he has without some outside force coming into play—especially with the possibility that you're carrying his child. We've known Bryn since we were both were five years old; you know he isn't acting like himself. "

And if that was true then maybe I'd been the one to betray Bryn and not the other way around. I was an immature hypocrite. Maybe I didn't deserve Bryn. The truth really did hurt. "So what do we—I mean *I* do?"

"How should I know? I'm just your subconscious," the old me said with annoyance. "By the way . . . happy nineteenth birthday to us."

I really did wake up after that. I lay in the cool dark room listening to myself breathing over the roar of my heart beating in my ears. This would be the first birthday I'd ever been apart from Bryn since we were five years old. No wonder it was also the first time I'd almost forgotten about it. Yep . . . happy birthday to me.

12

Terrance's whole body shook with thinly veiled fear as he approached the office door where his master was currently working on business. He was always working on some kind of business. And he would not be pleased with the news that Terrance was bringing him this day.

"Come in," his master's voice boomed through the thick oak, before Terrance had even raised his hand to knock. He only hesitated for a moment before entering. There was only so long he could delay the inevitable. "Tell me," his master growled as he scuttled into the lush room with eyes averted toward the ground.

"She's not dead."

"And what of our operative inside the human girl?"

"No news. She is either dead or being held captive. Either way she is currently beyond our reach."

"I see." His master's voice was much too calm. "You do realize this was your last chance, Terrance. I don't tolerate incompetence . . . at least not for very long."

Terrance dropped to the ground onto his knees. "No, please, my liege. I won't fail you again. I—"

"No, you won't fail me again." It was the last words Terrance heard before he was ripped from his host's body and pulled into the bright red stone where he would now make his home.

13

I *'m different, no doubt about that*, I thought as I tried to blend the rainbow clip-in extensions into my white hair. But maybe that wasn't necessarily a bad thing like I had originally thought. I had acted like a hypocrite toward Bryn, and like a child in general. A part of me had always known it, but didn't want to admit it to myself. Now was the time to ensure that my change would be for the better and not the worse. It was time for me to take responsibility for my own actions and choices and to stop hiding behind my fears and insecurities. How many times now had I declared that I would become the person I desired to be but only to backslide soon after? How many times had I blamed the actions of others for the bad choices I made? *Too many.* And the worst part was that I clearly knew better. "No more," I muttered to my scowling reflection. I let my emotions flow from chastising to hopeful in a slow trickle as I completed my morning routine and headed downstairs for some breakfast.

"You really should buy some better breakfast food," Nala complained as I entered the kitchen.

"I don't like breakfast food," I retorted. "Breakfast cookies and pastries I can tolerate though."

"The baby needs healthier stuff than sugar and carbs. It needs protein and—"

"I'll eat whatever I can keep down," I snapped. Who the hell did Nala think she was just coming in here and trying to tell me what's best for me and my unborn baby? She certainly had a lot of nerve.

"Well, that shouldn't be a problem anymore, should it?"

"It's probably a pretty good idea if you don't remind me of the little bitchy move you pulled last night," I said between clenched teeth.

Nala heaved a huge sigh. "Okay fine. I'm sorry. I just couldn't resist. I don't want you for an enemy, but I'm still not exactly your biggest fan."

I eyed her wearily before slumping down into a chair across the table from her. "Yeah, I get it. I guess I can kinda respect the honesty." She passed me a glass of orange juice and a breakfast cookie. "Today's my nineteenth birthday," I mumbled around a mouthful of oatmeal and raisins. I choked back a sob as I thought again how it'd be the first one without Bryn. And I wasn't about to think about the fact that it would also be the first one without my parents. I was still in big time denial about their deaths.

"Happy birthday . . . I guess," Nala said automatically.

"Yeah, there's nothing happy about it." Time to think about more important things I mentally chastised myself. "I had a vision about Cliff, that guy you met at my school, yesterday." She nodded her head in confirmation that she was following me. ". . . And in it he pushed one of the Riders out of his body." I paused to scowl down at my half-eaten cookie. "And yet he still has one inside of him. I don't know what it could mean."

She leaned toward me, her eyes gleaming a bright dragon blue. "How did he do it? How did he push it out of him?"

"I don't know really. He was having some kind of battle of wills while he stood looking in the mirror, and then . . . bam . . . out the little bugger came. Of course, Cliff passed out cold afterwards, and my vision ended."

Nala slumped back in her chair looking puzzled. "That doesn't really tell us much."

"No shit, Sherlock," I said as I picked up my glass of orange juice and drank it down with a crinkled nose. Orange juice wasn't one of my favorite drinks, but I was trying to get something healthy in my system for the baby. Maybe I should take double the dose of the prenatal vitamins I'd picked up at the grocery store. Or maybe dragons didn't need that kind of stuff. How was I supposed to know? I'd grown up thinking I was completely human. "I guess I'll just have to continue my fake schooling and deal with whatever it is my birth mother sent me here to figure out." I set my empty glass back down on the table and stood. "What about you? I guess you're going to be heading out soon?"

Nala shifted uncomfortably in her seat and flicked her gaze away from mine. "I think I'm just going to hang around here for awhile . . . if you don't mind."

A sudden bark of laughter escaped from my chest. "Afraid to face Khol, huh? You're not fooling me."

Her cheeks heated in embarrassment, which caused me to laugh again. "He's kind of scary if you haven't noticed. He might very well burn me to a crisp if I return without any real news of you . . . or with you."

"I wouldn't worry, his bark is much worse than his bite. I don't think he would actually kill you, for this anyways. I mean he let you go, didn't he?" Of course, when I had first met Khol he had scared me a little too, but that hadn't lasted long. And underneath it all he's just as human as I am . . . or thought I was . . . whatever.

She gave me a humorless laugh. "With *you* his bark might be worse than his bite, because he's a male dragon in love, but with me . . ." Her voice trailed off as she obviously pondered her demise at Khol's hands. "No thanks, I'll stay here."

"Suit yourself. Even if it is . . . well . . . you . . . I won't lie that having someone else here with me in the Murder House is slightly comforting."

Nala tilted her head at me with puzzlement much like a dog trying to understand its human owner. "Someone was murdered here?"

"Probably," I said as I turned to leave. "I guess I'll just see you later then."

"Yeah, okay." Nala's voice still held some slight confusion when I left her sitting in the kitchen.

"You look like you're feeling better today," Cliff's already recognizable voice stated from just behind me. When I didn't answer and continued shuffling around the contents of my locker looking for my math book, he continued on. "I hope you remembered to bring your meds today so I don't have to tote you around like yesterday. Not that I'm complaining or anything—"

"Look," I started without turning around to look at him. If I could just manage to treat him like any other guy I wasn't interested in and not like an alien leper, I'd be good. "I'm sure you're real nice and all." *For an alien,* I silently added. "But I have a boyfriend back home that I'm *very* serious about."

"Yeah, okay. Just tryin' to be friendly to the new girl is all," Cliff responded with cheer. His happy go lucky alien ass was really starting to get under my skin.

"Okay, good," I grated.

"Hey, Paige." I looked over to see Laila heading my way with a friendly grin on her face. "I'm so glad you look like you're feeling better." She paused long enough to briefly acknowledge Cliff, who I'd thought had already left. I guess the hairs on the back of my neck still standing on end should have been my first clue.

"Yep, I'm feeling much better." Hopefully those herbs that Nala had brought for me would do the trick. So far so good. "Although I kinda wish I could have missed some more school than a couple periods."

Cliff clearing his throat from behind me caused both Laila and me to swing our heads in his direction. Even though I was mentally prepared for the duel imagery of the Rider shining out from behind his face, I still had to fight the urge to gasp in horror. "I wanted to invite you, Paige," he paused. "And you Laila, to my End of the World party this weekend."

"Y-you're what?" I sputtered unable to contain my complete and utter shock.

"My End of the World p—" He started to explain but Laila didn't give him a chance to finish.

"We'd absolutely looove to!" she gushed with excitement. "Just text me the details. My number is still the same." I just stood there in stunned silence. I'd just been invited to a party themed *The End of the World* by an alien who was living inside a teenage boy, who in fact wanted to take over our world and use up all of its resources. Were the Rider's attempting to make some sort of sick joke? Laila elbowed me in my ribs. The pain caused me to refocus back in on the surreal reality that had become my life. "Right, Paige? We'd love to?"

"Um . . . yeah . . . sure," I said numbly. Of course, I knew on some level it would be the perfect opportunity to observe the Riders even closer than I was able to at school. And I knew that's the whole reason why I'd been sent here, to find out what I could about them, even if I wasn't entirely sure what I was looking for. But a part of me wanted to say *hellz no* and high tail it back to Bryn as fast as I could get there.

"Great." A huge smile spread across both Cliff's handsome face and the pinched alien residing underneath his skin. Well, at least they seemed to be in accordance at the moment. Something that my body and I didn't have in common. Despite the herbs that were supposed to help me with my morning sickness, I suddenly had an overwhelming sense of nausea sweep through my system. I had no other course of action but to make a mad dash for the bathroom. Yesterday was embarrassing enough with only one Rider as a witness, but half the school was not going to be privy to what I had eaten for breakfast.

I barely made it to the girl's room and dry heaved over one of the toilets when Laila's voice called out to me. "Hey Paige, sweetie. You okay?" The stall door squeaked open as she crowded in behind me. She gathered my hair up from my hand so I could better balance myself and locked the door behind us. "I thought you were feeling better." There was more than one unspoken question in her voice. "You don't have an ear infection do you?"

A feeling of ice slid over my heated skin. "What's that supposed to mean?"

"Oh, come on sweetie. I may be country but I'm not stupid. I've seen you rubbing your belly when you think no one's looking." I didn't know what to say. Should I try to deny it and risk alienating the only ally I had at this school? Or should I risk telling her the truth and maybe she could help me with my secret? "Does your guy back home know? What about your parents?"

Guess there was no point in denying it when she'd already figured it out. Or was I simply letting my fear of being alone on another level rule my decisions? "Everyone knows," I mumbled. "I was just kind of hoping to finish out here before I started showing." It was a partial truth, but it would do.

"Is that why you're here? Did your parents want you away from your guy?"

"I guess." My birth mom had wanted me on this mission by myself so in a way she'd wanted me away from my guy. "It's all just a bit more complicated than that," I said as I pushed myself up into a standing position and leaned against the stall wall.

Laila's big blue, and very innocent looking eyes, looked up at me with a mixture of pity and sympathy. "Does your guy want you to have the baby? Or is that part of the problem?"

I thought about how Khol had reacted when he first found out I was pregnant; as opposed to the angst Bryn had delivered me. It kind of felt like Khol wanted me to have the baby, and Bryn wasn't really sure how to react. "Which one?" I said without thinking.

Laila blinked up at me and gasped as if I'd just punched her in the stomach. "You mean—you mean—"

It was too late to take back what I'd just let slip out of my mouth unintentionally. "Yep. I don't know who the father is."

"But you said you were serious about your boyfriend back home."

"I am. Both of them." I laughed with a hysterical edge. "I'm in love with two guys, one who wants me unconditionally, and the other . . . well, the other I used to think did but now . . . I just don't know. And I don't know which one of them is the father of my unborn child." But what about my dream conversation with myself last night? Was the love I felt toward Khol enough to even be counted against what I felt for Bryn? Was I going to just discount what my subconscious was trying to call to my attention? I thought this morning I had made up my mind to stop with all the damn wishy washiness of my adolescence.

I could see everything processing in Laila's eyes, and like a light being switched on, I could also see when she fully accepted what I'd just told her. "Oh, you poor thing."

I scowled down at her. "I don't need or want your or anyone else's pity."

"No, of course not." She waved me off and unlocked the stall door. "My lips are sealed." She headed over toward the wall of sinks and paused. "Do you still wanna go to Cliff's party this weekend?"

I had to bite back a laugh, but a sincere one this time. She reminded me of Jenna so much. "I just can't drink is all," was my response. "But since we're spilling secrets, why are you so excited about being invited, and why are you being so nice to me? I mean you've kind of been hanging around with me, and not with a whole lot of anyone else since I've met you."

Laila's cheeks flushed briefly. "I—ah—well—most of the kids I grew up with around here . . . they're just different. It started happening sometime around middle school. At first it was just a couple of them, and I just chalked it up to people changin' as they grow up, but lately . . . I don't know, it's like I don't even know half of them anymore." Her shoulders slumped and she let out a huge sigh. "It sounds crazy, doesn't it? I mean some of them just creep me out somehow."

I reached out and touched her shoulder briefly, meeting her eyes in the mirror. "I don't think it's weird at all. But if they creep you out then why do you wanna go to the party?"

She started applying lip-gloss as she talked to me. I decided to try and avoid my own appearance for as long as I could. I was getting more used to the white hair, but I still wasn't a fan. "I'm just tired of feeling left out by the people who used to be my closest friends. They just stopped inviting me to their parties after this one night when . . ." Her mouth clamped shut in a thin line and her eyes took on a vacant look as she obviously relived the night she was referring to. "It just got really weird is all."

"Okaaay," I drew out as I lifted an eyebrow in question. "Care to elaborate?"

Laila made a big production out of stuffing her lip-gloss back into her bag and fussing with her hair before answering. "Not much else to say. It was weird."

I could tell she was lying, but I also could tell that was about all I was going to get out of her for the moment, so I decided to temporarily drop it. "But you're all gung ho to go to this party now? Aren't you worried it'll . . . get weird again?"

She gave me a nervous smile as she turned to leave the bathroom. "It was prolly just a misunderstanding of sorts, and I just overreacted."

I frowned at the back of her head before I started to follow after her. "Yeah, okay." I so didn't have a good feeling about this.

The next couple of days passed by with nothing out of the ordinary. How going to school, while pregnant with a child who I didn't know who the father was, while I tried to remain undiscovered by alien parasites hiding inside of my peers, had become ordinary was beyond me—but it had. Nala mostly kept to herself, except when she was attempting to push healthier food down my throat or stinky tea for my morning sickness. But my nights were filled with Bryn. Some were memories, and some were nightmares, but every night when I closed my eyes, I knew I would come face to face with his fathomless dark blue eyes and the man who owned them. I wasn't sure what it meant that the longer I was away from Khol, the less I thought about him and the more I did Bryn. I was starting to question how I had any romantic feelings for Khol at all after what happened between us. He had forced himself into my bed, and caused me to attempt to end my own life. Forgiving him, knowing what I did now, yes . . . but the rest . . . everything was just so mixed up in my head.

I was currently caught up in the memory of the first night Bryn and I had ever been together. It was so real I could almost believe I was reliving that night.

I could hardly wait to feel Bryn's arms around me, and I fully expected to be greeted with the same enthusiasm from him, and yet when I went to him, his arms stayed limp at his sides and his eyes regarded me with dark emotion. "What's wrong?" I asked studying his face for some clue. He didn't say anything; he just kept watching me, his eyes churning with something I couldn't read. When I looked closer, I could see his whole body was wrought with tension. "Bryn?" I licked my lips nervously, noting that his eyes followed my every move. He slowly stalked toward me, backing me up against the wall. His hands came to rest on either side of my head, balled into fists. And even though he seemed so angry, so dangerous, my breath caught in my throat and my pulse began to race with excitement. "Bryn?" I said again, my voice coming out breathy and low.

"I couldn't stand seeing you leave with him," Bryn practically growled, his voice so low I barely recognized it. "I had to fight everything in me to not come after you." His chest was heaving as he tried to keep himself calm. "You're mine. I won't share you."

"It's not real Bryn. You know that, I'm yours—all yours."

He stared at me a few more seconds, his eyes raging with so many dark emotions. "It felt real, Peej—so real. It felt like I was losing you to him."

I reached up and cupped his face, feeling his jaw tick with tension. "I'm here now. And I'm yours. Always."

He caught my lips with his, taking my mouth forcefully, dominating me like he never had before. I welcomed the feel of his jealousy turning into passion as he explored me with his tongue and mouth. Our clothes began falling away, and soon we were both left in just our underwear. Usually this was the point where Bryn and I stopped. We hadn't gone much farther than heavy petting and neither one of us had been completely naked in front of the other. Our physical relationship was just so new that we were both in awe of the simple things, like kissing and touching, but tonight—tonight Bryn didn't show any signs of stopping. And I sure as hell wasn't going to protest. I'd wanted to give my virginity to him since the first night in the woods. He was the one who didn't feel like it was the right time or place; he was the one who felt I needed more for my first time. Even though all I really needed or wanted was him—that's all I'd ever need.

"I need you, Peej," Bryn rumbled as his fingers deftly dipped down under my panties. I moaned as his long fingers explored areas where no boy had ever gone before.

"Yes," I gasped into his mouth. Bryn made quick work of getting my bra and panties off, lifting me up and setting me down on his bed. He joined me there, but not before sitting back to study me in all my naked glory. I fidgeted under his rapt gaze. "Bryn," I pleaded reaching for him. It was one thing to be naked with Bryn while we were kissing and touching but I didn't like him studying me while I just laid on his bed stark naked.

"You're so beautiful," Bryn whispered in reverence. He then came to rest over me, his pelvis cradled in between my legs. I attempted to swallow back my nerves as it really sunk in that Bryn and I were going to have sex. I locked gazes with him and his sea storm eyes pulled me under, washing away all my trepidations. "You still taking the pill?" Bryn asked huskily.

Reality check. "Yeah." My mom would be absolutely furious if she knew I was using the pill for its intended purpose and not just to regulate my period. Especially if she found out I was using it with Bryn on the heels of a date with someone she had set me up with. "What about your parents—"

"Not here," Bryn said as he dipped his head delivering me with more kisses before pulling away again. "You ready? I don't wanna hurt you."

"Yeah, I'm ready," I whispered, looking deep into his dark blue eyes. The way he looked at me in that moment, the love that emanated from him made me feel like the most beautiful and special girl in the entire world. Someone who looked at me like that deserved to have everything that I was, mind, body, and soul. So far he'd only received two of those three. Tonight he would have everything.

As he pushed into me, filling me in a way I'd never been able to imagine, I tried to mentally prepare myself for the pain. From all accounts, the first time for a girl was almost always painful, and I thought I was ready, but no amount of mental preparation could have readied me for the level of pain I was currently experiencing. I gritted my teeth and dug my nails into Bryn's shoulders, not wanting him to know how much it really hurt. But it was short lived, the pain I mean, and slowly, ever so slowly, as Bryn rocked back and forth inside of me, the pain began to be replaced by pleasure. A deep-seated pleasure that made me truly understand for the first time why people like Jenna were so sex crazed.

My entire world narrowed down to Bryn and me, and I could no longer tell where I ended and he began. Surely there was nothing closer to bliss than being in the arms of the man I loved, and sharing such intimacy with him. A feeling of warmth bloomed in my center, pushing outward into spasms of ecstasy. Bryn captured my face in his palms, forcing me to look at him instead of throwing my head back like I wanted. He didn't last too much longer after that, and I slumped down in his bed feeling completely boneless. Never, ever had I imagined sex would be so wonderful, or maybe it was just that way with Bryn.

I smiled up at him as he collapsed above me, careful not to put his full body weight on me. I ran my hands through his silky tasseled hair, and then down over his sweaty back.

He shuddered at my touch, leaning forward to kiss me with a slow languidness that spoke of shared intimacies, and unspoken promises. "I love you, Peej. More than I can even begin to explain." His voice was so low and husky it seemed to brush things on my insides, making me shudder in turn.

I gazed up into his eyes with adoration. "I love you too," I whispered, surprised at how husky my own voice sounded. I wished I could stay in his arms forever, forgetting about the outside world and all the problems it contained. But our love wouldn't be enough to protect us from our parent's wrath if they found us like this.

I must have frowned because Bryn's brow furrowed as he looked at me. "What's wrong? Did I hurt you?"

"No, Bryn." I bit my lower lip thinking about what we'd just done. "You made my first time more amazing than I ever could have imagined." He grinned at me, a look of pure male pride washing over his features. "I just wish I could stay here with you and not worry about everything else."

He rolled onto his back tucking me into his side so my head rested on his chest. "I hate this, Peej. I just wanna be with you. I wanna be able to touch when I want, to kiss you when I want. I wanna yell from the roof tops that you're mine." He pulled his fingers through my hair. "I don't wanna have to watch you go out on dates with other guys." I felt his fist ball up in my hair.

"It wasn't so bad tonight, was it? I mean, yeah, it sucked that I had to go on that date, but"—I lifted my head so I could look in his eyes—"look at where we ended up."

He frowned at me. "I'm sorry, Peej. I really wanted your first time to be more special, not in my bedroom because I was crazy with jealously over some guy that you're not even really dating. I just—"

"Shhh . . ." I brought my index finger up to his lips. "I'm glad it happened. I wanna give everything that I am to you, Bryn. The rest doesn't matter. Tonight was the best night of my life so far because I just shared something with you that I've never shared with anyone else. You own me now—heart, soul . . . and body."

"You own me too, Peej. Everything that I have—that I am—belongs to you and only you. Always." His lips sought mine out and our kisses began to become more fevered again.

Then my dream shifted to another night that held a first for me, but of a much different kind. It was the night that I was first been with Khol . . . so really my dream shifted to a nightmare.

"Khol," I croaked. "Khol—I'm ready." Am I really ready to die though? Could I really do this?

Khol appeared in front of me only a few inches away and pushed me back onto the bed and covered me with his body as he aggressively kissed me. He was obviously ready to get down to business, and maybe it was better that way, so I wouldn't have a chance to over think things and lose my nerve.

My body immediately responded to his heated kisses, even as my heart felt like a block of ice inside my chest. As he tore at my clothes, I found myself arching up to meet him, wanting, at least physically what he had to offer. Too soon, or not soon enough, we were both naked and Khol was claiming parts of my body with his touch that I swore only Bryn would ever know. I clawed and bit at Khol, wanting to hurt him in some way as he rocked into me, hating and loving what he was doing to me at the same time. Things with him were different than they'd ever been with Bryn. There was no soul deep feeling of connection. There was no feeling of being exactly where I belonged. All I felt was intense physical pleasure, which maybe would have been enough, if I didn't know what I was missing.

Intense heat seemed to seep out of Khol and wrap itself around me as the back of my neck started to burn. "You're mine," Khol growled as he looked down at me capturing my gaze. "Say it. Say you're mine."

"Yes," I said on the tail end of a moan, wishing I could deny the words, but I felt it—I felt his magic branding me.

"And I'm yours. Say it."

"Yes. You're mine." And then I arched up one last time before I blacked out.

I had let Khol claim me, I remembered as I slowly fought my way back to consciousness, and it left me feeling empty—oh, so empty. When I'd been with Bryn, I'd felt so good, so right . . . but being with Khol had been wrong . . . even if he had brought me pleasure. Maybe it wouldn't be as difficult as I thought it would be to take my own life after letting Khol claim me. Had Bryn felt our connection breaking? Surely he had to of. What must he think of me now, knowing what I'd done to make that happen?

I blinked my eyes open to find that I was alone, no Khol to be found. Well, isn't that nice, he finally got what he wanted and he didn't bother to stick around afterwards. I lurched from bed, stumbling toward the bathroom, not caring if I was naked or not, it didn't matter for what I was about to do. I shut and locked the door, and started the water running for the bath. As the hot water filled the tub, I scanned the bathroom for options. My eyes stopped when they ran over a small hand mirror. I snatched it up and broke it on the counter, picking up the largest shard. I had to do it—I had to do it now before I lost my courage. I stepped into the tub, hardly noticing when the much too hot water practically scalded me, and sank down in the nearly full tub. I set the glass shard on the edge. When the water covered me up past my chest, I turned it off, picked up the shard and leaned back in the tub.

I passed the glass shard back and forth between my hands, watching the lights glint menacingly off its surface. I had to do it—there was no other way. I refused to doom Bryn to a miserable life; my death would bring him happiness. Besides that, the emptiness that I felt knowing that I could never have him again was enough to make me want to end my life all in itself. But I wouldn't have done it for myself. I'd always thought suicide was the coward's way out, an easy escape from problems that would only make a person stronger if they stayed to face them. What would have happened if the hero of a story died before they had a chance to become who they were really meant to be? I never thought myself capable of doing such a thing, but then again maybe I wasn't the hero of this story. I wanted to live—even now as I readied myself for death—I craved life. There was still so much to do, so much to experience, the good and the bad . . . I didn't want to die now. No—it wasn't time for selfish thoughts—this is for Bryn. Everything is for Bryn.

I held the glass tightly in my right hand, so tightly that I drew blood, just not from the right place . . . yet. I pressed the glass to my left wrist making sure I cut deep and quickly, barely able to grip it in my left hand to repeat the process on my right wrist. I just had to hope it was enough. Dropping the shard and sinking back into the tub, I closed my eyes and waited for death—my death.

"No!" I heard someone roar with outrage, but it was far away, much too far away to care.

"Peej! How could you do this? How could you let this happen?" Another voice sounded from much too far away. "Save her!"

But I was just sleepy . . . too sleepy to care.

I came to in my bed, the sheets clinging to my sweaty body, and my hair plastered to my face. Why was my mind insistent on showing me things like that? I thought I had memories such as the first time I was with Khol and the night I tried to take my own life suppressed far enough down that I wouldn't be plagued with such nightmares. What was the point? What was my subconscious trying to tell me this time? It was clear that it had shown me my first times both with Khol and Bryn . . . as what . . . a comparison? Did I want myself to remember how I used to feel about the both of them as opposed to what I felt now? Did I want myself to remember the type of love I felt for Bryn that led to my attempted suicide solely for his happiness. *That was before he walked away from you*, a not so helpful voice in my mind offered. *No.* Suddenly it felt like an internal light switch had been flipped on. A feeling of resolution settled over me . . . finally.

Real love, true love . . . the kind of life altering love that Bryn and I share just doesn't go away that easily. That kind of love takes root in your heart and spreads throughout every fiber of your being. That kind of love makes you feel only half alive whenever the other person isn't around. That's what Bryn and I have, and it shouldn't matter that he walked away from me. It shouldn't matter that he was acting on some misplaced sense of duty to protect me—because he did those things out of love. He loves me just as much as he always has; he's just an idiot is all.

I laughed out loud. Of course, that part has always been true as well. It'd be different if he had cheated on me, or abused me, or some other unforgivable offense. I thought Bryn had been the one to break our relationship, but maybe the truth was that we had both done that. But the kind of love that Bryn and I shared could fix anything. Had *The Princess Bride* taught me nothing? I loved Khol, the man that he'd become for me, but I could never love him the way that I loved Bryn. I was kidding myself to think so. Bryn and I had promised each other always, and I wasn't going to let my own insecurities stand in the way of that, or his for that matter either. When I saw Khol and Bryn again, I would let them know my decision. I would let them know that it would be Bryn or no one for me . . . *always.*

14

I heard you cry out in your sleep again last night," Nala said conversationally as she stepped into the bathroom. She came to stand behind me as I worked on curling my hair. I was attempting to better blend the hair extensions into my crone style white hair. *Attempting* being the keyword.

I shrugged without taking my eyes off of my own reflection, and the tedious task at hand. "I had a nightmare."

"Every night this week?"

"Yeah, what of it?" It wasn't like she really cared about my mental health. Sure, she seemed to care about me and my unborn child's physical health, but that was probably just to protect her own hide. We both knew what would become of her if she let anything happen to me when she could have prevented it.

Probably sensing she wasn't going to get any more out of me about my nightmares, Nala wisely changed the subject. "Have you been drinking your tea?"

It was then I did meet her blue eyes in the reflection of the mirror. "No. And you know I haven't because it's plain to see that the supply hasn't been diminishing." Before she could say anything, I cut her off. "But the morning sickness symptoms seem to have passed, so I don't think I need it anymore." I resisted the urge to stick my tongue out at her when I was done talking. How very mature of me.

A flash of something I couldn't quite decipher crossed her face before she slumped casually against the door jam. Maybe just a little too casually. "It's probably best to be sure. You don't want to raise suspicions, do you?"

"I'm done with that heinous tea," I responded flatly. That stuff alone could serve as a form of birth control. Just let the would-be-mom get a whiff of that stuff and tell her she'd have to drink it every day to prevent morning sickness and she might rethink the whole wanting to have kids thing . . . forever. "Damn it!" I swore when I caught some hair in my bracelet for the umpteenth time. I set the curling iron down and pulled the pieces of hair out of the bracelet that were still attached to my head. Sadly, a few didn't make it and I let them drop into the sink.

"Why don't you just take that off until you're done with your hair?" Nala asked in a tone one might use to talk to a small child.

"I would if I could," I said, ignoring her condescending attitude and setting back in to finish doing my hair. It took me so much longer than when Jenna did it, and it never looked even half as good either. "If I take it off, Khol would be here probably before I even set it down." I sighed and turned the curling iron off. My hair was about as good as it was going to get—with me being the stylist anyways.

Nala looked up sharply at me. "What do you mean?"

Wow. She really was afraid of Khol, wasn't she? "Don't worry, my birth mother let me know that I wasn't to take it off at all. She—"

"Is that why he can't find you?" Nala interjected. Her face visibly went a few shades paler than it had been a moment ago.

I rolled my eyes. "Yes. But like I said, there's no reason to worry. My—"

"No," she interrupted me . . . again. *Rude much?* "That's not what I'm asking, entirely. *How* does it keep him from tracking you?"

I gritted my teeth and decided not to scold her for interrupting me—twice in a row. I guess she was just worried. "It breaks the connection that exists between Khol and me . . . He can't sense my emotions, and he can't track me. He's totally cut off."

Her eyes flared a brighter dragon blue before she looked away from me and mumbled to herself. "*All* connection to him. *Shit.*"

"What?" I said with alarm as I tried to interpret the dark expression on her face.

"Nothing," she said with irritation as she spun on her heel to leave. "Don't worry about it."

Before I had a chance to say anything else, the door to the room that she'd been staying in slammed shut behind her. I stared after her for a moment before letting my gaze drop to the shiny bronze bracelet that was fitted perfectly on my wrist. I let the fingers of my right hand run idly over the delicate markings I was convinced meant something, I just wasn't sure what. I wondered how much longer I'd have to wear it. Not that it wasn't pretty, it was just that I hated being forced to do . . . well practically anything.

My phone beeped signaling me that I had a text. I hit the unlock code and read the message from Laila. "Be there in 5."

"K," was my quick reply. I gave myself one more once over in the mirror before heading out of the bathroom. My hair looked somewhat presentable . . . At least it was better than the first couple of times I'd attempted to style it. My makeup also was done . . . adequately. I still hadn't figured out my new color palate completely, but that was only something time would fix. My black lace tee fit me snuggly, showing off the few curves I did have, but it wasn't too tight, and looked the right combination of dressy and casual when paired with the dark low-waisted jeans I had on. The dragon pendant from Khol sat at the perfect level to draw more attention to my cleavage than I probably wanted, but I refused to leave it behind. My outfit was completed with a pair of knee high, low heeled, black, zip-up boots. It was warmer this time of year than I was used to, but I wasn't wearing open-toes shoes going into a nest of Riders. What if I needed to run, or kick, or something? One did not wear open-toed shoes of any kind when heading into enemy territory of the alien kind. If there was a how to survive a party with alien Riders somewhere, I'm sure that rule would be in it. Once I was satisfied that I looked the best I could under the circumstances, I made my way outside to wait for Laila on the front porch of the creepy Murder House.

I was only outside for a minute or two when a big black pickup truck pulled into the driveway. The window rolled down, and Laila's blonde head peeked out. "Well, are you coming, or what?" she said with excitement laced into the tone of her voice.

I shut my mouth and shook my head. What had I expected, a Volkswagen Bug or something? She might remind me of Jenna at times, but she most certainly wasn't her, not by a long shot. I went and opened the door to the massive truck and pulled myself up into it, barely managing to shut the door before Laila was burning rubber to get out of my driveway and to the party. I for one would have preferred a more leisurely pace; I wasn't one to rush off to the end of the world . . . even if it was only the theme of a party. Once I had my seatbelt in place, I turned to eye Laila's outfit. She had gone with a cute little red dress and cowboy boots. Ugh. I knew it seemed to be the style down here, but I cringed every time I saw a girl rocking out cowboy boots with a skirt. But then again, maybe I should have tried a little harder to blend in. I tried to picture myself in similar attire and cringed. Nope . . . never going to happen.

"You look nice," Laila said interrupting my inner fashion diva. "Just how far along are you anyways; you don't seem to be showing at all."

I bit my lower lip. That was the million-dollar question, wasn't it? If I actually knew how far along I was then I would know who the father of my unborn child was . . . maybe . . . There was still that whole dragon versus human gestation difference thing. Not that it mattered anymore though, I'd already made up my mind that I would be with Bryn, no matter who the father was. I just hoped Khol and Bryn both would go along with that, especially if Khol turned out to, in fact, be the daddy. "I'm not exactly sure." I decided to go with another partial truth. "If I knew exactly then I would know who the father is."

Laila nodded, keeping her eyes on the road. "Yeah, I guess that makes sense."

I slumped down in my seat, hating that Laila had reminded me of my "who's the daddy" predicament. Not that it was ever entirely from my mind lately, but even still, I didn't want to focus on something I couldn't do anything to change. "Yeah, um, talking about that doesn't really put me in the partying mood."

Laila's cheeks flushed a dark crimson that I could easily see with only the aid of the streetlights we were passing under. "Sorry," she mumbled.

"It's okay." We then sat in an awkward silence that lasted until Laila flicked on the radio and I let out a loud groan. "Please, no. Not country. I think my morning sickness is going to make a dramatic comeback." Laila glanced at me before looking back at the road and we both laughed. I'm guessing turning on the radio hadn't broken the awkward silence in the way that she had planned, but it had gotten the job done in the end. "So how much longer?" I glanced at the clock on the dash and realized we'd only been driving for five minutes. It seemed like much longer. I guess the feeling of dread that had settled over me made time feel like it was dragging on.

"We're almost there. This isn't that big of a town."

"I've noticed," I grumbled. In comparison to Pittsburgh, Spring Hill made me feel like I was practically out in the middle of nowhere. A perfectly good place for a nest of Riders to take up residence, I mentally noted. *No one will hear you scream.*

"That's Cliff's place, up on the right," Laila said a few minutes later. Even if she hadn't pointed it out to me, it would have been kind of hard to miss with all the cars parked out front. She pulled neatly into a spot at the end of the row and turned the truck off. As she slid from her seat and hopped down to the curb, I took a moment to gather myself. I could do this. I had kick ass powers inside of me that I didn't even fully comprehend yet. *Yeah, and you don't know how to use them either,* that stupid little annoying voice in my head added. I was really starting to hate that voice. I clenched and unclenched my fists before unbuckling my seatbelt and sliding from the truck cab. Laila was waiting for me on the sidewalk, reapplying a peachy gloss to her lips with the aid of a tiny compact. With a soft snick she closed it, dropped it into her small messenger bag and looked up at me. "You think about how you're going to explain not drinking without sounding lame?"

"Medication?" I looked at her with doubt.

Her face scrunched up as she considered that option as a viable lie. "I guess it's the best you've got. And with what happened the other day, it could just work." She then fidgeted with the hem of her skirt one last time before turning to lead the way to Cliff's.

My legs seemed to protest my intentions with every step I took, my feet suddenly feeling a thousand times heavier than normal. I felt like I should be reciting some verse from the *Bible* or something. *Yea though I walk through the valley of death, I will fear no evil . . .* Wait . . . how did the rest go again? I brought my hand up to encircle the dragon pendant, for a moment its warmth was comforting to me, that is, until I actually stood at the threshold of Cliff's house. If felt strange going to a party without Jenna, and without Bryn at least waiting for me inside somewhere. The last party I'd actually attended had been the night I'd nearly been raped by a guy who I didn't even know, and I had finally figured out my true feelings for Bryn. It had been a turning point in my life, and this party had all the signs of being another kind of turning point for me. I just hoped that it would turn me in a positive direction when all was said and done.

I could tell Laila was almost as nervous as I was because she hadn't said a word to me all the way up the front walk. I wondered how she would feel if she knew what she was really walking into. We both hesitated at the front door, and it was me who finally found the courage to reach for the doorknob first. My breath caught in my throat as I turned the knob and pushed the door open. But just like any other normal high school party, we were greeted by loud music and even louder talking. I'm not really sure what I expected, but it all seemed entirely *too* normal. Laila clutched at my arm as we entered, and damn if she wasn't latched on tight enough to draw blood.

"Hey, ladies," Cliff drawled, as if appearing from out of nowhere. Creepy much? As if having a Rider inside of him wasn't bad enough, he had to pull that weird stalker-ish thing guys do that's only cute when you actually like them. Bryn and Khol were both very skilled at it. "Was wondering when you two would show up," he said while he looked at me, making clear who he really was addressing. "You want something to drink?"

"Yes," Laila said.

"No," I said at the same exact time. When Cliff raised his eyebrows at me, I felt the need to explain. "Medication, remember? I really don't wanna get sick again."

Cliff smiled at me good-naturedly. "Right. Don't want you ruining any more of my shoes."

I lifted my head up to glare at Cliff and the stupid Rider inside of him that were both seemingly amused with their little comment. "Come on Laila; let's go get you something to drink." I tugged her along, not really sure where I was going.

"Awe, come on Paige. I didn't mean nothin' by that," Cliff said as he followed behind us. "Besides, the kitchen is the other way."

Without acknowledging him, I pivoted on my heel, taking Laila with me and headed in the opposite direction. "This is going to be a long night," I mumbled under my breath. I sent up a silent prayer that I would find what I was looking for and that this would all be worth it.

I stopped short when I got to our destination, all the hairs on my body standing to attention—every single person in the kitchen had a Rider inside of them. *Every. Single. One.* "Oh, God," I said as I swiped my sweaty palm over my mouth in horror. There was no way I was going to be able to handle this.

"Are you not feeling good again?" Laila whispered to me under her breath.

"More than you know," I whispered back through gritted teeth.

"You gonna be sick again?"

"I'm way beyond that point." I forced myself to stand up straighter and to don an air of false confidence. "Now let's get you that drink." How's that saying go? Fake it until you make it? I wasn't sure if I was that good of an actress, but I was damned sure going to try to be.

"Okaaay," Laila said, drawing the word out to let me know she didn't exactly know what was up with me. *That would make two of us.*

As we strode toward an ice chest obviously filled with various kinds of alcoholic libations by the way everyone seemed to be orbiting around it, Cliff scrambled to get ahead of us. "Hey, what can I get you then, Paige? A coke, or sweet tea, or water, or something?"

My lips turned up in a wry smile. Oh, how sweet, the alien wanted to play host to me. Too bad my whole planet had already been doing that, and I was so over it. "Nothing, thanks."

"Natty Lite? Don't you have anything left besides Natty Lite in here?" Laila said with annoyance as the sound of ice sloshing around reached my ears. I almost wanted to laugh, the more things change, the more they stay the same. Were teenagers, no matter where in the country, whether they were fully human or playing hosts to aliens, forced to drink the beer cast offs of society?

Cliff frowned down a Laila. "You know all the good stuff always goes first; maybe if you would have gotten here earlier you could've had something else."

Laila finished flicking the ice off a can of Natty Lite and cracked it open, and lifted it to her mouth. She proceeded to chug it all down in almost one go. Huh. And maybe her solution was the same as mine always had been, to use quantity to make up for quality in beer. But then again look what almost happened to me the last time I'd attempted to actually apply that flawed logic as a solution. "I need to go to the bathroom," I said to both Cliff and Laila, hoping that Laila would be a good girlfriend and offer to come with me, and Cliff would be a good host and direct me to the nearest one. Too bad neither one of them wanted to fulfill those particular roles.

"I'll wait for you here," Laila said as she made goo goo eyes at a cute boy and his little friend inside of him.

"I'll show you where to go," Cliff said with a smile on his face. *Ugh.*

"Fine," I grated. I suppose that Laila wouldn't be much help anyways. I was seriously outnumbered and she was a non-gifted human who had absolutely no idea what was really going on right under her nose.

"Come on." Cliff tried to link his arm with mine and I sidestepped him, not wanting to come into contact with his bare skin again. The bold move made him frown at me.

"Do I need to remind you again that I have a boyfriend back home?" I punctuated my sentence with the best death glare in my arsenal.

It didn't even faze him. "Can't blame a guy for trying," he said with a laugh.

"Actually, yes I can," I retorted with ice dripping from my voice. I trailed along behind him, wishing I could use my dragon magic to fry him to a crisp, but I knew it was just the Rider I wanted dead, and not poor Cliff, at least not the real Cliff. When we got to the top of a huge set of winding stairs, Cliff sauntered down to the end of the hallway and turned the light on in the bathroom for me.

As I moved to walk past him, he stuck his arm up to rest his hand on the edge of the doorjamb to completely block my way. "Aren't you gonna thank me for taking you to this bathroom where you don't even have to stand in line?"

"Ummm . . . Thank you," I said crisply, and tried to duck under his arm, but he wasn't having any of it. Or maybe it was the Rider that wasn't having any of it.

Cliff's features suddenly seemed to completely take on the appearance of the alien within. It was a shock that made me stumble back and gasp. "Cliff has been difficult to hold on to from day one," the Rider snarled at me as he grabbed a huge clump of my white hair at the back of my head. "But I have a feeling if we get one of us into you, and the two of you make nice with us"—he smiled a big toothy grin at me—"then Cliffy here will be a lot more easy to manage."

Riders couldn't possess dragons. I still wasn't really sure why, but if they tried to put a Rider in me they would know something was different and my cover would be completely blown. I couldn't allow that to happen. I twisted abruptly and managed to wrench myself out from under Cliff's tight grasp, losing a clump of hair in the process, and slammed him into the wall. His head hit at a wrong angle, or just right for me, and he passed out cold. He probably hadn't been expecting that. That made two of us . . . or should I say three?

I stood there for a second, my chest heaving from the sudden adrenaline rush, before my brain finally caught up with what had just happened. Now what the hell was I supposed to do? "Think, P.J., think," I whispered hoarsely to myself. I glanced back down the dark hall just to make sure someone hadn't come up behind me when I wasn't paying attention. Much to my relief the coast was still clear. But I knew I had to do . . . something . . . fast.

Okay, first I should probably check to make sure that Cliff was in fact still sucking in oxygen. I tentatively stepped over his slumped body, my heart pounding in my chest, half expecting him to suddenly sit up and attack me like in some grade B horror movie villain. But he didn't, and the rise and fall of his chest let me know that I hadn't killed him. I heaved a sigh of relief, short lived, as I heard footsteps coming up the stairs. *Shit.* In a moment of panic I grabbed Cliff under the arms and drug him into the bathroom, it was harder work than I would have thought, and as soon as he was far enough in, I shut the door behind us and locked it. Great—now I'd managed to trap myself in an even smaller space with the hostile Rider. *Go me!*

I looked around the small second story bathroom for some kind of . . . I don't know . . . inspiration to help me out of my predicament, but none came. I was about one panicked second away from ripping off my Khol repelling bracelet so that I could call him for help. The only thing stopping me was that I didn't seem to be in any immediate danger . . . yet. Well, that and I didn't know if my pride could take that kind of blow. I was kind of attached to the idea of doing things on my own now, and besides if I was going to be with Bryn, I couldn't keep relying on Khol for everything without killing Bryn a little more each time. I was beginning to understand why Bryn was so upset about me always relying on Khol instead of him, when I should have chosen him, or the best option . . . myself.

A knock on the door made me feel like my heart was going to explode out of my chest and I tried to sound calm when I answered. "Someone's in here," I squeaked. Yep . . . I sounded like the epitome of calm. *Nothing suspicious going on here . . . nothing at all.*

"Cliff in there with you?" a male voice asked while I heard a decidedly masculine chuckle at his question. *Shit.* Two Riders outside the door, and me stuck in here with a third. *Think, P.J., Think.* My eyes finally settled on the window. I bit my lip with determination. There really wasn't any other way. I stepped over Cliff's still unconscious body and pushed the medium sized frosted window open. I hoisted myself up onto the ledge and looked around for options to climb down to the ground on: a tree, a drainpipe, a vine . . . something . . . anything . . . but there was nothing. I heard a loud groan come from the bathroom floor as Cliff started to come to. I had to make a decision on what I was going to do . . . fast.

"Cliff man, you in there?" the Rider outside the door asked with suspicion in his voice. Cliff groaned louder in response. "Hey," the Rider said. "What's going on in there?" The door handle began to rattle as he tried to turn the locked knob without any luck. It looked like I was going to have to jump. Hopefully, I'd just sprain an ankle or do something pretty benign, but at least I would get away relatively unscathed, all things considered. I wondered briefly if I should try to tuck and roll or just jump feet first. Or maybe—

"Not so fast," a very angry Rider growled from Cliff's body as he grabbed me by my shoulder. I let out a startled scream as I teetered forward toward the ground and instinctively reached back to grasp Cliff's hand. But instead of keeping me on the ledge, the sudden movement sent us both careening forward. With nothing else to do but fall, I clamped my eyes shut and wished I had never left the house tonight. Why, oh why, couldn't I have spent a nice evening at home at the Murder House? Spending time with ghosts isn't as bad as becoming one. Suddenly a weird—familiar—feeling of dizziness overtook me, and instead of feeling the impact of the hard ground shortly before my emanate demise, I landed with an oof on what felt like a bed. Of course, I felt Cliff crash into me half a second later.

"What the fu—?" Cliff exclaimed as I opened my eyes to find the purple and white pattern of my bedspread that I had been using at the Murder House under my nose. I quickly reeled around, picked up the lamp from my nightstand, and knocked Cliff out cold again. As he slumped down to the ground, I found myself wondering for the second time in one evening if I had killed him.

My bedroom door slammed open, hitting the wall behind it to reveal a battle ready Nala. She paused to take in the scene of Cliff unconscious on the floor, and a freaked out me standing over him with what was left of my lamp and relaxed a bit. "Who's he, and what happened?" she asked a little too calmly.

"That," I started, surprising myself with how normal I sounded, "is the Rider who was going to blow my cover by trying to force one of his buddies into me because his host has some kind of thing for me." I inhaled and exhaled a couple of times trying to get fresh oxygen to my brain. "And I have absolutely no idea what happened. One minute I'm hurtling toward the ground to my death, and the next I'm here."

It was then that Nala's face took on the look of surprise. "You transported yourself and him here?" she said incredulously. "You're too young to have that kind of control."

"Hey," I snapped with indignance. "I'm the same age as Bryn and he can already do it." And then everything sunk in. I had . . . finally . . . been able to use the super cool dragon power I'd been drooling over since I first found out what I really was. Too bad I had absolutely no idea what I had done to access it, besides having a near death experience. And cool or not, that wasn't something I was willing to replicate, even for a power that awesome.

"Alright. Fine. I really don't want to get into to it with you about your powers right now. The more important issue is, what exactly do you plan on doing with your new little friend, now that we have him here?"

That was a good question . . . a very good question indeed.

15

So what are you going to do with me?" the Rider inside of Cliff asked in an exasperated tone.

"I don't know yet," I said, resuming my pacing from one corner of my room to the other. Cliff, and the alien leech inside of him, was currently tied to a wooden chair that Nala had brought up from the kitchen. We'd used rope and duct tape to secure him there . . . lots and lots of duct tape. I guess that goes to prove that duct tape really is all-purpose.

"Well, aren't you going to question me or something?"

"Look," I said as I came to stop directly in front of him, "if this is so hard on you, then why don't you just ooze on out of Cliff's body and leave him alone?"

The Rider made Cliff's handsome face grimace at me in response, "It's not that simple."

I crouched down in front of him and peered up with curiosity at the Rider inside of Cliff. The alien inside seemed to have almost eclipsed him completely since the moment he came to in my room. "So why don't you try and explain it to me then."

He narrowed his eyes at me with hatred. "No."

This all seemed a bit surreal. Was this actually happening or was I having some kind of weird dream? If felt real, it felt like I was awake. And yet the fact that I was having this conversation with the Rider inside of Cliff while he was duct taped to one of my kitchen chairs seemed a bit . . . ridiculous. I guess I had to stop repeatedly questioning the fact that my life had turned into one surreal moment after another. "Really? You just asked me if I was going to ask you questions, and—"

"I didn't say I was going to answer them," he snapped with more irritation, like I was an annoying little gnat circling his head.

"Fine. If that's the way you wanna play it, then I'm about ready to enroll you in Torture Class 101." But could I actually torture Cliff's poor body? I had no doubt that my conscious would have no problem letting me cause some major damage to just the Rider, but he wasn't just the Rider at the moment. "Why are you still in Cliff anyways? I saw him push you out. I saw you leave."

"How do you know that?" The Rider's jaw dropped, or I guess Cliff's jaw dropped. Everyone kept telling me to think of a host and the Rider within as one and the same, to which I used to be able to do pretty easily. But with one currently residing inside of Jenna, and with having the vision of Cliff pushing this Rider out, it was beginning to be more and more difficult.

I let a slow smile creep across my face. It was obvious the Rider had figured out I was a dragon, but I was under the mistaken impression that he had also come to the conclusion of who I was specifically. Guess I was wrong. Time to fill him in. "I *saw* it in a vision."

He just stared at me, shock playing across his face. "Impossible. You're a dragon."

I leaned back and flopped into a sitting position on the floor in front of him before crossing my legs casually. "Yes,

I'm a dragon." I smiled brightly at him. "But I'm also a Seer, and a very powerful one at that."

"The dragons only have one Seer, and she's a gifted human. And she should be dead by now," he blurted out, seemingly unable to stop himself.

All amusement drained from me. "I am that Seer. And clearly I'm neither human nor dead." Of course, until recently even I had thought I was human, at least partly, so I couldn't really expect the Riders to be privy to any information that said differently. I rose up from my sitting position on the floor and came to stand as close as I would dare to the Rider. "But I'm hoping you'll be soon . . . dead that is."

"What are you doing here?" the Rider asked as he clearly tried to hide the fear in its eyes. "Did you come here for me? Because of who I am?"

I could feel my face scrunch up in both shock and confusion. "Who you are? I don't know who you are, besides Cliff that is."

He let out a dark laugh. "Well, isn't this perfect." He paused and I could tell he was trying to weigh what he should say to me next. "Okay. If you let me go, I'll get my father to back off of you guys, to leave you alone. I mean a lot to him . . . in both my forms. And he doesn't really care about you guys, not really, just the threat you pose. If you promise to leave us alone, we'll do the same."

It was my turn for my jaw to drop. Was he kidding? There was no way he actually thought I'd go along with that, could he? "You can't be serious. You killed our families, slaughtered my people, are trying to destroy our world . . . and you want us to simply look the other way? Maybe I hit you on the head too hard," I muttered, the last part more to myself than him. Could Riders suffer brain damage if their host did?

"My father felt threatened . . . and we're not trying to destroy your world. We like it, actually."

"No. You've destroyed worlds before. Decimated them for their resources like the parasites you are and then moved on to the next world you planned to victimize. And how you've been treating our world . . . *my world* . . . definitely proves you plan on doing the same here."

"Mistakes," the Rider pleaded with his voice and eyes. "We didn't know any better. We were just trying to survive. But we like it here—want to stay."

"Well you're not!" I bellowed, finally losing control of my temper. I could feel my dragon fire magic spark to life just under my skin, practically begging for me to release it on the Rider. But I fought the urge because I knew, even through the haze of red that was tinting my vision, that I didn't want to hurt Cliff.

The Rider's eyes widened to the size of saucers as he finally realized how much danger he was really in. "We can make a bargain. I swear. Just don't hurt me."

"How many have begged for your mercy? How many of my people begged before you slaughtered them in cold blood? Men, women, and children, all of the same, just because of who we are. This is our planet and you can't have it!" Flames crept up into my fingertips, and I stretched out my palms in Cliff's direction.

"That was my father! Not me! We're not all the same! Some of us just want to stay—to live!" the Rider exclaimed as sweat trickled down Cliff's frightened face. "Please . . ."

"Tell me," I growled. "Tell me who your father is, and what his end game is."

"Sena—Senat—Senator Bill Wexington is my father's human host . . . and my real father is the one inside him . . . our leader," the Rider stammered.

What were the chances? I had both Senator Bill Wexington's son, and the son of the lead Rider both as my prisoner. Actually—I chuckled darkly to myself—I knew none of this had happened by chance . . . My birth mother had seen it all and planned for it to happen. There was no other explanation.

"Senator Bill Wexington is your father?" He seemed to be the center of all of this from the beginning. One of my first big visions had been of the alien rider taking possession of him. He also seemed to be the one leading the charge that was pro-gun control and anti-American citizen's rights—or anti-human rights, if I really wanted to be accurate. Maybe if I could take him out, then the rest of the Riders wouldn't be as difficult to manage.

"Yes," the alien made Cliff's head bob in affirmation. "He'll make a deal for me—trade—"

"Tell me," I growled, my throat feeling raw. "Tell me what he's planning."

Cliff's crystal blue eyes blinked at me slowly a few times before the Rider began to speak again. "He wants control. He wants the humans as slaves. We won't kill off your world. We want to stay, to live, like I said, but we want—"

"To rule," I finished for him. It was a story as old as time itself. The struggle for power. How cliché. Couldn't they at least come up with something new? I never quite understood it myself, but then again, I've heard that those with power usually didn't pay much mind to it, and those without, or with a little, made it their focus, or sometimes obsession. I clearly have always had power, and now I had more than I'd ever dreamed of, and more than I'd ever wanted.

"Yes," Cliff's full lips responded with the fowl sound of the Rider's voice. "So you see, it doesn't have to involve you, if you don't want it to. We'll leave you alone to do whatever it is that you do, and we'll do our thing. The humans are no concern of yours, not really."

A low animalistic growl erupted from my chest. "Until not too long ago I thought I was human. I was raised to think I was human. I still *feel* human." I tried to keep my fire from going to him, from burning him alive, because I didn't want to hurt Cliff, but beyond that I knew that keeping this particular Rider alive for the moment would do our cause more good. He was full of information, useful information, I reminded myself. "The people who raised me, who were the only real parents I ever knew . . . were human." But it was hard . . . harder than I thought to not just act on my murderous impulse. I had to leave . . . leave the room now . . . or he would die . . . they both would die.

I slammed out of my room and ran down the hallway, my dragon fire magic dripping down from my fingertips. "Nala!" I screamed. I needed help. I couldn't handle my emotions and all of my new raw power together. "Nala, please!" But she didn't come. I knew she was afraid. Afraid because she was a Water Dragon, afraid that my fire would consume all of her up and leave nothing but ash. I dropped to my knees as things around me began to burn . . . the carpet, the wall . . . my own clothes. I had one of two choices: I could reach down inside of myself and find the strength of will to get myself under control, or I could rip the small—hot—very, very hot blackening bracelet from my wrist and call on Khol for help. The latter was more appealing . . . simpler . . . but . . . but *Bryn.* His name swam through my mind as I tried to decide what to do before I burned everyone and everything down around me. If I wanted him, wanted to be with him the way that I truly desired, I was going to have to stop relying on Khol. I had to trust in myself, in my own strength of will. The old Dragon Queen, my birth mother, wouldn't have given me her powers if she didn't think I could handle them. I had the strength in me somewhere; I just had to find it . . . for Bryn. *Always for Bryn.*

I conjured up an image of his face in my mind's eye for focus. I pictured his dark blue eyes glittering with amusement as he laughed at something silly I'd done. His full firm lips would curve up slightly at first, and then his patented smile complete with dimples would spread across his perfectly chiseled jaw line. I wanted him to look at me like that again, to laugh easily in my presence like he used to be able to do. I wanted to banish the new, hardened Bryn from my life forever, because I had made him that way, I had changed him. I wanted us back, and I would do anything . . . anything, including burn down this world to have a chance with him again.

And just like that my dragon fire magic pulled back into me and took all of the fires it had started with it. I was surrounded by blackened and still crackling . . . well, everything . . . but nothing was actually burning anymore. I laughed hoarsely. What do you know? I'd actually done it . . . all by myself. No. That part wasn't true. I'd done it with Bryn, because he was as much a part of me as my own heart. I could never let myself forget that again, never let anyone or anything come between us again. Or maybe I'd done if for Bryn. I was too tired to care at the moment though, all that mattered was that I had done it; I had stopped my fire from burning the creepy Murder House down around me.

A contented smile spread across my face as I collapsed to the ground and my mind went as black as the carpet my face pushed into.

"I'm so thirsty," I mumbled from the desert that was my throat.

"Using your fire magic will do that; it won't ever burn you though, but I guess you found that out the hard way." A familiar voice rumbled from nearby. "Here, drink this."

My eyes snapped open to the sight of Khol. How'd he find me? What was he doing here? "Wha—what—how did you find me?" It was then that I noticed that I was not in fact in the Murder House any longer, but lying in Khol's large comfortable bed.

He handed me a glass of what appeared to be ice water, and I took it with shaky hands. I watched him with wide eyes over the rim of the glass as I greedily gulped down the best glass of water I'd ever had. When I'd finished, I lowered the empty glass to my lap and gripped it tightly. What would Khol's reaction be now that I was back? Would he be angry I was gone? Or would he be ready to pull me back into his arms to pick up where we left off? I was hoping the former because he'd be easier to deal with in that mood when I told him I'd chosen Bryn.

He eyed me warily, his green eyes blazing with unreadable emotions. "I don't know what you're feeling," he said as his mouth dipped into a frown.

"It's the bracelet," I said as I tapped the tiny intricately made bronze bracelet on my left wrist. "My birth mother gave it to me to wear so you couldn't track me."

Khol's nostrils flared with anger. "I see. Will you be taking it off now that you're back then?"

I bit my lip and looked at my hands still gripping the empty glass in my lap. "No. I'm not ready to take it off just yet."

Deafening silence engulfed the room, and I didn't need to be able to read Khol's emotions to know that he was not happy. I decided to change the subject and quickly. "So how did you find me?"

"You used enough magic to announce your presence to all of dragon kind," he responded flatly.

"Oh." I hadn't really thought about that. Of course, with all that dragon magic I had used, Khol probably zeroed in on me in seconds.

"What did you do with the Rider? The one I had at the house—the one—"

"We have him here," Khol interjected. "He's important then, like I thought?"

I did meet Khol's electric green eyes then. "Oh yes," I breathed. "Very important."

Khol leaned forward, his face growing more intense, "Tell me."

"His father is the lead Rider, and his host is none other than Senator Bill Wexington. He's the son of both the lead Rider and the Senator."

A tight smile turned Khol's lips up slightly at the corners. "He is very important then." He suddenly came to me in a burst of speed almost too fast to track with my eyes, and took me in his arms, inhaling sharply as if in pain as he crushed me to him. "I went out of my mind not knowing where you were, not being able to sense you." He pushed his nose into my hair and inhaled. "I've missed you so much."

"Khol—I . . ." This was going to be harder than I had originally thought. I loved Khol, I really did. He just wasn't Bryn. Despite that, my body responded to Khol's, and a feeling of liquid heat bloomed inside of me. But the difference now was that I wouldn't let myself get swept away in those feelings. I wouldn't let the ease of our relationship rule my decisions. No one ever said love was easy.

I felt Khol's body tense around me and he pulled back from our embrace enough to meet my eyes. His bore into mine, and after a moment's time, but what seemed like forever to me, he backed away from me completely. "I see." His voice cracked with emotion.

"Khol—I—please—I'm sorry. You know I love you—you do. And you've got to believe me. I never would have done . . ." My voice caught in my throat as my mind skidded over the memories of the intimate moments Khol and I had shared. "I never would have . . ." I tried again, but this time was stopped short by the look on Khol's face. It was a mixture of hurt and anger. And my heart cracked just a little for him. Why did he ever have to fall for me? Why did things have to be so complicated?

"So, you're back to wanting Bryn again," he said without question. "And if he still doesn't want you?"

"He wants me," I whispered. "He's just afraid that being with me will result in my death."

Khol's face had lost all emotion, and he looked at me with a mask of neutrality, which was worse because it told me how much he was hurting. "And if it does? Result in your death?"

"Then it'll be my fault, and none of yours. I should be able to protect myself." And that was the truth of the matter. No one was ever truly safe, not really. And relying on someone else for security would result in my suffering no matter which way I looked at it. I had to rely on myself for my own protection.

"So my little Seer has finally become our little queen." Khol gave me a smile that didn't touch the sadness in his eyes. "I told you that you'd find the strength in you one day."

I stood and went to him, cupping my hand to the side of his face. "Thanks to you."

He brought his large hand up to cover mine and leaned into my touch, meeting my eyes with intensity. A familiar feeling of electricity shot through my system. I always felt sparks when Khol touched me. "I can't lose you . . . again." His voice was hoarse from raw emotion. "He doesn't deserve you."

I tried to pull away from him then, but he held me to his face with his strong fingers. "I don't care what you think," I said as anger began to build in me. "I can't help that I've loved him practically all of my life. I need him almost as much as the oxygen I breathe! I loved him before I even met you!"

I could feel the muscles in Khol's jaw spasm as he ground his teeth together. "And yet you came to my bed. And you trembled so sweetly under my fingers and tongue." His words were soft but there was no mistaking the underlying cruelty that they meant to inflict on me. "You had no need of him to help you breathe when I let you do the same to me. And you happily made love to me with your mouth."

My lower lip began to tremble as tears gathered in my eyes. I knew this wasn't going to be easy, but I hadn't expected Khol to be cruel, to use all of my fears against me. He knew I felt slutty for doing what I did with him, and for still being involved with Bryn. There was no way he didn't know with his close emotional connection to me. He was just trying to hurt me like I was hurting him . . . and it was working. "Don't," I squeaked. "Please don't say those things to me."

"You mean the truth?"

I opened and closed my mouth not knowing what to say. He was right; of course, nothing he was saying to me was a lie . . . not really. It was then he captured my lips with his, and as I gasped in surprise, he swallowed down all the breath in my lungs. I struggled against him, even as his body made mine hum with excitement. I was attracted to him, still . . . and just because I loved Bryn more didn't change the fact that I loved Khol too.

He pushed me back onto the bed and pushed my arms up over my head, holding me in place as he continued his assault on my senses. I couldn't help but moan when he ground himself into me. Even when he had essentially blackmailed his way into my pants by threatening Bryn's life, Khol had always brought me pleasure. Why would now be any different?

"Khol—stop—please," I begged when he freed my mouth only to begin kissing a trail of fire down my neck and other more sensitive areas.

"I won't lose you again," he growled.

It was with those words I knew how truly desperate he had become to have me for keeps. He was about to do what he swore he would never do to me again. He was going to take from me without asking—he was going to claim me against my will. As in the past with Khol . . . it wouldn't be rape . . . not really . . . but it wasn't exactly what I wanted either. At least not mentally. Or maybe this is what it means when someone says another person seduced them? Was Khol seducing me? As my body arched up into his touch, I was pretty sure I had the answer, and I was not happy.

"Don't do this to me, Khol," I hissed. "You promised."

"And you promised to wait—to wait until the child was born. We all agreed." He freed me from my shirt and bra, and while he still held my arms over my head with one hand, his callused palms skimmed roughly over my naked flesh, eliciting a moan from me. And I hated him for it.

"You were going to cheat. You admitted it—and I changed my mind," I grated as I felt my dragon fire magic push up through me as my anger began to heighten. How dare he pull this crap with me again? Maybe he hadn't changed as much as I thought he had. "Khol, stop, before I make you." My voice had changed, dropped to a low animalistic growl. "I don't wanna hurt you."

Paying no mind to my words, Khol tugged at my pants, tearing them from my body. I lay before him now, with only a tiny lace thong keeping me from being completely naked—something in the past that would have been sexy, but now—*I was pissed.*

An inhuman scream erupted from my chest as I pulled the strength from somewhere to push Khol off of me. In fact, not only did I manage to push him off of me, but I threw him clear across the room to where he landed in a heap on his ass with a dazed expression on his face. I pulled myself up to my full height and let my fire magic explode from my palms.

Khol, with almost no effort at all, captured my magic in his own palm and smiled at me. "This little display of power—it only makes me want you more," Khol rumbled as his eyes raked over my nearly naked self, causing goosebumps to erupt all over my flesh. "You're acting more and more dragon with every passing moment, and that means I'm the one you belong with."

"I belong with Bryn."

"He's too human. And beyond that, he's a Black Dragon. Your powers clash. Your flames would consume him and leave nothing behind. Even weaker Red Dragons are no match for you." Khol paused and offered three words to me in a hushed voice, "Think of Drake."

I knew what he was referring to—when I had first discovered my dragon fire magic I'd nearly killed Drake—a Red Dragon. "I would never hurt Bryn. I love him too much."

Khol raised one of his eyebrows at me in question. "Like Jenna."

"That was different. That was—"

"Over me." Khol's voice held a note of triumph, like making that point alone would win me over. All it did was make me angrier.

"Maybe you're too dragon for me. Maybe I need someone with more human-like emotions," I retorted, knowing it would bother Khol deep down. He'd never loved anyone the way that he loved me before, and there was a vulnerability he wasn't used to inside of him because of it. He wasn't sure he knew how to treat me, not really.

"Enough," he seethed. He locked his fire backlit eyes with me briefly before he leapt suddenly through the air with lightening speed, pinning me against the wall with his rock solid body. He dipped his head to whisper in my ear as I turned mine away from him. "He doesn't have a second form. You do." My whole body began to shake with fear. Khol knew how much I was afraid of being able to shift into a dragon. He'd been very careful to not show me his other form, or to let anyone else for that matter, as to not freak me out now that I knew I was fully dragon. I guess this meant we were playing for keeps, pushing an entire elevator's worth of each other's buttons.

"No. It doesn't mean I have to change, not ever. Not if I don't want to." Yep, that's right, I fully intended to rely on complete denial when it came to shifting into a dragon. I refused to lose that part of the illusion of my humanity.

Khol chuckled low and dark in response. "You won't have a choice. It *will* happen. It's just a matter of when."

His words sunk in slowly and when they finally hit home, I cried out as if I was in physical pain. "No! Why didn't you tell me that before? Why should I believe you now?"

"Because I didn't want to scare you. But now it's obvious you need more than just a simple dose of reality. Things won't work with him. I don't understand why you insist on trying." Khol's voice had dropped down to a barely audible level, and I could hear the pain that had been hiding under his anger. I had hurt him deeper than I ever had before, because this time he had dared to hope for it all.

My anger slipped away, causing a dull ache in my chest. "I can't help the way that I feel," I croaked. "I'm sorry."

"What changed? What changed while you were away?" Khol's voice sounded so small, and so brittle.

I closed my eyes tightly and let the fresh tears that had been gathering in the corners of my eyes spill down my over heated cheeks. "I don't know. Things just seemed to become clearer to me somehow."

"It's that damn bracelet. It keeps me from you, and you from me. Your birth mother has clearly been meddling in our lives. I should have known from that letter. I should have known from . . . everything." He reached up with one hand and started to bend the bracelet off.

A chill ran down my spine. He was right; my birth mother had been meddling in everything since before I was even born. What if the bracelet did more than just make me untraceable and unreadable to Khol? What if it was messing with my head somehow? "What did the letter say?" I asked on a shaky exhalation. But Khol ignored me and focused on removing the bracelet. "Khol, tell me please. I deserve to know."

"She wanted me to be prepared for a change in you when you returned. She wanted me to give you some space," he growled while he still struggled with the piece of jewelry. "I thought she meant—I don't know—not that you would come back and suddenly not want me any longer." He abruptly released me and turned away from me. "It's welded on. We're going to need a special tool to get it off," he said with frustration oozing through his entire body as he stood perfectly still.

"What? What the hell?" How did it become—wait—it was my fire magic—I distinctly remembered the bracelet growing really, really hot back at the creepy Murder House. "I reached up and clutched at the dragon pendant Khol had gifted to me. It was perfectly fine. "Why didn't the pendant—"

"It's been charmed to be fire magic proof. It was made for our kind specifically," Khol answered before I could finish my question.

"Oh."

"Get dressed. We have more important things to worry about right now." I didn't know how to react. One minute Khol had been ready to force himself on me, and the next he's acting like I was the one who was focusing on our little love triangle to the detriment of everything else. "I'll be outside when you're ready." He stalked out of the room without so much as a backward glance at me.

"Okaaaay," I mumbled to myself. Not that I wasn't ecstatic for the reprieve from Khol, but I wasn't sure exactly what had just happened. Had Khol accepted that I wanted Bryn and not him? I highly doubted it, and yet he had walked away . . . literally. Maybe he'd just realized we *did* have more important things to worry about at the moment and the rest could wait.

I harrumphed to myself as I located my discarded clothes and pulled them back on. I for one was ready to get back to dealing with the Rider inside of Cliff instead of focusing on my messed up love life. Because screwed wasn't even a good enough word to describe my situation at all . . . not by a long shot.

16

Terrance blinked his human host's eyes in complete disbelief as he settled back into the familiar body. When he was ripped from it, he had thought it would be the last time he would exist outside the red stone that imprisoned him. He knew many others that had been placed there by his master to never return. He looked up questioningly at his master and immediately averted his eyes in submission.

"They have my son," his master growled with fury. "Consider this your last and second chance at this life." There was a long pause before he spoke again and Terrance didn't dare so much as to twitch a single muscle. "Get him back no matter the cost."

Terrance rose and left the room without a single word. He didn't need to say anything. His master knew that he understood what was truly at stake. And he had no intention of losing his freedom again.

I knew I needed to focus on the Rider inside of Cliff and getting any kind of information we could out of him. The opportunity we had was priceless, and yet all I really wanted to do was to go to Bryn. I needed to tell him how much had changed in the short time I'd been away. Well . . . at least from my perspective. I was still pregnant and didn't know whether he or Khol was the father, but none of that seemed to matter in regards to wanting to be with Bryn anymore. But what could I say to him this time around that I hadn't already said before? He'd told me that love wasn't an issue, and that love, in fact, was what was motivating him to give me up . . . for my own protection. I just had to make him understand somehow . . . make him see that it wasn't his job to protect me.

What I really needed was to talk to Jenna—the real Jenna anyways. I hadn't allowed myself to think in much detail about her being possessed by a Rider while I was away. I had too many other things to deal with and it was just easier to pretend what had happened with her was all a really, really bad dream. Yep . . . I was not only the new Dragon Queen but the queen of denial as well. I was suddenly overcome with the irresistible urge to visit her. I missed her more than I ever thought possible. Sure, she's completely self-absorbed at times, sex obsessed, and utterly annoying but—she was Jenna and I loved her. I knew if I asked well—anyone—to take me to see her that they would disagree with that line of thought and prevent me from doing so. The only way I was going to get to see her, I knew, was if I found her on my own. Now . . . where would I stash her if I were Khol?

About fifteen minutes later, a very annoyed me still hadn't figured out where Jenna was. Maybe if I could find Jeremy, I could force it out of him. I wondered if having a Rider in Jenna had dampened his newfound devotion to her? He had to know it wasn't really her that had sent him to deliver her cookies of death to me. I heaved a huge sigh and was just about to give up when I spied Jeremy, speak of the devil, coming down the hallway. Isn't that the way it always is . . . you only luck into something just when you're ready to give up?

"Jeremy!" I called out, hurrying toward him with excitement.

He looked up at me, and a smile spread across his face slowly. "I'm so glad you're back." He came to me and wrapped me in a bear hug, swinging me around, causing me to giggle despite myself. Yep . . . I'd missed Jeremy too. Even though he had started out as just another guy trying to play tonsil hockey with me, since his feelings for Jenna had developed, we'd been able to relax into a real friendship, at least I felt that way. "Have you figured out a way to fix Jenna?" he asked with hope filling his caramel colored eyes as he set me back down on my feet.

All feelings of elation instantaneously drained out of me. "Not yet." I paused to study the ground before gathering the courage to meet his eyes and the disappointment that shone out at me from them. "But I know I will. My birth mother said I could, and she's never wrong apparently."

He nodded, letting some hope settle into his tense features. "Okay. So what's the plan then?"

"I wanna see her Jeremy. I know you're probably gonna say it's a bad idea but I just miss her so much, and I just—"

"Yeah. Okay," Jeremy interjected, thoroughly shutting me up. I'd been prepared to argue with him to get him to tell me where she was. I was shocked at how easily he agreed. He must have read it on my face. "She can't hurt you, and she knows she has a Rider inside of her. It's almost like she has a split personality or something. Jenna—the real Jenna—there aren't even words to explain how awful she feels about—"

"Trying to kill me," I said dryly.

"Yeah," Jeremy said softly, like he was partly to blame or something.

I reached up and touched his arm. "But she's okay besides that? I mean no one is mistreating her, right? Khol promised he'd protect her." And yet another instance of me turning to Khol for aid. But then again he was the Red Dragon Lord, and I was the Dragon Queen. Technically, I could ask any dragon for assistance and expect them to give to me.

"She's safe but . . ." Jeremy's voice trailed off and his brow furrowed with concern. "She's not doing well. The animals . . . well, they won't talk to her and she's just—"

I gasped, cutting him off. "Oh God, no. I never thought about that part—either way." A Rider with the ability to talk to and in a minor manner control animals—we could have all been so screwed. "I'm sure once the Rider's gone, they'll talk to her again."

"That's what I keep telling her," Jeremy mumbled while studying the floor. He then suddenly looked up at me, as if he forgot for a moment he wasn't alone and gave me a weak smile. "Come on, we'll go see her now before anyone else . . ." He raised his fist up to his mouth and forced a cough. "Khol," he said with a smirk, and he turned and started walking back down the wall in the direction I had seen him coming from, "tries to stop you."

I couldn't help but laugh as I fell into step beside him. "He is a bit controlling, isn't he?"

Jeremy stopped in his tracks and raised his eyebrows up to practically his hairline. "A bit?"

I rolled my eyes at him. "You know what I mean."

Neither one of us said anything else for over the few hundred feet it took to travel until we paused in front of a huge wooden door. As Jeremy pulled it open, I only hesitated for a second before following him in. Inside, much to my surprise, looked like a bedroom with prison bars in front of it. Like someone had just installed bars as an afterthought. And I suppose, that's probably exactly what happened. Talk about a whole new definition to being sent to your room.

I trailed along behind Jeremy and scanned the room for Jenna. Only when we were standing right up next to the bars, did I notice her sprawled out on the bed, staring up at the ceiling. She looked so tiny, lost, and forlorn, laying there with black messy hair and light brown roots. I was overcome by the urge to run to her and hug her, but of course, I couldn't for obvious reasons.

"Jenna," Jeremy said in a soft tone. "Someone's here to see you."

I heard Jenna heave a huge sigh. "I told you, I don't want any visitors. Please just go away." Her voice was so flat and utterly hopeless sounding, lacking all of the usual life that Jenna always seemed to have in her, it was if someone had sucked out her very essence. My stomach knotted immediately, and I felt bile rise up in my throat.

"Jenna," I said. "I wanted to see you. Please won't you talk to me?"

She sat up suddenly and came running toward the bars with a huge smile on her face, and she was still, in that moment, my best girlfriend I'd known forever. But as she got closer and the duel imagery of the Rider inside of her shined out from behind her pixie face, I involuntarily took a step back and let out a strangled scream. My reaction halted her dead in her tracks and her face went ashen. She blinked back tears that were gathering in her deep brown eyes as she looked at me.

"I'm sorry!" I blurted out wanting desperately a do over. "I knew what to expect, it's just that . . ." What could I say? Seeing an alien living inside of you kind of freaked me out? Well of course—duh. "I—I'm sorry." Maybe I shouldn't have come to see her after all. I thought I could handle it, but maybe I was wrong.

Jenna's eyes finally filled to the brim and the tears spilled out and rolled down her face, her lower lip trembling. "You know I would never try to kill you. I mean—*I* would never try to kill you. And the animals—they won't talk to me anymore. I know it's in there—I can feel it but I can't see it! Can't control it when it starts implanting things in my head!" She wailed the last part and dropped to her knees.

Tears of my own began to flow freely down my face and I desperately tried to think of something to say to comfort her. "I'm going to find a way to get it out of you—I promise."

"What if you can't? Or what if even when it's gone it leaves some kind of—I don't know—darkness behind?" Her whole body began to shake as she sobbed. "I tried to kill you. It made sense at the time. It convinced me that you were to blame for all of my problems . . . losing my family . . . being here . . . just everything." More huge sobs wracked her body. "It made total sense—to kill you—my best friend."

"Jenna—I . . ." I looked at her beseeching eyes and began to wonder if it was so easy to convince her I was to blame . . . because I was. I swallowed to try and combat the sudden dryness of my throat, the bile that had risen up had left a burning sensation in its wake. I then turned to Jeremy with wide eyes and shook my head in panic. "I'm sorry—I thought I could—but I can't." Those were the only words of explanation I managed to get out before I turned and ran from the room—ran from Jenna, my best female friend who had an alien inside of her.

Once outside of the room I continued to run, not really sure where I was going, letting my feet lead me blindly. Where could I go? Not to Khol. I knew I could find comfort in his arms, but that would be the easy fix, and short lived at that. Not to Bryn either. I wasn't sure how he would receive me at the moment, and I didn't think I could handle being turned away from him in the state I was in. So I continued to blindly run, my tears smearing the world into bright water colors before my eyes, until I found myself outside in one of the many gardens surrounding the compound and I collapsed under a huge tree.

As I brought my knees up to my chest and hugged them to me, I realized that I'd never been so utterly alone in my life. Sure I might have felt this alone in the past, but I was just being overly dramatic—a truth that I felt down to my core in that moment. Now—now I actually was alone. I had no one to turn to—no one who understood me the way that I needed to be understood. Because that's what I really wanted . . . understanding. Isn't that what everyone wants on some level? That's why sometimes love just isn't enough, because if there's no understanding, then a lack in communication will drag the relationship down. Look at what had happened between Bryn and me. I just couldn't make him understand that it's not his job to protect me, that I only want him to love me.

I sat beneath that tree until no more tears would come, and the air began to grow chilly with the onset of dusk. But I had nowhere else to go, so I stayed until all there was left to do was sleep.

17

I dreamt that I was in a maze, not knowing which way was out, and as I ran around one of the corners, I saw Bryn. He smiled at me, giving me one of his patented lopsided grins complete with dimples, and turned to run from me. He glanced over his shoulder and called out, "This way Peej." As if I was supposed to follow him. And of course I did. Or at least I tried. But bands of steel held me around my waist, keeping me from moving from the spot I stood. I yelled at him to wait but he didn't seem to hear me. I struggled against the bands, and when I looked down I realized that they weren't bands at all, but arms. I whirled around in a panic to see who was keeping me from following Bryn, half expecting to find Khol, but instead I found Drake. He grinned at me and whispered harshly, "You belong with my lord. And I'll make sure he gets you." That's when I screamed.

"It's okay, it was just a nightmare." A heartbreakingly familiar voice murmured from underneath me. My eyes snapped open and I inhaled sharply the scent that I'd come to think of as home . . . Bryn! His hands pulled through my hair, smoothing it back away from my face. "Peej," he whispered my name like a little prayer as I swept my eyes up the line of his chest to meet his fathomless dark blue eyes. My whole body tightened with need, and I pushed myself up so I could slant my lips over his. I needed him, needed to taste him, needed to feel his skin underneath mine. I'd never been so singularly driven to possess Bryn in such a way in all of my life. It was as if I couldn't have him . . . all of him . . . as soon as I could manage . . . I would just shrivel up and die.

As I pushed my tongue into his mouth, demanding him to accept me, I pulled myself up so I could straddle him. He immediately responded to me, a low growl rumbling in the back of his throat as his hands threaded into my hair and pulled me tighter to him. I frantically ground myself against his growing need, wishing that there were no clothes separating us, wondering if I could possibly wait one moment longer or if I possessed the skill to just burn them off without injuring him. "I need you . . . now," I gasped into Bryn's mouth as he lifted his hips up to meet me while I continued my frantic gyrating rhythm. I swore I'd never need anyone again . . . especially a man . . . but I did. I needed Bryn in that moment more than I needed oxygen in my lungs to breathe. It's exactly what I'd told Khol, and it was true. I was so empty without him and I needed him to fill me up, to make me feel . . . *more.*

And then he just stopped . . . everything. "No. Peej. We can't do this," Bryn croaked raggedly as he grabbed my wrists to keep me from holding on to him and slid out from under me.

"I need you, Bryn. Please," I begged as I looked up into his tormented face. "I don't wanna be with anyone but you. It's been you, and only you for as far back as I can remember. It'll be you—always."

His sea storm eyes suddenly began to churn with anger as he regarded me darkly. "You never seem to have a problem getting cozy with Khol. It seems to me you want him plenty."

My mouth dropped open and any sort of reply stuck in my throat. Bryn's lips turned up into a cruel smile. "Even the first time when I was sent away, you couldn't seem to keep your hands off him."

White-hot fury coupled with adrenaline shot through my system. "Nala—that's all I have to say about when you were sent away—Nala." I ground my teeth together. "And as for the rest"—unbidden and unwanted images of the intimacies I'd shared with Khol played across my mind's eye—"you practically put a bow around me and handed me to him." It was true, if Bryn hadn't walked away like he did from me, and he had just let our—even if it was semi-permanent—mate bond reform then I never would have so much as kissed Khol.

"A willing gift," Bryn growled.

I rose up onto my knees so I could reach him, swung my arm through the air, and slapped him across the face with as much force as I could manage. "I love you—you stupid asshole!" And I was showing him in a very peculiar way at the moment.

Bryn blinked his dark lashes over his shocked blue eyes at me, all anger draining from his face. "You hit me," he said as he brought his hand up to cover the small red spot blooming on his perfectly chiseled jaw. "I can't believe you hit me," he mumbled numbly as he continued to stare at me.

"You deserved it," I said with conviction.

Bryn shook his head slowly and the shock turned into some emotion I couldn't quite read. "I think you should leave."

I raised my chin at him petulantly. "No," I replied simply.

"No?" Bryn said incredulously.

"No," I said again.

"Then I guess I'll just have to make you," Bryn retorted as his face morphed into a mask of zen. All cold clean lines, and no emotions . . . at least none I could read. Which was beyond frustrating because I used to be able to read him so well, or at least I thought I could. He reached for me, and I slipped out from under his grasp, reached up and smacked him across his other cheek this time.

His arms immediately dropped to his sides and he gazed at me with renewed shock. "You hit me again." Thanks, Captain Obvious. Next would you like to tell me that the sky is blue?

"Yeah, I did. And I'm gonna keep hitting you until I smack some sense into you." Did I really just say that? When did I become so violent? *Since Bryn started refusing to see reason*, that helpful little voice whispered in my brain. As if to punctuate my point, I reached up and hit Bryn again. This time he just stood there as still as a statue, his big blue eyes blinking in confusion at me. His lack of reaction only angered me more. So I hit him again . . . and again . . . and again. He continued to just stand there. *What the hell?* The sound of my palm meeting his face, first on one side and then the other was the only sound besides our harsh breathing. I just couldn't seem to stop myself. *Crack, crack, crack* . . . a steady rhythm was taking shape, and I seemed to be a slave to its dance.

Finally Bryn reacted. He moved with the speed of a dragon and Guardian mixed as one as I abruptly found myself pinned under his body on his bed. His eyes blazed the fiercest dragon blue, and even though I couldn't see them, I was positive mine glowed just as brightly. What would he do? I absentmindedly wondered, too focused on his perfectly formed face, and how even contorted with rage, it was the most beautiful one I'd ever laid eyes on. "You may be quick to give me away Bryn Aries O'Bannon, but make no mistake—you always have been and always will be mine," I spat at him with more harshness in my voice than I intended.

A low growl erupted from his chest and before I really registered what was happening, his lips came crashing down on mine. He covered me with his entire body, pinning me with his weight down into his mattress. I moaned my approval as his tongue plunged into my mouth, hot and wanting. This is what I needed; this is what I'd been waiting for. As he ground himself into me with wild abandon, I lifted my hips up to meet him with each thrust. His clothes needed to be off . . . like yesterday. I was more than happy to help him with his not being naked issue. I tore at his clothes with a desperation he seemed to match, and within what seemed like the blink of an eye, Bryn loomed over me, naked and ready to finally give me what I needed . . . him.

But he paused, despite the raw hunger I saw in his eyes as he looked down at me. "Peej—we shouldn't—why won't you just—"

"Let you go?" I snarled at him. "Never. I'll never let you go. You promised always and I'm here to collect."

Bryn's pupils noticeably dilated further and he looked at me with wonder. "Always," he murmured, and as the word left his mouth, I could almost see the acceptance wash over his face. He finally understood . . . He finally realized he belonged to me and when he promised always, there would never be any going back. We didn't need to be mated as dragons for that to be the truth between us. Being mated to him would merely be an added bonus. He brought his lips back down to mine in another onslaught of need, and in one quick motion he came to find his home . . . inside me. I cried out as the pleasure of feeling him again rippled through my system. "I love you Peej . . . always." Bryn's voice was a guttural sob as he began to build a blistering pace.

And that's when I felt it . . . my magic . . . my new stronger magic flowing up to wrap around us. I just instinctively knew that this time, our mate bond would be complete . . . the real deal. No words were needed between us like when Khol had claimed me; Bryn's soul and mine were linked together on a much deeper level. I cried out at the pure joy of knowing he was finally and completely mine. Our session was much quicker than normal, but then again we hadn't been together in quite some time and our current need was completely primal. Even still, the familiar feeling of ecstasy began in my center and pushed its way out through my body before I fell to pieces in his arms shouting his name to the world. I heard Bryn call out my name with his own release just before I slipped into darkness.

18

You don't look well," I said, knowing there was no way to tell Bryn that tactfully. "Were you sick or something?" I thought back to the vision that had me so worried about him when he woke up as if from a nightmare covered in a sickly sweat.

"I haven't been sleeping very well," Bryn replied as he ran the tips of his fingers down my naked back, eliciting a shudder from me. "But I have a feeling that's all going to change soon." I didn't have to look at him to know he was smiling.

I inhaled deeply, letting his delicious scent overwhelm my senses as I lay with my head on his chest, my hand making lazy circles across his skin. "I had a vision about you. I was worried."

"I'm fine . . . now."

"So sex is the cure-all for you then?" I asked with a giggle.

"With you it is." His voice went all dark and seductive on me.

I tried to ignore the things his voice alone did to my insides, and persisted with my line of questioning. "Are you sure? It just feels like something else is going on."

"Like what?" I could hear the exasperation in his voice. He knew I was like a bulldog when I got something in my head. I'd learned from the best . . . Jenna.

"I don't know. I just feel . . ." Very conspiracy theory is what I wanted to say. But about what? I guess it went back to when the Riders broke into the compound and shot me. How did they find me so quickly and without any resistance? I just couldn't shake the underlying feeling that there was a traitor amongst us. But who? " . . . I don't know. Maybe I'm just being paranoid."

"Who could blame you for being paranoid? With everything that's been going on lately . . . how the hell did a Rider get into Jenna anyways?" Bryn added one more thing to my list that had me thinking conspiracy theory again. There was something else going on right under my nose, I knew it. If only I could get my powers to work the way I wanted them to, then I'd be able to figure it out.

"Let's go," I said, pushing myself up and out of bed. "We have a Rider to question."

As I bent to pick up what was left of my clothes, I felt Bryn's body heat behind me as he lifted my hair up off of my neck and kissed where I knew his mate mark had finally sunk all the way into my skin. "Mine," he murmured as he wrapped his arms around me and pulled me against him.

"Bryn," I chastised, even though I wanted nothing more than to lose myself in his embrace for just a little bit longer.

"Yes, my queen," he said, and I could feel his smirk against my bare skin as his tongue darted out to lick the back of my neck this time.

"Bryn, I mean it. I—we have responsibilities. To our world." My words sobered him up and he let go of me, leaving me to sigh over the loss of his warming touch.

Just as I finished pulling my shirt over my head, Bryn's door slammed open to reveal, not Khol as I half expected, but his second in command . . . Drake. His face was contorted into a mask of rage as he looked back and forth between Bryn and me. “You just couldn’t stay away from him, could you?” he growled, his eyes flaring brighter. He then looked at me with bewilderment. “Why? Why would you choose him over my lord? You’re our queen, you deserve better than a baby dragon.” And before I had a chance to really process what he was saying, Drake was across the room, pinning Bryn against the wall. “My lord won’t kill you—but I will.”

“NO!” I screamed, moving with speed I didn’t even know I possessed. But before I could reach Bryn and Drake, Khol appeared.

“What the hell is going on?” he bellowed.

Drake immediately released Bryn and dropped to the ground in front of Khol. “I was protecting my lord’s interests,” Drake said, not sounding the least bit sorry. If anything he sounded proud of his actions.

Khol took in Bryn’s half-undressed state as he leaned against the wall gasping for air, and he met my wide eyes with question. “Tell me,” he whispered.

“I—I’ve chosen,” I stammered, my voice not sounding even half as confident as I wanted it to.

“I see,” he responded with absolutely no emotion whatsoever. A huge lump formed in my throat and my stomach knotted up as I waited to see what he would do. I wasn’t worried for Bryn’s safety, not with Khol anyways, because I knew Khol would never do that to me. He would never try to kill Bryn like he had once before, because ultimately it had resulted in my near death. “Drake,” Khol said between gritted teeth with menace, “Explain yourself.”

“I believe I already have,” Drake spoke with his head bowed and his eyes averted to face the ground. “I was protecting my lord’s interests.” His head then snapped up to meet Khol’s dark gaze head on. “Even when my lord wouldn’t do it himself.”

Khol took a step back as shock played across his features. "What have you done?"

"Khol?" I said with uncertainty. I knew I was missing something. What did Drake do besides just try to choke Bryn to death? I had to know. I moved quickly to Drake's side before anyone could protest and reached out to touch him. I silently willed my powers to cooperate with me. I needed them to show me what I was missing—what Drake had done. I gasped, as I was thrown head long into a vision as soon as my skin made contact with his.

There was so much information, and one revelation after another played out in front of me in quick secession. I only really grasped the major points: Drake arranging for the Riders to kill Bryn. I wasn't their target at all; Bryn was the one they were aiming for. It seemed Drake was enraged when I had almost lost my life in the process. He knew how it would affect Khol. The herbs Nala was giving me for my morning sickness had a little something extra added in, courtesy of none other than Drake. Before I left he had been putting that little extra something into my food. It was meant to strengthen the bond between Khol and I—Nala knew, of course. She hadn't given up on having Bryn for herself at all. And Bryn was being . . . poisoned. Slowly . . . very slowly by Drake as a back-up plan. Not only that, but Drake had been giving Bryn herbs in an effort to foster some kind of connection between him and Nala. He had planned to stop the poison as soon as Nala could manage to bed him and gain him as a mate. Nala was not privy to that part of the plan. She never would have gone along with Bryn being poisoned. Bottom line . . . Drake was determined that Khol would have me for his mate. But nowhere did I see that Khol had anything to do with it, or any knowledge even hinting of what Drake was up to.

As the vision faded away, I let go of Drake and dropped to my knees. "We trusted you."

Khol slid his arms around me and lifted me up before I crumpled fully to the ground. He turned me to face him, his eyes beseeching mine. "What did you see?"

I closed my eyes before responding, knowing what I was about to tell him would only cause him more pain. "Drake is the traitor. He arranged for the Riders to kill Bryn. He's been putting poison into his food, and he's been giving me herbs to strengthen the bond between us—so I would choose you." I thought back to the visions I'd had about Khol after my attempted suicide and when he had been with Shannon. How could I have been so stupid? Those visions were showing me Drake's reaction to those events. They were a foreshadowing of events to come. "Nala helped."

I opened my eyes to see Khol's face constricted into hard lines with the force of his agony. I had just informed him that his most trusted dragon—his second in command—had betrayed him—and to top it all off—my feelings for him had been helped along—pushed by magic. That's why when I had donned the bracelet from my birth mother cutting off my connection with Khol, my feelings for Bryn had pushed back to the forefront of my heart.

Khol let me go and I crumpled to the ground, my eyes tracking his every move as he stalked toward Drake with deadly intent. Drake raised his chin defiantly at Khol as he came to stand in front of him. "I did it all out of love," Drake said softly, his voice the only indication of his true fear.

"I know," Khol said as he reached out with lightening speed and snapped Drake's neck. I screamed as I watched Drake's lifeless body fall to the floor in what seemed to be slow motion. And before I could even blink, Khol had ignited his fire magic to burn the remains of Drake. "Macon," Khol called out as he stood watching Drake burn. Almost instantly, Macon appeared beside Khol, his face showing shock of his own as he looked down to see Drake's burning body. He dropped down on one knee and bowed deeply before Khol. "You are my second now, Macon. Don't disappoint me as Drake did." Khol then turned to me. "I'm sorry." Pain played across his face briefly before he disappeared before my eyes.

As soon as he was gone, I started to sob. I hadn't betrayed Bryn willingly; magic had been used on me. How could I have not known? And Bryn . . . he hadn't so much as touched Nala despite the magic that had been used on him. He had been stronger than I'd been able to be with Khol. I had come close . . . very close to letting Khol have me before I was sent away on my mission in Tennessee. And then it would have been too late. I would have never have had another chance with Bryn again. I looked up to meet Bryn's burning blue eyes and he came to me and swept me up in his comforting embrace. My Bryn . . . my mate . . . my home. "Bryn," I murmured. "I'm—"

"Shhh . . ." He rumbled. "I know." I wanted to ask him if all was forgiven. I knew we had finally mated but that wouldn't change the fact that he might continue to be bitter about my seeming eagerness to hook up with Khol. And okay, I had definitely been eager, but as it turned out, it hadn't been entirely my fault.

"Why didn't you sleep with Nala? How did you resist?" Another topic probably best left for another time, but I had to know.

Bryn tilted my head back toward him with the aid of his long index finger. "Because I love you. Not her." It was both the most perfect and worst thing he could have responded with. The most perfect because him telling me he loved me so unconditionally was something I was worried I'd never hear, and it was the worst because I hadn't treated him the same in kind. I hadn't loved him unconditionally at all.

I slipped my chin off of his finger and crushed the side of my face to his chest. "I don't deserve you." And in that moment I knew that I didn't, that Bryn was more than I ever deserved to have.

"No, you don't. But I guess we're stuck with each other from now on." I could hear the smile in his voice as he teased me like he used to. God, I'd missed him. I clutched him even harder and pushed my nose into his chest so the only thing I could smell was him, and not the lingering smell of burnt flesh. "Let's get out of here," Bryn murmured as he tightened his arms around me in response. "I don't want a reminder of what just happened." And with that, a familiar feeling of weightlessness surrounded me and I knew Bryn had transported us with his dragon powers out of his room. Not that he needed that room anymore, I thought smugly, because he was mine and he would be back in our room, with me . . . where he belonged.

"Peej," Bryn rumbled, and I could feel his words more than hear them. "I'll never leave you again—I swear—I'm here—always." Tears began to freefall down my face. I couldn't believe I'd almost lost him . . . again. And in some way, even though Drake had manipulated me, I'd willingly participated in the destruction of our relationship. "Hey," Bryn tried to console me as he continued to hold me tightly to his chest and tenderly stroked my hair. "Don't. Don't think about what could have happened."

I pulled away from Bryn reluctantly and looked up into the face of the man I loved, the face of a fallen angel—my fallen angel. "We thought everything had been settled before, both in the dragon realm and after. Who's to say something won't rip us apart again?" Another huge sob escaped from my constricted chest as I allowed myself to say my worst fears out loud. Who was to say if Bryn was really and truly mine? I'd dared to believe it before and look where that had gotten me. I had been shattered into a billion pieces.

"We'll be more careful. Trust no one but each other. It's the only way to survive this apparently." He reached out and pulled me back into his arms. "I don't care if that baby is mine or not, I'll love it like it was." I didn't think it was possible but I started to cry harder. I'd wanted to hear those words from Bryn from the beginning, to hear him say he'd never really walk away from me, that it had all been one huge mistake—and it had been. Thanks to Drake. "I love you Peej."

"I love you too," I croaked. He then tilted my head back and claimed my lips with a tenderness that spoke of a forever kind of love . . . our kind of love . . . *always.*

19

I had Bryn back, that was something that only in my wildest dreams had I dared to hope for. And we had the answers to what had happened between us. Despite everything that had happened . . . me becoming the next Dragon Queen, Jenna getting possessed by a Rider, me going to Tennessee on a solo mission, me hooking up with Khol, me finding out I was pregnant . . . well, Bryn and my relationship felt stronger than ever. We had weathered the storm and come out on the other side. He was my true mate now, our marks wouldn't be disappearing anytime soon, unless one of us died, and I was just too happy to allow myself to think about that grim reality. With Bryn by my side, I could make everything else right again. Because I had also learned that the person I needed to depend on the most was me. Bryn was my partner—my mate—but it wasn't his job to take care of me, even though he certainly seemed to want to.

"Do you feel okay?" Bryn tried to hide the worry in his voice. "You still don't have morning sickness, do you?"

I laughed into his chest, where I was currently splayed across. We decided to have just a little bit more alone time before facing the real world again. Both of us had been dealing with a little too much of that lately. "No, I'm fine."

"God, Peej, you have no idea how much it was tearing me up to knowing you were pregnant and me not being there for you. At least not in the way that I wanted to be."

It was almost weird how easily I was moving on from everything now that I had Bryn back. He made me feel anchored to reality in a way that no one else probably ever could. Sometimes it felt like if I didn't share things with Bryn, they really didn't happen, or didn't mean anything. I guess that's because he'd been the most important person in my life since I was five years old. "I don't wanna think about any of it, Bryn. Let's just pretend none of it happened."

"Peej—that's just not realistic."

"Fine. If you can't pretend, then lets at least not talk about it." I frowned into his chest. Why rehash all the unpleasant things that had happened between us lately when we could simply be enjoying what was between us now?

Bryn didn't say anything for a few minutes, and I knew he was thinking about if he should just go along or argue with me. He heaved a huge sigh, causing my head to move up and down with his chest. "Alright. You might have a point."

"I always have a point." I sat up and grinned at him.

"Yeah, but I didn't say it was a good one." Bryn gave me his patented lop sided grin complete with dimples, his eyes glinting at me with mischief.

My insides melted for him. I'd dreamt about that smile, combined with that gleam in his eyes . . . quite literally. I was suddenly hit with an overwhelming desire to have my unborn child wear that exact same smile. "I want the baby to be yours. So badly, Bryn," I said around the huge lump that had formed in my throat.

Bryn's face clouded over. "Yeah, me too." He then guffawed. "Us parents . . . at nineteen . . . who would have thunk it?"

"Certainly not me. I always thought if anyone, Jenna would be the one to get pregnant this young."

"Yeah, you and me both, Peej."

Not wanting to let our conversation turn anywhere darker, I knew it was time for us to get back to reality. I always hated this part. "We have a Rider to question." I pulled myself up and out of his embrace with reluctance and began getting dressed.

"You mean *you* do," Bryn grumbled as he too started pulling his clothes on. I stopped and stared at his chiseled body. Even though Drake had been poisoning him, Bryn still looked mighty fine . . . mighty fine indeed.

I bit my lip with worry. "Are you sure you feel okay? I mean Drake was poisoning you. I think that maybe we should have Khol use his healing powers on you or something." Would Khol have to touch Bryn, kiss him? That would be veeerry interesting, I smirked to myself.

"You've got to be kidding me," Bryn growled low. "Khol's done enough. I'll be fine. The poison will pass out of my system. Besides"—and he grinned at me mischievously—"I can think of plenty of ways to *work* it out of my body and none of them require anyone but you."

I chose to ignore his remark about Khol and laughed. "That doesn't even make sense, Bryn. I'm going to label that innuendo as failed."

"It's not failed because you got what I was going for," Bryn protested with false indignance.

"Yeah, okay, whatever." I rolled my eyes at him as I turned to leave the room. It felt so good—beyond good—to be able to talk to Bryn like this again. I'd missed him so much. He might be more, but he was still my best friend—my best friend with tons of extra benefits. "By the way"—I stopped and met Bryn's gaze with narrowed eyes—"if you ever try to leave me again." I paused for dramatic effect. "I'll more than just slap you." I don't know why I felt the need to tell him that at that moment, but I did. Maybe on some level I felt most things we could move on and not talk about . . . bury our heads in the sand . . . but not that.

Bryn gave me a tight-lipped smile. "We're mated now. Nothing to worry about."

I bared my teeth at him, feeling every bit the full-blooded dragon that I was. "If something happens—like before—if you walk away from me—you'll regret it."

Bryn's brows furrowed together as he studied me. "Are you threatening me, Peej?"

"Yeah, I guess I am."

Bryn's full lips turned up slightly at the corners showcasing his dimples. "I wonder if it's the whole being mated thing, but I kind of think it's hot, how you're reacting to the thought of me leaving."

I quirked one bemused eyebrow at him. "Seriously?"

"Yeah." His eyes darkened to show the sudden heat in them that was burning for me. "I know I was stupid, Peej—beyond stupid. But you know I did it all out of love for you."

I flicked my gaze to the floor, not wanting to get caught in the magnetic pull of his sea storm eyes. "That almost makes it worse," I mumbled.

Macon appeared in front of me, causing me to jump about a mile. One would think I'd be used to dragons popping in and out around me by now, but I wasn't. And I could only sense the ripple of power letting me know someone was about to appear if I was paying attention, and not fully focused on Bryn. "My lord sent me to bring you to question the Rider known as Cliff. He wanted to remind you that you also have queenly duties that go beyond seeing to your mate Bryn." Harsh. But then again I guess Khol reserved the right to be a little mean to me after everything we'd been through together.

"Lead the way," I said, somehow managing to curb my sarcastic tongue.

Bryn and I trailed along behind Macon silently hand in hand. The tension between Macon and us was palpable. I had the feeling Macon wanted to say something to me but just couldn't bring himself to broach whatever subject it was. I was sure it either had to do with Jenna, or the fact that Bryn and I were mated . . . again. Either way, I was glad he didn't want to go there at the moment.

When we came to a huge wooden door, much like the one that Jenna was stashed behind, Macon pushed it open and stepped back to allow us entrance. We both slid past him, and I for one didn't make eye contact.

"It's about time," Khol's annoyed voice greeted us as soon as I crossed the threshold. I looked up to meet his eyes and beyond his annoyance was a world of pain. I had completely crushed him by choosing Bryn. I knew that on some level, but seeing it was something else entirely. I dropped Bryn's hand as my face heated. How could I be so callous? I didn't have to rub it in Khol's face, did I?

"Hey," I said as my entire face flushed. I was a horrible, horrible person. But then again I couldn't really be considered a person so . . . I was a horrible, horrible dragon. I then looked over to see a tied up and bloodied Cliff. "What the hell? What did you do?" Oh, please don't tell me that Khol has been taking out his anger on Cliff. I was still holding onto the hope that we could return him to his normal life once we figured out a way to get the Rider out of him.

"What needed to be done," Khol responded coldly.

Yeah, okay. I could tell by Khol's face that there would be no arguing with him over this. If I had wanted it to go differently then maybe I shouldn't have stayed in bed with Bryn and been there to protect Cliff's body instead. "Did you get any useful information at least?"

"Nothing exceptionally useful." Khol strode over to stand inches away from Cliff, who flinched away from him with fear. "The time for questioning is over."

"Okaaay," I drawled out. "So why am I here then?"

"We need to figure out how to remove a Rider from his host." Khol waved his hand over Cliff's head as if I should have known that. "Here is the perfect candidate for us to experiment on."

"What?" I was so not using poor Cliff as a guinea pig.

"Would you rather use Jenna?" Khol asked as his mouth pushed into a thin line.

"No! Of course not . . . It's just . . ." I shook my head with dismay. ". . . Poor Cliff."

"Every war has collateral damage. You, as a queen, should get used to that fact."

"And I guess Cliff is a better choice than Jenna for that," I mumbled to myself. I lifted my head and met his steel gaze square on. "What do I need to do?"

"What else can we try?" I ground out with frustration. We had spent—Khol, Bryn, and myself—the last couple of hours trying to force the Rider out of Cliff's body with everything we could think of. I just didn't understand it. My birth mother said it was possible, and she said I was the one to do it . . . But how? When neither Bryn nor Khol responded to my question, I repeated it with more vehemence. "What else can we try?"

"I don't know," Khol replied with exhaustion as he scrubbed a hand down his face. "I just don't know." Bryn just remained silent as he stared at Cliff, his dragon blue eyes blazing brightly.

"Well, we can't just give up!" My voice climbed a few octaves.

"No one's giving up," Khol grumbled. "Maybe we just need a break, to take some time to think about this.

"I want that thing out of Jenna now!" I would not cry again. I would not cry again. *Right.*

Bryn put his arm around my shoulders and pulled me into his side. "I know," he murmured as he brushed his soft lips against my temple. "I know."

"Fine. We'll take a break." I stood, breaking all contact with Bryn and stalked toward the door. I was letting my anger take hold in me so I wouldn't feel the anguish of not having the answer to save Jenna yet. But I would find it if it was the last thing I did.

"My lord!" Macon burst through the door nearly knocking me over. "We're under attack!"

"The Riders?" Khol asked but it sounded more like a statement.

"Yes."

"How did they breach our wards?" Khol swore under his breath. "Someone had to have led them here."

I was supposed to be queen but I didn't have the experience and scope of knowledge to deal with this kind of thing, so I looked to Khol for answers. "What should we do?" I tried to hide the panic in my voice and failed miserably.

Khol was already leaning down to untie an unconscious Cliff when he responded. "We retreat, and re-gather ourselves. We have something they obviously want very badly, but we're not in a position to use it to our full advantage when we're on the defensive."

I had no idea what that meant exactly. "So we run away?"

Khol grimaced. "I would prefer a different choice of words, but yes."

"We need to bring Jenna with us!" I ran from the room, not waiting for anyone anyone's response.

"Peej!" Bryn was close at my heels. "I'll help you!"

I nodded my head at him but didn't turn to acknowledge him. I was on a mission. I had to get to Jenna before the skeevy Riders did. Just as I made it to the door of Jenna's prison, Jeremy came barreling out with her slung over his shoulder, unconscious. "What's the plan?" he blurted out as soon as he saw us.

"Well, you already have the first part covered. I guess the next step is to get the hell out of Dodge," Bryn answered for me.

"We'll use a Gate," Jeremy said and he turned and led the way down the long corridor.

Anxiety built up in my mind. What if we didn't make it? Pushing my worry down I sped along quickly behind Jeremy, hand in hand with Bryn. I only stumbled a few times trying to keep up before Bryn scooped me up in his arms. I didn't bother to protest because I knew he was right. We'd move faster with him carrying me.

We finally made it out of one of the back exits and scurried toward the forest and to where Jeremy would open the Gate and escape route. Strange how we hadn't seen one single Rider on the way out. In fact, we hadn't run into anyone on the way out. I hardly had time to register my sudden feelings that something was wrong before we burst into the clearing... and came face to face with a horde of Riders.

We stopped short just as Khol appeared beside us with Macon, who was carrying a still unconscious Cliff. It was evident in that moment that our little crew had run straight into a trap.

"Give me my son," Senator Bill Wexington snarled.

"Nala," I felt Bryn growl. And sure enough she was standing a little bit behind our dear Senator.

"You set us up," Macon chimed in angrily. "We were never under attack."

Nala sneered at Macon. "No. But I convinced everyone that we were and all the rest of your allies high tailed it out of here. You're all alone now."

"Why?" Bryn demanded, his question obviously directed at Nala.

Her face softened when she shifted her gaze to his. "We belong together, can't you see that? I knew it from the first moment I laid eyes on you."

"She's our queen. You can't kill her," Khol snarled at Nala.

"Why not?" she screeched sounding like a child throwing a temper tantrum. "We've gone all these years without a queen, we can manage without one again. I would have been happy to let her live, but she couldn't keep her hands off him."

I tightened my arms around Bryn possessively, too shocked to feel the full strength of my anger at Nala for what she'd done.

"Enough!" the Rider that was Senator Bill Wexington interjected. "You can work all of that out after I get my son back."

"Not going to happen," Khol said, his voice burning with menace. "Not unless you agree to leave our world."

The Senator's lips curled up in what was supposed to be a smile, at least I thought. "We'll see." He waved his hand and my mouth dropped open when I saw who stepped forward from behind some of the Riders. It was a Gatekeeper, and it had a Rider inside of him. It was Evan Thompson, the star of my long ago fantasies back before all of this had begun with the Riders. *Holy Shit!* He began moving in a similar fashion that I'd seen Jeremy move before to open a Gate. Although in my opinion, Jeremy did it with much more grace. *Yep . . . because that matters right now.* When he finished and the Gate shimmered open to the right of us, more Riders stepped through. "As you were saying?" the Senator asked as he tilted his head at Khol. I felt Khol's power snap through the air as he readied for attack. Bryn set me on my feet and he too tensed for what would happen next. I didn't have to look at Macon and Jeremy to know that they were doing the same. We wouldn't go down without a fight. "Just give us my son and we'll leave you alone." The Senator tried using a more placating tone. "We have no interest in the affairs of dragons. Just the humans."

"I want Bryn," Nala demanded. "You promised if I helped you that you would get rid of her." She raised her index finger and pointed at me.

"I'll never be yours, Nala. You're not the type of woman I could ever want," Bryn said with cold indifference. "You think after I've had a queen, I'd want you?" Way to twist the knife, Bryn. I couldn't help the smile that tugged at my lips. *That's right . . . He's mine bitch!*

The Senator sighed demonstratively. "Alright. Let's see what else I have in my little bag of tricks that might convince you to see things my way." He motioned again with his hand and some dragons, a few from every faction appeared on their side. The effect of the battle lines being drawn was not lost on me. And before the shock of him having dragons on his side could fully sink in, the mac daddy of surprises stepped forward . . . Bryn's father walked into the mix.

"Dad?" Bryn's voice wavered in question. "I thought you were dead."

The Senator spoke up. "Seers and Speakers are useless with one of us in them, but Gatekeepers and Guardians . . . oh yes . . . they work quite nicely. So, I decided to keep a few of them around . . . just in case I could use them for a rainy day."

"Don't worry, Bryn," I whispered under my breath. "We'll save him and Jenna both."

"It's time you found out Bryn, you're not my son," Bryn's father said out of nowhere with malice. "Your mother couldn't conceive, and then we were given a gift. At least we thought it was a gift at the time. I never thought you'd shame me the way that you did by taking up with P.J. when it's against our laws. But I guess you're not even fully human. No wonder whoever left you for us didn't want you." *What?* I immediately thought of when my birth mother had told me that Bryn, another dragon, at least part dragon, growing up so close to me hadn't happened by chance. She told me that he was there for a reason. "I'll enjoy taking you out myself just for the heartbreak you caused your mother. She was so ashamed of how you disregarded the most important law of being a Guardian. May she rest in peace. It's your fault she's dead after all. Yours and hers," he hissed and his eyes briefly met mine.

Everything seemed to happen at once. It wasn't like it is in the movies. I saw Bryn's father launch himself at Bryn, but I couldn't track anything else that was going on after Nala slammed into me, causing me to fall to the ground. She scrambled to get on top of me, and sat with all of her body weight on my chest and began to choke me. I desperately reached for my fire magic but was having difficulty pulling it up when black stars began to dance in front of my eyes. Not only that but I felt a slow trickle of water moving up to cover my face. Dazed, I registered that Nala must be using some kind of water power to try and suffocate me faster. I gasped for air and came back with a mouth full of water. My vision grew darker and my thoughts slower. I knew she was drowning me.

Then suddenly the pressure released and I sat up to gasp mouthful after mouthful of fresh air as I saw Khol push his fire magic into Nala. She let out an ear-shattering scream before all that was left of her was ashes. *Good*, I numbly thought. I stood and scanned the clearing for Bryn, who was currently rolling around on the ground with his father. Bryn was at a huge disadvantage because it was obvious he didn't really want to hurt him. His father clearly didn't feel the same way. "Help him!" I screeched at Khol.

"Enough!" Senator Bill Wexington's voice rolled over everyone. "Hold him," he ordered Bryn's father, who stood with Bryn and brought him into a headlock. The Senator met my eyes, "Him for my son."

I didn't even hesitate. "Okay. Just don't hurt him." The Senator then nodded at one of the Riders standing beside him who walked slowly over to Cliff's prone unconscious figure and picked him up. Khol came to stand behind him so he couldn't make his way back to the Senator just yet. "Now release Bryn," I said with false calmness. My insides were finding a new definition for panic.

Bryn's father released him and Bryn walked steadily back toward me. Khol then gave the Rider holding Cliff a rough push to get him going. I reached my shaky hand out to Bryn, needing to feel his skin under my fingertips. He gave me a tight smile, and I knew he was thinking it was his fault we were losing Cliff as a bargaining chip—that he should have been able to best his father—that he couldn't even protect himself—how would he protect me and my unborn child? I could read all of his tormented thoughts in his eyes but I didn't care just as long as he was safe. As soon as my hand gripped his, I heaved a sigh of relief. "I love you," I mouthed to him. None of the rest mattered. We might be down, but we weren't out just yet. I would make him understand that eventually. We were finally bonded as *Anam Caras* and together we could take on the world.

Bryn's father suddenly appeared directly behind him. The Rider inside of him shone so brightly it almost eclipsed his host's features. He met my eyes and grinned down at me. It was in that instant I knew what he meant to do. "No!" I screamed, my whole body going ice cold instantaneously. I reached for my fire magic, but it was too late . . . all too late. I watched, completely helpless to stop it, as Bryn's father, the man that had protected my mother and my family for as far back as I could remember, snapped the neck of his only son. The sickly cracking sound it made rang out in the clearing like thunder in my ears. "No!" I heard myself scream as I watched Bryn's hand slip from my grasp as his body fell forward and slumped to the ground. *Life over. My Life is over.*

"Like I said, he wasn't really my son."

Silence engulfed me. I tried to go to Bryn but someone caught me around the waist and began to run toward the pulsating gate with me in tow. I struggled against my captor, wanting nothing more than to curl up with Bryn's body and to die right alongside him. Sound came back to me in a rush. Someone's hysteric screams pounded against my head. Was that me? I didn't know and didn't care.

When whoever was carrying me got me to the Gate, they jumped in without pausing. Ice ran over my skin and the air was sucked from my lungs. I didn't stay conscious for much more than a moment as the magic of the Gate pulled me down into blackness.

ACKNOWLEDGEMENTS

This is the part where I get to thank all the people who made this book possible. As usual I'm hoping I don't leave out someone important. *gnaws on nails*

First I'd like to thank my amazing Hubby, who is supportive and patient beyond the realm of what I imagine any normal man is . . . dah dah da duuuh . . . Super Hubby! (I think that's just going to be standard text in every acknowledgment from now on.)

Next I would like to thank my parents for encouraging my love of reading and crazy imagination during my most impressionable years. (Check on averting pouty parents syndrome again. Phew.)

Then of course there's my lovely squad of beta readers for this book: Kristin Bingham, Jamie Degyansky, Kellee Fabre, Jessica Johnson, Sarah Ashley Jones, Shona Lawrence, Bieke Paesen, Lauren Reidy, and Tabatha Ventura. You ladies rocked it . . . Dragon Hussy style! You know I love all of you!

Also a very special thank you to Lauren Reidy, a.k.a. Ren Reidy, a.k.a. the Dragon Hussies founder, a.k.a. the beta who I almost left out of the acknowledgements. *cringes* That's what I get for writing these types of things when I'm going on practically no sleep. But see, Ren, now you get an extra special thanks, so it's not all bad, right? Plus maybe I can stop gnawing on my nails, worrying that I'm going to forget someone because I almost nearly did. Eeep! You know I love you girl!

Of course I need to thank Lindsay Tiry for her amazing cover design, and Jordan P. Fremgen for his amazing logo designs for The P.J. Stone Gates Trilogy. Both artists extraordinaire! Although I think Lindsay might need to check for gray hairs after all the emails I sent her with "notes" about cover ideas. I hope she's ready for book three. I know I am. Muahahaha!

I also need to thank my editors Greta Maloney, Tara Chevrist, and Matt Larkin. You guys rocked it as well!

Of course I'd like to thank Dragonfairy Press, because I can't thank them enough! Especially Kenya Wright and Alicia Wright Brewster to be specific. I love you guys!

And last but certainly not least: I've said it before and I'll say it again and it still won't be enough . . . Thank you to all the book bloggers and fans who keep me going! I wouldn't be anywhere if not for you guys! I love each and every one of you!

—D.T. Dyllin